THE
ROAD HOLE
BUNKER
MYSTERY

WILLIAM MEIKLE

The Road Hole Bunker Mystery

Copyright © 2023 by William Meikle

ISBN: 979-8-9876847-3-3

Cover by Kent Holloway

CHAPTER
One

THE DAY STARTED like many another.

I dressed, I made coffee, I sat at my desk trying to magic up a client through the power of my will. All I managed to magic was a headache.

Outside my window rich men played golf; chatting, back-slapping and giving high-fives as they rolled putts across the pristine Eighteenth of St Andrews Old Course. None of them showed any signs of needing my services.

Five weeks. Five weeks of staring at the walls and trying not to scream while the money drained out of my account like a river working its way up into a spate. The only thing close to a client had been old Mrs Malcolm wanting to pay me a tenner to find her cat.

I'd been so desperate I'd taken her up on the offer.

I spent two days sitting through hours of stories of gangs of kids stealing cats to sell to far-eastern clothing manufacturers, of Chinese shops with bulging freezers, and even weirder tales of devil worship and ritual kitten slaying.

The cat stayed lost, and I never got paid.

I thought, not for the first time, how much money I could get for selling the flat that doubled as my office. Unfortunately, I only rented it, and I only had it because I'd done so many favours over the years for Tom in the museum below. Favours could only be strung out for so long, and my hold on the flat, the office, the business, had become tenuous.

I spent five minutes trying to roll a cigarette, but the paper and tobacco wanted to lead separate lives and refused to become anything that even resembled anything smoke-worthy. I felt cranky; so much so that I seriously considered making a dive for the whisky bottle, even though it was only an hour since breakfast.

The front door creaked; always a precursor to footsteps on the stairs. I got the crumpled mess of paper and tobacco into my top drawer and just had the time to straighten my tie when she walked in.

My heart fell.

A tourist stood in the doorway. A large, too colourful tourist with aquamarine tracksuit bottoms and a pink sweatshirt that hung voluminously over a figure a hippo might have been proud of on a bad day. She carried a sheepskin bag over her shoulder, big enough to hold my luggage for a two-week holiday. A pair of red tortoiseshell glasses hung from a gold chain round her neck, and her hair had been dyed a shade of blue only ever seen on the head of ladies of a certain age. She had that puffy, red-faced look that heavy people get after climbing a flight of stairs.

I knew how she felt...they got to me like that after a session on the whisky.

"The museum is downstairs," I said.

She looked at me blankly.

"The museum... it's downstairs...ground floor for hickory, haberdashery, mashies and memorabilia."

"This is 'Old Course Investigations', isn't it? You are John Royle?" she said in an American accent, Southern States by the sound of it. She had, or had access to, money, if her rings were any indication.

She smiled, and my estimation of her went up several notches. On a second look she proved to be older than I'd originally thought, somewhere in late middle-age, but she'd taken care of herself. Her skin was smooth, her teeth the perfect white we've come to expect of Americans rich enough to travel. Only the crow's feet at her eyes and the soft folds at her neck betrayed her.

"Yes, I'm Royle. All investigations undertaken; no job is too large; no fee is too large."

She looked around, taking in the torn linoleum, the battered desk and the old leather armchairs on either side. "You don't put up much of a front, do you?"

I tugged at my ear and gave it my best Bogart reply.

"There's not much money in it...not if you're honest."

"Now who's the museum piece?" she said. "That line is older than me."

"Yep. And not half as pretty," I said.

That got me another smile.

"I bet you say that to all the girls."

"Only the ones that want to hire me."

"I haven't decided yet," she said. "Go ahead. Impress me."

"What with?" I replied. "I have an extensive knowledge of malt whiskies, film noir, card games and local blondes. What do you want to know about?"

"Do you work hard at it?" she asked, looking me up and down. "The image I mean?"

I wore my 'work' clothes; black high-waisted trousers with the watch-chain running from the belt loop to the pocket, black braces attached to the trousers by large wooden buttons, thick white cotton shirt and a kipper tie that reached only two-thirds down the front.

"The suit came from Oxfam, the pocket-watch from my grandfather, but the rest is all me."

She looked around the room, laughing.

"Where's the big-busted secretary?"

"It's her day off... she tires easily."

That got me another laugh, so infectious that I joined in.

"So, which is it?" she asked, "Spade, Hammer or Marlowe?"

"It depends on how tough I'm feeling," I said. "Today I'm a pussycat, so you get Marlowe. He gets a better class of women."

She giggled, like a much younger woman. It looked like something she'd been practising for a while.

I motioned her over to the desk, but she went to the window and looked out.

"Nice view," she said.

"Aye. Luckily, I don't have to pay for it."

She still showed no sign of sitting down. I let her take her time. Some came in here and blurted out their stories like vomit over my desk. Others had to be left to get there at their own speed.

I knew it wouldn't be long now. She'd cased me out; I hadn't frightened her too much; now she was preparing to tell me why she was here.

"Look at all those men out there, all that expensive equipment, all those elegant clothes, all that *money*...and all because someone once had an idea to chase a ball around a field with a stick."

She shook her head.

"My father was mad for the game, and his father before him, for as far back as the family remembers. There they'd be, out in all weathers—although in Texas that's not much of a problem—tramping around the only bit of green grass in the county, trying their dangest to get a little ball into a little hole. I've never understood why they do it."

"It keeps them out of trouble and away from the womenfolk," I said. "Besides, it's not just the golf you're paying for in this town. It's the history; the tradition."

"That's my brother's department," she said. Suddenly she looked like she might cry. Once more I motioned her over to the desk.

Finally, she moved.

She sat in the armchair opposite me and sighed loudly. As did the chair... it had been a while since anyone had stressed it so much, and I worried that it might give way. That got me wondering about my insurance cover, and my mind wandered so far that I had to focus to catch up.

"I need to rest," she said, "I've been all over the town this morning. All those cobbles are bad for my ankles. Why do you people have to walk everywhere?"

"That's an easy one," I said. "Have you ever tried to park anywhere in this town? It's bad enough now, but just wait till the summer. The place is clogged up worse than Times Square at New Year... Can I offer you a coffee?"

She looked down her nose at me.

"Not if it's any of that so called mellow shit that looks like pond water and tastes worse," she said.

"I know what you mean," I said. "Half the cafés in town think that coffee comes in glass jars. Nope. I've got the real stuff in the kitchen. Can I get you some?"

"No, what I really need is a cigarette."

I liked her better all the time. I got the tobacco and papers out of my drawer, surreptitiously throwing my last failed attempt in the waste bin under my side of the desk.

To be fair to her she sat patiently and watched me try to roll a cigarette for more than thirty seconds before she offered to take over.

"Pass the makings over here sonny," she said, laughing. "It's a lost art these days, but I was doing this before you were born. I was taught at my grand-daddy's knee."

I tried not to be too embarrassed as I watched her put the cigarettes together. She had fast, nimble fingers and we were soon lit up and puffing merrily at each other.

"I like a man that likes to smoke," she said. "It reminds me of my youth."

"I like a woman that likes a man that likes to smoke," I said.

She smiled.

"I hope you're not casting me in the Sidney Greenstreet part," she said. "I know I've put on a bit of beef, but surely I'm not that big?"

"Nowhere near," I said. "You can be Mary Astor."

"As long as you don't slap me if I start whining," she said laughing.

We both sat back. An unspoken signal went between us.

It was time for business.

HOW DID YOU FIND ME?" I asked.

She blew two perfect smoke rings, one through the other, before replying.

"I looked in the phone book. I didn't like the sound of Adams Detection Agency, and you were the only other one."

Actually, I was the only one...Adams Detection Agency was one of mine as well, a second line for people who might be put off by the golfing connotations of 'Old Course Investigations'. In the past ten years the second line had taken precisely five work-related calls, none of them leading to a client; such is the power of golf, here in its hometown.

"So, what can I do for you?" I said.

"We're over here doing some genealogy research..." she said, and my heart sank. She saw it in my face and raised a hand.

"Oh no, I don't need any research done on the family tree. Well, not on the older part anyway. It's my brother, Hank. He's gone missing."

"That's not easy in this town," I said.

"I noticed that. I've only been here for a few days and already I know the life stories of half the people in the hotel."

"How long has he been gone?" I asked.

"The last time I saw him was yesterday lunchtime. I went to that cute little ice-cream bar, he went for a beer, and I haven't seen him since."

"It's not unusual in this country for one beer to stretch a wee bit, Miss...?"

"Courtney. Elsa Courtney. And I know all about Scotsmen and booze. But you don't know my brother. One beer, he likes. Two beers and he'll puke up like a baby. No, it's bad. I can feel it."

Sudden tears sprung in her eyes, and she took a little handkerchief from her sleeve and fluttered it around her cheeks.

I wasn't so easily fooled, but she didn't know that.

"I got really worried this morning," she continued. "When he didn't come down for breakfast, I got the maid to let me into his room... his bed hadn't been slept in."

"You should really try the police," I said. "Recently missing persons is more their line."

"Humph. Fat lot of good they were. Sitting on their rear ends seems to be all that's in their line. I've been round there already this morning. First, they made me wait for half an hour in a draughty room, after which they looked me up and down and decided I was a stupid tourist. They told me not to worry my not-so-pretty little head, and that was about that. They said Hank would find his way home...hell, Hank can't even find his ass with both hands."

That almost caused me to choke on my cigarette.

She nearly laughed.

"We Texan gals like to call a spade a spade," she said. "I hope I didn't offend you."

"Ms Courtney, you couldn't offend me if you danced naked on my desk singing 'The Star-Spangled Banner'."

"Don't tempt me sonny," she said, and winked. Suddenly it felt like flirting with a friend's mother. I decided not to tell her about the whisky in the drawer. I had a feeling she'd take it straight from the bottle... and that there wouldn't be much left when she put it down.

"Do you know which bar he went to?"

"No," she said, shaking her head. She dabbed at her eyes with the handkerchief again, but it looked even more like an act this time. "But there can't be that many can there?"

"Obviously you haven't been paying attention on your walks round town," I said, "We've got nearly as many bars as we have golf courses. And we have a lot of golf courses."

"Will you help me?" she asked.

"I'm thinking about it," I said. "Your brother... he wasn't depressed or anything?"

"What do you mean?" she started. Finally, the penny dropped. "Thinking about offing himself? No, he wasn't the type. In fact, he was happier than I've seen him for a while. That's what makes me think that something's happened to him. He would have been in touch somehow. We're very close."

"How long have you been in town?"

"Just since Thursday. Hank's been mixing golf and a hunt for our ancestors."

"Ancestors?"

She sighed loudly.

"It's his big thing this year. Last year it was fishing. He's at that age when he doesn't know what to be doing with himself. He found that there used to be a Scots branch of the family, and he's been chasing the story for months now. He was really ticked off in Edinburgh when they couldn't find a Courtney tartan."

"Where were you doing it, this research?"

She blew more rings at me.

"Anywhere we could. Parish records, council offices, the University, graveyards. Hank was a demon for it. And on Friday he said he was finally getting somewhere. He was as excited as a puppy."

"Any idea what he'd found?"

She shook her head.

"He wouldn't tell me. But he was buzzing and happy and just...energised. I haven't seen him like that in years."

"That was Friday. Anything else over the weekend?"

She pretended to think for a bit. She had trouble keeping up the act.

"Not that I can remember."

"How about you?" I asked, "Do you have business in the town?"

"No, not me. I only came along for the ride and the shopping. We're scheduled to go back to Edinburgh later in the week."

There had been a lie in there somewhere, I'd spotted that much. I let it stand. If I turned down everybody who sat in that chair and lied to me, I'd never have any clients.

"Are you going to help me?" she said.

"You're good," I said, doing Bogart again. "Mainly it's the tremor in your voice and the soft puppy dog eyes when you say, 'Help me'."

She forced a smile.

"Well, will you help me?"

"My instincts say no, but my bank manager says yes. I can have a look round for him. Do you have a picture?"

She shook her head.

"You won't need one. He's a lanky drink of water, six foot three and less than one hundred and sixty pounds, going bald, blue eyes, about sixty but dresses thirty years younger, and he's the 'orniest sonovabitch you'll ever meet. He's loud, Texan, and likes to let folks know it. He plays five card stud as if he'd like to be Steve McQueen and he carries a Bowie knife down his snake-skin cowboy boots. Like this one," she said.

She took a key ring from her bag and showed me a small replica knife. Even at just over an inch long it looked mean and nasty.

"He shouldn't be too hard to find," I said, smiling.

"You'd think so," she said. "But I've asked around this morning, and nobody's seen him."

"I know some places you might not have tried," I said.

"I'm sure you do sonny," and she winked again. She had the act under control once more.

Now came the hard bit. I cleared my throat nervously

"I cost five hundred a day, plus any expenses."

She peeled a wad of fifties from a purse and counted off five hundred as fast as a bank clerk. She passed it over without a murmur.

"I should have asked for more," I said.

She smiled, and suddenly I thought of sharks.

"You wouldn't have got it. I'm in the Excelsior," she said. "Room 312."

She stood and looked out of the window for a long second before turning to leave.

"If I find out he's been playing golf all this time I'll have his guts for gaiters."

She checked herself in the small mirror on the wall, smoothing her hair and straightening her glasses. There was a parting shot coming... there always was, and I wasn't to be disappointed.

"Just find him," she said. "There's a grand of a bonus in it for you ... don't worry, I'm good for it."

I knew that much. There had to have been at least five thousand pounds in that purse.

I began to dream, of the 'Bogart' case, the one that would make my name and bring rich, good looking, women flocking to my office looking for a shoulder to cry on.

After a while I went through to what passed for my bedroom and got my suit jacket out of the wardrobe. A battered fedora sat on the top shelf. For maybe the thousandth time I put my jacket on, lifted down the fedora onto my head, practised tugging my ear in front of the mirror, then put the hat back in its place. I'd bought it in a charity shop five years ago, and never yet had the nerve to wear it out in the street; I was willing to take the cliché just so far.

I went back to my desk and fondled the money while smoking a poor excuse for a cigarette, then put the cash away in my wallet.

Duty called.

CHAPTER
Three

OLD TOM WAS OPENING up downstairs as I closed the office door behind me and turned to go down the tight staircase. Tom was over seventy, but his bad back had him almost bent double, and with that and a lifetime's exposure to wind and weather, he looked more than eighty. He weighed eight stone when soaking wet, and he was almost bald, his head covered in liver spots like a map of an archipelago. With that, and the hooked Roman nose that dominated his face, he looked like a vulture; until he laughed. Then he looked like everybody's favourite uncle.

"I heard your visitor leaving. I thought she was looking for me," Tom said.

"She's too big for you," I said. "She'd snap your spine like a toothpick."

"Too garish more like. I'd have to wear sunglasses. Is she a client?"

"Looks like it. Probably not for long though. It's only a missing relative gig. I'll probably find him in the first pub I look in."

"Well then, better make that the last pub you look in," the old man said and cackled.

"Are you coming in for a coffee?" he said.

"No. I'm on a case."

"About bloody time too," he said. "I was getting fed up with you rattling around up there all day. And if I hear that Benny Goodman album one more time, I'll be up to strangle you."

"Sorry Tom. It's the one I always turn to when I'm bored. But now I've got a client, it'll be Gene Krupa, Jelly Roll Morton, maybe a wee bit of Coltrane."

"Not Coltrane," Tom said, "Please. As long as it's something with a tune I don't really mind. Besides, the punters think it adds to the ambience."

He laughed loudly; he laughed louder and more often than anyone I'd ever met.

"How about you?" I asked. "Are you busy this morning?"

"A minibus from Argentina this morning, and three army colonels from Singapore this afternoon," he said. "Not busy, but lucrative."

He laughed again, the bass booming in the confines of the hallway.

'The History of Golf' museum was his retirement project. It wasn't really a museum, but it did contain plenty of history. It was mainly a display of all the items he had gathered in a lifetime's obsession with the game and its memorabilia, but Tom brought something that the bigger museums lacked ... Tom had the stories, and the experience of living and working first-hand with the biggest names in golf.

Tom worked as green-keeper on the Old Course for most of his working life until a bad back forced him to retire five years ago. But he just couldn't keep away, and once he got permission for the small museum there was no stopping him. Soon he had a steady trail of the more knowledgeable tourists beating a path to his door.

Over tea, biscuits and the occasional wee whisky, Tom told his stories; of the day Jack Nicklaus hit a hole in one on the Eighteenth, the day Arnold Palmer lost a match but won the hearts of a nation. There were older tales, of Tom Morris, of the first Open championship, and further back, to the beginning of the game itself.

He came out to the front door with me and took a deep breath.

"Fog later," he said, "Then a clear night. Mark my words."

"How do you do that?"

"Years of practice," he said. "And the BBC Weather forecast."

He suddenly looked serious.

"I'm not sure about your new client," he said. "There's something not right about her.

"Come on Tom. You're no judge of character. Remember the vicar you told me was 'nothing but trouble'?"

Tom was about to reply, but I wasn't going to let him off that easily.

"And remember that nice boy two years ago...the one you sent up with your personal reference? The one that pulled a knife on me?"

He looked sheepish.

"I'm serious John. I have a bad feeling about her. Don't take the job."

"Too late. But look on the bright side...I'll have enough money to pay the rent for months to come."

"Does that mean you'll be settling your bill?"

"Not so fast. Maybe I can interest you in barter? I could set you up with a spreadsheet?"

"And what would I need one of them for?"

"To keep track of your business, your taxes, stuff like that."

"The taxman owes me one hundred and three pounds. I owe the VAT man two grand; my turnover went up three point five per cent last year and I've made sixty pounds so far this morning. And you still owe me two hundred forty pounds. As I said... what would I need a spreadsheet for?"

"Maybe you could count the number of folk that come into the museum?

"There's been six hundred and twelve this year. And that doesn't include repeat visits. See John. I notice things. And I'm telling you...there's something about that woman."

I didn't take old Tom seriously. Like I said, he'd been wrong before. But even bad guessers get one right at some time.

CHAPTER

Four

MY FIRST STOP in town was to the corner shop for a pack of Camels.

Mrs Baxter was in her usual place. Apart from the occasional funeral, I don't think she'd left the place in more than forty years. She didn't like me...I think she thought I was somehow 'disreputable'.

As I stood in the queue, I watched her work. She knew all his locals by sight if not name and would have their 'orders' made up in advance. I knew she remembered them from what they bought every day. The boy at the front was 'A Daily Star and twenty Benson and Hedges'. The woman in front of me was 'A pint of milk, four bread rolls and a packet of M&Ms', and the little old man in front of her got a brown bag which she told me contained a Hustler and a Penthouse.

She raised an eyebrow as I passed her a fifty and checked it against the light. I tried not to be offended as she counted my change out, slowly.

"I come in here every day you know?" I said.

"We can't be too careful," she said, and gave the fifty another long look.

I held the pair of twenties she'd given me up to the light, taking my time.

She was affronted.

"I would never give you a fake note," she said.

"You can't be too careful," I replied, and left her spluttering behind the counter.

Once outside I ripped open the pack, fired up the Zippo and stood in the doorway sucking in tobacco, just savouring the taste of my favourite brand for the first time in a fortnight. Then I hit the streets of St Andrews.

I love this town, with its mixture of the ancient and modern, the hotchpotch of diverse interactions as the tourists collide with the locals while trying to avoid the academics. Golf brings the money, the University brings the culture, and the locals keep the wheels of sport and academe running smoothly. And all of this in a small town perched on a promontory on the edge of the North Sea, tucked away from both the industrial decay of Scotland's central Belt and the awesome sweeping beauty of the Highlands.

It was spring, so the tourist numbers were still relatively manageable, and you could walk in the streets without banging into people who stopped suddenly to marvel at the latest must-see view. As I got to the main town centre the traffic got heavier, but no more than in any other small town on a Monday morning. The High Street was busy as always, but it was mainly local traffic, old ladies and the few students active enough to be up early after the weekend.

The supermarket was already doing good business, and the money burned a hole in my pocket as I thought of salmon steaks and tiger prawns, sirloin and pepper sauce, roast lamb and just about anything except the tinned mackerel that had been my recent staple diet.

The usual smattering of golfers milled around the specialist shops, eyeing up too-expensive clothing with R&A badges sewn on, and clubs that cost more than I currently had in my pocket.

Today's batch of eager shoppers seemed to be mainly oriental. I remember hearing in a bar once that a coach-load of Japanese golfers could feed a shopkeeper's family for a year if they were in the right mood.

A man stood outside a shop swinging a club with the head the size of a small football while little old ladies dodged skillfully around his swing. In any other place the police would have been after him for brandishing a dangerous implement but here nobody batted an eyelid.

And everywhere knots of local pensioners stood, passing on gossip, at all available corners. A tall Texan wouldn't stay lost in a town this small for long...not unless he didn't want to be found. And even then, I knew some places worth hiding in, places where a Texan with a penchant for poker might get himself a game.

I cut through an alley, a short cut only known to locals, and came out in North Street. There was a minor traffic accident on the far side of the road. It looked like a student had backed his Jeep into a local man's mini. But there were no harsh words being spoken. The student had his chequebook out. Money makes the world go round they say.

In St Andrews it goes round fast.

OLD GEORGE LET me in to the Halt Bar when I gave the Indian sign on the window.

I'd been coming here since I was not long out of school, some twenty years before. The décor hadn't changed much; the urinals still smelt of stale beer and piss, the carpet still needed a clean, and old George still had a cigarette dangling from his lower lip.

A long mahogany bar ran the length of the far side of the room, high stools spaced along its length. Between me and it sat an array of tables of different shapes, sizes and ages, some formica tops, some mock burnished copper, some scratched and stained wood. The chairs stacked on the tables were the same mishmash, plastic, pine and padded leather. Along the three walls ran a leather bench, ticking escaping in places, other rips badly patched with black tape. The wallpaper had at one time been floral flock but was now stained yellow with nicotine and the windows, over a hundred years old and inlayed with adverts for long defunct breweries, hadn't been cleaned in living memory.

As you can imagine, the pub doesn't get much tourist traffic; it is tucked away in an alley, and tourists are seduced by the bigger, more modern bars on North Street itself. That is one of the reasons they stay away. The sign in the window might also have something to do with it. George put it up himself years ago, and it is fading now, but its message is clear.

"This is a bar. That means we sell alcohol. We may also sometimes sell you a packet of crisps or a mutton pie and beans, but we do not guarantee to have any food on the premises. If you want food, I suggest you go to a restaurant. But if it's booze you're after, come on in, we've got plenty."

Some days passed without a single non-familiar face entering the bar. George had got adept at studying the few tourists who stood outside and read the note. He could always tell when they'd turn away, or when they'd come in. It was a knack he'd learned over the twenty-five years he'd stood in the same spot.

Back when I'd first met him, he'd been one of the few publicans who would never allow anyone under age anywhere near his bar. I'd tried to sneak under his radar several times, but he was too wily, and I always ended up getting shown the door, usually with a well aimed boot in my backside. Even then we teenagers knew that the Halt was where the dark side of the town did its business, a place away from learning or golf where real life happened. And George was at the hub of it all, the man who knew what was what.

Grey hairs showed at his temples now, and he carried a bit of extra bulk around the waist, but he still knew more about what went on in town than anybody else. He made a nice sideline in tipping off both cops and criminals, and he ran the biggest card game for miles around in the quiet room in the back.

"John. Good to see you. The usual?"

Normal opening hours didn't apply to George; something to do with the favours he put the way of the local police.

"No. Better not," I replied sadly. "I'm working."

"A word not often used in your vocabulary," he said, laughing.

"Not recently anyway."

The ruin of last nights drinking still covered the bar. A young girl made a slow job of clearing it up.

"Get a move on lassie," George shouted.

"Students," he said to me, "Intelligent maybe, but they're as lazy as you are."

"I'll have you know I tidied up just last year," I said.

"That would be round about the time of your last bath then?"

"Oh no, it was much closer than that."

He smiled.

"So where have you been hiding? The lads have had nobody to fleece for a couple of months."

"I've been out of funds," I said, "But I'm not here to play, I'm on a case. I'm looking for a poker player. Do you have a game on?"

"Not today, and nothing booked this week. We had a big game in the back room over the weekend...a thirty-six-hour stretch. Some of the lads got cleaned out, and it'll be a while before they're back."

"I'm after a Yank, a Texan."

I described my quarry the same way his sister had.

"Aye, I've seen him," George said. "He was here for most of the session. He managed to wind up Davy Clark and Willie Brown. You know what the Texans can be like, claiming ancestry over half the country and bragging about how big the ranch is? He didn't make any pals. Not even when he offered to pay for their round if they went round the auld course with him. He left when the game ended, about eleven yesterday morning. He said there was a golf course waiting for him."

George took a drag on his cigarette and let the ash fall to the carpet where he brushed it in with his foot.

"What's up anyway? Why are you after him?"

"His sister thinks he's in trouble. She's paying me to find out how much."

"Well, he looked like the kind that trouble follows. And he took a lot of money off the lads; off Jim Crawford in particular."

"How much money are we talking about?"

"I'm not sure, but there was ten grand on the table at one time, and the Yank had away with most of it."

I whistled. Jim Crawford didn't like to lose, and ten grand might just be enough to work that dislike up into a temper. I'd seen Crawford in a temper, and it wasn't pretty.

"How did the big man take it?"

"Oh, he was fine at the time, but after the Yank left, he drank a lot of whisky and it started to work on him. You know what he's like with a drink in him…we had a job keeping him quiet."

"And when was this?"

"Late yesterday afternoon. I had to stop his drink after a while, and he wasn't best pleased when he left."

"What time was this?"

"It must have been about half six. He was cursing and swearing about getting even. I hope he didn't get up to anything stupid."

"Jim Crawford? Stupid? I wish I had a pound for every time I've heard those words in the same sentence," I said.

"Aye, so do I…Maybe then you'd settle your bar tab."

"That'll be any day now, George. I promise, any day now."

I passed him a cigarette, which he placed behind his ear.

"You said he wound up Willie and Davie. Were they playing?"

"Aye, there was the two of them, Crawford, the Yank and

Sandy Thomas. It was Crawford that lost most of the money though."

A thought struck me just as I was leaving, and I turned back.

"Is the Yank a drinker?

"Oh aye, he's a Texan. Have you ever known them to be tee-total? He drank me out of bottles of Bud…I'm just waiting for a delivery to stock up in case he comes back."

CHAPTER
Five

WEAK SUNLIGHT CAUSED me to squint on leaving the bar. I was sorely tempted to turn straight round and take up George's offer of a beer, but five hundred a day buys at least some legwork.

I decided against bearding Jim Crawford straight away. Approaching the big man in a temper was not something to be undertaken lightly, and I needed more ammo before I went accusing him of anything.

I knew where to find Davy Clark and Willie Brown...the same place they were every morning, rain or shine; taking their 'constitutional' on the beach before the pub opened. I checked my watch ... ten-thirty. They'd be up at the far end of the point, near the nature reserve, arguing about the relative merits of Palmer and Nicklaus, Woods or Singh. I had half an hour before they'd be back in town, plenty of time to shake another branch of the contacts tree. I headed for the newspaper office.

I had a 'mole' in the Fife Free Press; circulation thirty thousand and falling. Dave Turner and I met years ago when we were stupid enough to take on Willie and Davy at three card brag. We lost fifty quid, but each gained a friend, so I guess we were up on the deal.

Climbing the steps to the office reminded me just how long I'd been coming here; the walls were covered in headlines from the paper. In amongst the local traffic stories and plans for the reinstatement of the railway line were some that caught my eye, like a newsreel of my last ten years; Woods wins the Open, William comes to town, Palmer's last dance, Dylan's degree of success. All fine headlines, but all repeated in a thousand other papers across the world. Dave thought of himself as a reporter, and what he wanted was a big story, all to himself. In reality all he reported on were local fetes and flower shows. The nearest he came to a scoop was when a prince of the realm was spotted 'incognito' after hours in one of the local pubs...and the royal security guards soon made sure the story never got anywhere near the papers... not even the local ones. Dave had been on the FFP news desk for ten years, and his frustration was starting to show. Recently he'd been spending more time in the town bars than at the paper, and local chins were starting to wag. If he didn't watch himself his reputation would be nearly as bad as mine.

His desk dominated the top of the stairs, and Dave sat, crouched, peering at something on his computer. He had his head down, and his bald spot had doubled since I'd last noticed it. His chin hadn't seen a razor in three days, and his tie told the story of his last two breakfasts. At least his shirt was almost clean, but it hadn't seen an iron for a while. He looked tired, older than usual; the bags under his eyes would have carried my week's shopping.

He checked his watch when he saw me.

"You're early," he said. "They don't open for a bit yet."

I'd never paid Dave for info...not directly. But it had cost me a small fortune in beer over the years.

"I've not got time for a beer this morning," I said, "I'm working."

His eyebrow headed up in feigned astonishment.

"Working? Before noon? Somebody text Reuters."

He put a pen in his shirt pocket, point downwards, and it immediately started sending out a blot of ink in the corner. Dave either didn't notice or didn't care…I suspected the latter.

"I need some info," I said.

"The going rate is two beers for each fact at this time in the morning. How many do you need?" he said.

"I'm after a big Texan."

"Aren't we all dear," he replied calmly. "Let me guess? Six feet three and looks like Boris Karloff on a diet? And loud with it?"

"That sounds like my man. I take it you've seen him?"

"He was in here on Friday morning. He made one of our juniors cry with all his shouting and bawling. I would have thrown him out, but he had a scary big knife. He kept asking to see our records. He was *most* put out when I told him we only went back fifteen years."

"He was after something older?" I asked.

"Much older. He was looking to go back a couple of hundred years and more. I sent him over to the Uni' library. Andrew Foulkes is the man to point him in the right direction."

"Foulkes? The fellow with the cape and the walking stick?"

"That's the man. He's the chief archivist, and what he doesn't know about the town's history doesn't need telling. I've used him before when I needed some back info for a story. He's steady and reliable. I sent the Yank over there round about eleven on Friday. Why, what do you need him for?"

"He's gone missing."

"Missing?"

"Aye, missing. As in, not present, cannot be found, nowhere to be seen? *Comprendez*? His sister went to the cops, but you know what they're like, so she came to me. I'm on a new case."

Dave perked up at the first sniff of a story.

"Something juicy, I hope? If there's a scandal involved, I can trade you back some of the beer you owe me."

"Down boy…at the moment it's just a missing brother gig."

"But maybe he's done more than just make a lassie cry." Dave said. "I saw him, remember. He was a big scary fellow."

"Don't start writing any headlines yet," I said. "He'll be off spending his ill-gotten gains. He took a load of money off Jim Crawford in the Halt. Rumour is it could be anything up to ten grand.

Dave whistled.

"The big man won't like that much."

"No. We both know that. Seemingly it was a thirty-six-hour session, so if I've any luck at all I'll find my man sleeping it off somewhere and magic him away out of Crawford's way before any damage is done."

"I wish I was ... sleeping that is," Dave said, running a hand through his thinning hair.

"Rough night?"

"No, rough morning... the night was fine," he said with a small smile. "I went out in the afternoon for a quiet pint and ended up in Anstruther at midnight."

"How did you get there?"

He shrugged.

"No idea. I must have killed those brain cells off."

"You'll not want any more beer just now then?" I said, although I knew already what the answer was. Dave had hollow legs when it came to ale. He confirmed my suspicions.

"Oh, I'm sure I could manage one or two. Hair of the dog and all that happy shit..."

I checked my watch. It was ten till eleven.

"Listen, if you do me a favour I'll stand you a round. I've got to see Willie Brown and Davy Clark. They'll be thirsty, so I'll be in the Halt over lunch. Could you phone the Uni' for me and ask Foulkes if the big Yank turned up? Find out what they talked about and there'll be an extra beer for you."

"Free beer. How can I refuse? How long do you want with the 'Chuckle Brothers'?"

"Give me until twelve. It'll take them that long to get to the point."

I GOT HIJACKED in the street outside the newspaper office.

"Have ye found my cat yet son?"

My heart sank.

A very small old lady stood behind me. She wore all black, her skirt so long that it almost trailed on the pavement. The clothes were heavy, like thick velvet, and when she crossed a patch of sunlight coming through between the shops, she seemed no more than an empty, black space.

As she got closer, I saw a light, a vitality, in her eyes, and although wrinkles creased her face and neck, she still showed plenty of signs of having been a beauty in her younger days. Her eyes were bright blue and piercing but she had been crying recently... the skin under her eyes looked dark and puffy, and there were red rims showing. She stood no more than four foot eleven tall in her flat black shoes.

"I've got a tenner if it'll help?"

She held out her hand and offered me a note.

I grabbed it and pushed it back.

"I don't need any money Mrs Malcolm," I said. "I only get paid if I find your cat for you."

Her hand felt smooth and cool and slid in my palm as if it had been slightly greased. A strong smell rose from her clothes... mothballs and lavender. I guessed the black velvet wasn't her usual daytime apparel.

"Thanks son."

I turned to go, but she grabbed my arm and pulled me back.

"You widnae happen tae have a cigarette on you?"

"I didn't know you smoked."

"I've started again recently."

She took a cigarette as if it was a pill that might save her life.

"My man didnae like me smoking, I've hardly touched the baccy in near on forty years, but I used to love a smoke. Now he's passed on I might start up again."

She wasted no time getting back in practice. I had barely lit her up before she was sucking away like an industrial strength vacuum cleaner. Only occasional wisps of smoke appeared when she breathed out... the rest she somehow, magically, seemed to soak up.

"Cancer. That's what took Tommy. Seventy years of God-fearing abstemious living... and look what it got him. Two months ago, he found a lump under his left arm... just a wee thing, not any bigger than a pea. He wisnae even going to tell the doctor, but when I saw it, I knew what it was all right. The doctor hummed and hawed and sent him for tests. They opened him up in the hospital... and shut him straight away again. It was downhill all the way from then."

She looked up at me, heavy tears filling the bottom half of her eyes.

"In the end, the drugs did for him, and he just slipped away... a wee smile on his face as if he'd heard some private joke. The nurses let me spend an hour with him after he passed on, then I went to phone the boy. He was living in a bar. I remember the time..."

This was a Scotswoman of-a-certain-age in full flow. Experience told me it could take a while. Any sentences that started with those four words had to be nipped in the bud quickly before they spread.

"Mrs. Malcolm...I'm sorry. I've got to be getting on..."

She waved her cigarette at me. A small snowfall of ash spread across the black velvet.

"Bugger," she said.

It was as shocking as a fart in a church.

"I'll never get that out. And I had it cleaned specially. Twenty-five pounds the cleaner took... I would have washed it in the bath if I'd known it would cost that much. When I was a lassie…"

"Mrs. Malcolm….I've really got to be going."

I turned away. I looked back, and she still stood there. She suddenly looked lost and lonely. I made a mental note to myself to find some time to look for her cat.

CHAPTER
Six

I WALKED QUICKLY down to the car park at the west end of the beach. The usual batches of tourists were getting their pictures taken by the Eighteenth green in front of the old clubhouse. I knew at least three local photographers who made enough money March through October to afford to spend the winter in sunnier climes, just taking pictures of thousands of inane grins in these few square yards of ground. And of course, the club got its cut…the club always got its cut.

A clutch of expensively dressed businessmen putted on the practice green, serious and intent while local caddies stood around, cigarettes hanging from lower lips, warming up their fake congratulations in a hope of bigger tips. Buses disgorged tourists outside the Golf Museum and a queue snaked away from its doors down towards the sands.

If I'd had time, I'd have directed some of them round the corner to old Tom's little museum instead. He didn't have the big flashy exhibits, but he told better stories and knew more history than the drones showing you round the official building. Plus, another favour like that would do me no harm in my quest to save the flat. I promised myself I'd hijack the queue if I got a chance later and headed down to the sea wall.

The wind blew the flags out to horizontal above the club-house, and loose sand scudded along the beach. The sea had receded with the tide, exposing the wide flat sands. At the far end of the beach sports kites filled the air, swooping and soaring like giant gulls as students bunking off lectures fought each other in the sky. Down on the sands closer to town people walked dogs, students jogged, and a single windsurfer practiced falling into the water.

Far out to sea a fog bank hung offshore, waiting for the tide to turn. I knew it wouldn't be too long before the town was engulfed in candy-floss grey; Old Tom was rarely wrong, and fog was never far away at this time of year.

I'd timed it just right. Willie and Davy were walking off the beach. Willie's hands waved animatedly as he explained something. The only movement from Davy was the occasional nod of the head.

Willie Brown was the older, and more garrulous, of the two. Willie stood straight, his former military career showing with every rigid stride. In the past year or so he'd developed a slight stoop, but he fought against it. He wore a heavy tweed suit, black shoes shined to a mirror sheen, and was never without a tie, even on the hottest summer days. He had an anecdote for every occasion and never used one word where two would do. He'd been old as long as I'd known him, but his blue eyes were still clear and piercing, and little got past him.

In contrast Davy Clark was almost taciturn. He shuffled beside Willie, a small, rotund, man, with the air of a bear snuffling after food. He always looked rumpled, even on the rare occasions he had to wear a suit and favoured an old brown overcoat that was at least as old as me, and just about in as good a condition. He spoke only when spoken to, and his soft brown eyes looked casual, but he had a mind like a steel trap. I'd been trying to beat him at chess for fifteen years now, and I hadn't yet won.

They did this walk every day, a three-mile round trip, even though they were both of them well over seventy years old. I once asked them when they had started, but they couldn't remember, apart from saying that it used to be only at weekends until they were both retired. I joined them sometimes, not talking much, just listening, soaking up the anecdotes and banter they shared so casually together. The only time their arguments got heated was when talked turned to golf, and even then, they both knew that neither was ever going to lose their temper over something that was only a game.

I sat on the sea wall, lit up a Camel, and waited for them. They had almost walked past me when I spoke.

"Hello gents."

Willie stopped suddenly, as if he'd walked into something. He looked towards me, squinting in the sun.

"John Royle?" He turned to the other man, "Look Davy. It's Tom Royle's boy."

"I can see that," Davy replied. "I'm going deaf, not blind. Morning, John. It's a fine day."

"It is that Mr Clark."

Willie and Davy had been 'Mr Brown' and 'Mr Clark' to me since I was a boy. They'd been drinking partners of my father and had been around in my life for as long as I could remember. My first memory of them was of them telling my father off for leaving me standing outside the Halt while he got drunk inside. Many a time I'd stayed with Willie and his wife in the evening while my mother worked her guts out to make enough money for Dad to drink and piss away. Both Willie and Davy were like uncles to me…no, more than that…they were the father I should have had if the world had been perfect.

I had fallen into daydreaming again, a bad habit I always picked up during prolonged periods without a case.

"You'll get piles sitting on that cold wall," Davy said.

"Are you just going to sit there, or are you after something?" Willie Brown added.

"I thought I might buy you a drink," I said. "Can I not buy a couple of pals a beer now and then?"

"Ah, so you're after something," Davy Clark replied.

I knew they could see right through me. I never had been able to lie to either of them.

"I only want some gen about your wee game this weekend."

Davy Clark put his finger to his lips.

"Shhh. The wife disnae know about that, and if one woman in the town hears, the rest'll know by tomorrow. We'll talk in the pub."

I didn't bother asking which pub. The men were George's most regular customers in the Halt...every day, same seats, different arguments.

They restarted their conversation as if I'd never been there. They were on golf again today, and I had little to contribute to that one. I left them to it as the three of us strolled at old-man's-pace back to the bar. They were in no hurry. They knew that they were in their twilight, and they took every day as if it would be their last. We stopped at the edge of the car park to watch the cormorants on the rocks, wings spread to catch the sun.

"Hogan would have slaughtered any of the nancy-boys today if he'd had the equipment," Willie was saying.

Davy thought about it for a while. "No, you're wrong there. Woods has got what it takes up here," he said, tapping his forehead. "And you're forgetting that courses have changed over the years."

Willie wasn't going to let that go.

"You're ignoring Hogan's strength...he'd be able to...."

I tuned them out and spent some quality time thinking how I was going to spend the five hundred. My current debts totaled some eight hundred and forty pounds, but that wasn't what I was thinking of. I was considering buying that 1940's coffee machine I'd seen in the antique shop on South Street. It was a snip at £199.99, and I'd still have plenty of change left over.

When we got to the Sea Life Centre we stopped again. Davy

suffered a heart attack a couple of years ago, and since then needed a rest at this point before tackling the small but steep incline up past the war memorial.

"I've always meant to ask you," I said as we inched up the hill, "Why don't you go round past the clubhouse and up Golf Street? There's hardly a hill at all there."

Willie looked at me as if I was mad.

"We *always* go this way. It's the way our walk goes. Anything else wouldn't be right."

Davy nodded. It was one of the few things they were in complete agreement on.

As we passed through the town centre and into North Street Willie and Davy were still at it.

"Anyway, Palmer would have taken them both in his prime," Willie said.

Davy shook his head," No, Palmer wasn't that good. Too inconsistent. Let me tell you…"

I tuned them out again. Golf never interested me. When my contemporaries were learning the game and getting ready to seal deals in clubhouses across the country I was smoking behind the caddie's shed and trying to get my hand up the skirt of any local girl who'd let me. Over the years since I'd tried my hand at swinging a club, but I never managed to hit the ball, and flailing at air didn't feel like a whole lot of fun. Then I discovered beer and public houses, and the lure of club and ball passed me by completely. Besides, golf wasn't the only game in this town, not by a long way.

We got to the Halt as George was officially opening up. Willie and Davy stood aside to let me go first. Protocol had to be observed. I was buying.

The girl had finished her cleaning up and was now standing at the far end, staring vacantly into space, chewing gum like a cow at the cud. George went back and stood at the near side of the bar, chewing at the end of his cigarette.

Willie looked at the girl, then back at George.

"I don't fancy yours much," he said to Davy.

"At least mine doesn't look like a concrete mixer in action," Davy replied.

The girl heard him, and her mouth snapped shut. She threw Davy a glare that would have killed if it could.

Davy gave her a small wave.

"Don't worry hen," he said, "I hope it gets better soon."

The girl's glare turned to bemusement, and Davy was away across the bar before she could think of a rejoinder.

Willie and Davy headed straight to their seat in the corner. I motioned to George, a circular movement with my finger pointed down, and headed over to join the old men. Three beers arrived a few minutes later, but the old men didn't notice. The argument was coming to its usual conclusion.

"Away ye go you daft auld bugger," Willie Brown said. "You wouldn't know a decent golfer if you saw one."

"Naw," Davy Clark said, "I suppose I've been too busy shagging your wife to be paying attention for all those years. That must be why I'm going deaf... it's all that screaming she's been doing in my ears."

They lifted their beers, said "Cheers", and another argument was over. If I hadn't known that Willie's wife died ten years ago, and that Davy held the older man up at the funeral, I might have expected Willie to be offended. But it was a running joke between them, and one that caused them great amusement when it was overheard by someone not in on it.

We sipped our beers in silence for a bit. Willie raised his head first.

"Did you hear? Old Mr Bryant passed away...in the middle of Coronation Street. He had a good innings though. Ninety-three he was. When I was younger hardly any man lived beyond sixty-five. Apart from auld Jock Weir...they say he was a hundred and six. He died back in '41, so he was born before Victoria came to the throne. Imagine the changes that man must have seen in his life. Mind you, I haven't done so bad myself. I remember when..."

It was time for me to get my questions in, and I'd have to be fast, for I recognised the opening. Another circular argument, probably about when television came to St Andrews, would be along any minute.

"I need to ask you about the Yank and your wee game over the weekend," I said, then sat back and let them go at it. I knew I'd get my info somewhere in the ensuing conversation, and I'd probably be entertained in the meantime.

Willie started.

"It was all George's fault," he said. "We were in here on Friday morning when he asked if we fancied a game that night."

Davy's first interruption came as quickly as I'd expected.

"No. It was Sandy Thomas that asked us to play, not George,"

"You're wrong there, and not for the first time." Willie said. "Sandy didn't come in till dinner hour, and I'd already been to the bank to get stoked up with cash in advance by then."

Davy quietly conceded defeat on that one, but I knew that wouldn't last long.

"Sandy hung about for a wee while then left. He had a golf match booked ... the Yank and three others."

"Two others," Davy said.

"I'm sure he said three," Willie replied.

"No. He said there were three gents playing."

Willie thought about that then nodded, conceding the point. It was one-all, but the game was far from over.

"I went home in the afternoon and got spruced up..."

"Spruced up?" Davy said laughing. "Is that what you call a change of shirt and a clean pair of underpants? You need to get that incontinence seen to ... either that or let me sit down wind."

"Just let me tell the story," Willie said, "And we can discuss your hygiene habits later. We'll tell John here about your collection of nasal pickings."

"Those were capers," Davy said, laughing.

"So you say," Willie said, trying to keep a straight face himself. "But they looked like bogeys to me."

"You might be right after all," Davy said, "They're certainly salty enough."

I took a long sup of beer to avoid laughing. Once I started, I might not be able to stop.

"Sandy brought the Yank in on Friday afternoon after their round," Willie said. "They got here at five o'clock."

"Quarter-to," Davy said. "He bought a round while old Mike McMaster was still here, and you know that Mike leaves at five-to on the dot."

Willie nodded again. Davy was in the lead.

"He was a big spender, your Texan," Davy said. "He was buying double malts like they were going out of fashion."

"That's right," Willie replied. "And he bought Sandy plenty. But that was only after he knew that Sandy would be playing poker that night. Not much got past the big man. Davy and I spotted that early. We went through into the back room with them at half-nine."

"No," Davy interrupted, "It was half ten."

"It was half nine," Willie said, "The news had just finished."

"Aye, but the news starts at ten these days, you senile old bugger."

Willie was a couple of points behind, and he wasn't very happy about it. He was getting tetchy.

"Listen, am I telling this story or you?"

"No, you started. Away you go." Davy said.

"So we went through to the back room," Willie continued, "Me, Davy, Crawford, the Yank and Sandy Thomas."

"No," Dave interrupted. "Sandy came in a wee bit later. He was finishing off a game of pool."

Willie thought about it while moving his false teeth around behind his lips.

"Aye, you're right for once in your life," he said begrudgingly. "So anyway, we went through to the table. George had it all set up just right. Crawford had first deal. I only got eight high, and I folded early, but Crawford won the first hand, about fifteen pounds I think…"

"Seventeen fifty," Davy said.

"Nope. It was definitely fifteen. Do you want me to go through the whole hand?"

Davy sat back in his chair. He was far enough ahead to feel smug.

And away we went again.

Over the next hour I discovered that it had been a legendary session, and that the Yank had taken close to eight grand off Jim Crawford. I also discovered many other things, including that Willie's grandfather had fought in the Zulu wars, that Hank-the-Yank said he came from a family once rich but fallen on relatively hard times, that Davy's niece was now a lawyer in London, that seemingly Raith Rovers had been crap on Wednesday night and that Jim Crawford thought the Yank had been cheating.

"Did either of you spot anything?" I asked. They'd both been poker players for longer than I'd been alive, and they could spot a potential shark before anybody else even knew there was blood in the water.

"No," Davy said.

"It looked kosher to me," Willie added, "But then again, I didn't lose eight grand."

"Besides, Jim didn't say anything at the time," Davy said.

"That's right," said Willie, "It was only later, when the whisky started talking for him, and he got to thinking how he was going to explain it to that blonde he's shacking up with this year."

I hadn't met the new Mrs Crawford, but I'd heard she fitted the model of the previous three; much younger than the big man, small, pneumatic, blonde and needing another brain cell to make up a pair. It was said in the town that Jim had to travel to find a wife because he was after somebody less intelligent than he was, and he had to go a long way to find them.

I sat back and lit up a cigarette. It was beginning to look like Jim Crawford was my best hope of finding my man.

"So, when did it all wrap up?" I asked.

"About eleven yesterday morning." Willie said.

"Thirty hours plus," Davy added, shaking his head." Not quite a record."

"No," Willie said. "That was in 1981, when we avoided the Royal Wedding? We had that busload of Germans in the back room. Remember the big fellow? The one with the belly and the bad teeth? Man, he was just about the worst poker player you ever saw. I'll never forget that last hand when I had ace high and..."

I'd heard that story before and interrupted before we got in too deep. It was a good story, but it took most of an hour in the telling with these two, and I just didn't have the luxury.

"And what time did the Yank leave?"

Willie looked at me as if I'd just slapped him. It was considered bad form for anybody apart from Davy to interrupt an anecdote. Then again, I was the one buying the beer, so he owed me something.

"The big man left straight away. He wasn't much of one for idle chit-chat."

"No," Davy agreed, "And we'd had enough of him going on about how much money his family were worth once upon a time."

"And what made it worse he claimed to be Scottish," Willie added. "I ask you; what kind of Scotsman would carry a name like Hank Courtney? He said he was away to play golf."

Davy looked as if he might contradict the other man, but he changed his mind and sipped at his beer. All of our glasses were getting empty by now, and the old lads weren't showing any signs of moving from their seats. I motioned to George for another round.

"Did he take much off you pair?"

"Nah," Willie said, "We saw him coming. It was obvious he knew what he was doing from the first hand, so we played it canny. I lost about a tenner...well worth it for thirty hours entertainment."

Davy nodded, "I was down about two hundred at one time and beginning to sweat, but I took some money off Crawford as well late on, and I came away slightly up."

"It was that last hand that did it," Willie said. "It had been back and forward all day on Saturday. The Yank was a bit up off Crawford, but only a couple of hundred. And it stayed that way for a long time. All night the Yank played it quiet, folding when we thought he might have a good hand. Then he seemed to wake up."

Davy took up the story.

"He was good, I'll give you that. He started to take money off Crawford, steadily, for a couple of hours, until he was a couple of grand up. And for Crawford, the red mist came down. He threw money into the pot, raising the stakes until they were sitting in front of more than eight grand."

"It was like something out of a film," Willie said, his eyes sparkling with the memory. "Smoke filled the air. There were empty bottles everywhere, and a big pile of cash on the table. Crawford sweated like a pig, but the Yank was cool as a cucumber. It came down to the last hand. Crawford showed two pair and thought he had it, but the Texan laid out a royal flush, calm as you like."

"I thought Crawford would go for him," Davy said, "But the Yank had made sure we'd all seen yon big knife he carried. He picked up the money and was off and away while we were still stunned by the amount he'd won."

"And what about Crawford? When did he leave?"

They both looked blank.

"No idea son," Willie said. "We stayed for a couple of pints then went to get some kip. We're no' as young as we used to be.

The big man was hitting the whisky hard by that time, but I don't know when he left. Ask George, he'll know."

I'd already had that info from George. My quarry's movements were beginning to fall into time slots, but I still had plenty of blanks to fill in.

DAVE TURNER ARRIVED JUST in time to save me from a long story about the night watchman, the student dressed as Jesus Christ and the sudden re-appearance of several hundred-weight of coal. I'd heard it before, and although the old chaps told the story well it was beginning to wear even thinner than the "German on Royal Wedding Day" one. I left the old men to it and met Dave at the bar.

"Did you talk to Foulkes?" I asked after I'd bought him a beer. He drained half of it in one smooth gulp before replying.

"Yep. He saw your man on Friday morning, but he couldn't help him. The Yank showed him a document, some old deed or other that the Yank is hoping will prove something about his past. Foulkes was dismissive... but then again, he's dismissive about everything. He pointed the Yank towards the parish offices in Cupar. He also informed me that the Cupar Office was shut on Friday, so the earliest your man could be there was today."

I had more than enough to do without tracking across Fife. I decided to concentrate on filling in the blanks over the weekend. Hadn't my client said that the man had been missing for a day already? Surely she would know if he was meaning to go to Cupar? I left Dave to his beer and went to the phone.

The receptionist at the Excelsior put me through at only the second attempt.

"Ms Courtney. It's John Royle."

She started talking before I'd even finished saying my name. She sounded anxious, jittery even.

"Have you found him? Have you? Please tell me that he's okay. I'm going frantic with worry. I even had room service deliver me a packet of cigarettes. I'm going to be blaming you for that... I was smoke free for ten years before today."

"Sorry, but you didn't exactly fight very hard. Listen, I need to check something with you. Was he meaning to be in Cupar today?"

"Cupar? No. We were scheduled for Kingbarns Church graveyard."

"Is that another wee lie Ms Courtney? I've been to some of those places I told you about. You should have told me about the card game. And the drinking."

She sighed heavily.

"Yes, I should have, but then you wouldn't have taken the case. You'd just think he was off on a bender"

"You're probably right. And he might still be. So, when <u>did</u> you last see him. Really. And no more lies."

"As I told you, yesterday morning. He came in from the game, happy and excited. He gave me a big bundle of money to look after for him. 'Things are looking up,' he said. He was going out, to meet somebody. That's all I know. I swear it."

She sounded like she might burst into tears.

"Was he going to play golf?"

"He might have been," she said. "He played on Friday afternoon, and he said he had something lined up for Sunday."

She was getting more distraught by the minute.

"Just keep yourself busy," I said, "And try not to worry. I'll call when I get anything."

She started to say something but was interrupted. I heard a distant knocking, somebody at her door.

"I have to go," she said, "Just find him. Please? He's all the family I've got."

CHAPTER
Seven

WHEN I GOT BACK to the bar Dave finished off his pint and looked expectantly at me. He waved the empty glass in my face.

"Was it worth a second?"

"Only if you can confirm where the Yank was on Friday afternoon."

"Strange you should ask that," he said with a smile. "He was out on the Old Course, with two guys I didn't know, Sandy Thomas was caddying for him. I walked past the Eighteenth as they were coming in, and I recognised him from earlier."

George piped in at that point.

"That's about right. The Yank came in here about five, and said he'd had a good round. He bought Sandy a few double malts, and that's when he found out about the game. Sandy was here as well on Friday night for the session."

Another bit of the jigsaw had fallen into place. And for once it looked like my client might have been telling me the truth.

I bought Dave that second pint. Auld Willie came over to ask George for the cribbage board.

"Do you want to join us, lads?" Willie said. "Davy's feeling flush after Saturday night. Do you want to help me take some of it off him?"

"I'm in," Dave said.

Willie looked him up and down.

"You look like you can count to fifteen, but can you manage all the way up to thirty-one?"

"Easy," Dave replied. "There'll be three pairs of hands holding the cards and my todger holding the table up."

"Must be an awfy wee table," George said.

I strategically made my excuses and left. For one thing, Davy hardly ever lost at crib, and for another, I knew that one more pint would be enough to keep me in the bar for a while and knock me off the case for the rest of the day. My clients deserved more. They didn't always get it, but this time my better judgement won...just.

I'd run out of time. There was no option left but to approach Crawford and find out what he knew.

IT WASN'T something I was looking forward to. Crawford and I had a history that went all the way back to our schooldays.

We had originally been in the same class all through primary school. Back then he'd been bigger than the rest of us, but he'd never been a bully. That started when we went to the High School, and he found some other guys as big as he was. The usual schoolyard gangs formed, and his was the biggest and the toughest. Soon he ran protection rackets, demanding money with menaces and beating up smaller, smarter kids just because he could.

My first run in with him happened when he picked on one of my friends. It proved to be an unequal fight, and unfortunately, I'd come upon it late. Joe already lay on the ground counting his teeth when I arrived, just in time to see Crawford swing his foot back for a kick. I jumped at him before thinking, and the next thing I knew he pinned me to the wall, slamming my head against the bricks. I blacked out while he pummelled me black and blue. That bought him a week's suspension, and me a mild concussion, three days in bed, and a further beating from my father for getting involved and 'affronting' him.

It was while I lay in bed with a sore head that I learned my first lesson about fighting. If you're taking on a bigger, stronger opponent, you'd better have some sneaky moves ... and it pays to hit him first. The next time I used a cricket bat. I sneaked up on him from behind and hit him as hard as I could. It almost wasn't hard enough, and I needed to hit him twice. Blood spurted, shockingly red in his blonde hair, and I couldn't lift the bat a third time. But I'd hit him hard enough with that second blow; this time it was him that ended up with the concussion and me with the suspension. Both of us were off school for weeks. When we got back, we kept away from each other for a while, but he had just too much rage in him to forgive and forget.

A month later it came down to an all-out fistfight in the school playground. I actually had a fit of guilt about almost breaking his head. I went up to him and offered him my hand.

"All square Jim?" I asked.

He took my hand, pulled me towards him, and head-butted me, mashing my nose into my face and bringing the warm coppery taste of blood in my mouth. I kneed him in the crotch, and he fell back. After that it was all flying fists and feet. It ended in blood, tears, a broken nose each, and suspensions for both of us. The janitor told me days later, when we were sharing a fag round the back of the Games building, that it was the best scrap he'd seen since Foreman vs Ali.

After that Crawford and I held an uneasy truce. We stayed out of each others way, made sure we moved in different circles. After we left school he spent a spell in jail for aggravated assault, and when he came out his temper had been brought under control. He'd started working in one of the local garages, and eventually became the owner. The only place we met was on the neutral ground of the Halt, and even then, we usually kept to separate ends of the bar apart from occasional bouts of name-calling when one or other of us had too much to drink. He still called me "Squinty" due to the fact I had a lazy eye at one point as a boy. Usually I just called him a "big shite".

But I still always saw that raised foot over Joe's bloody face every time I looked at him and that image filled my mind as I walked up Scotlandwell Road towards Crawford's house.

He might have been big, and not the brightest bulb in our class, but he was tenacious, and he worked harder than anyone else I knew. I held a grudging respect for how he'd managed to build up his garage business over the years, enough so that he could afford one of the select Victorian townhouses that lined this leafy avenue.

It hadn't all been clean money. I knew that he offered paint jobs and number plate changes, no questions asked, in one of his backstreet shops, and there were rumours in the town of small boats being unloaded off the West Sands late at night, with cargo intended for big city dealers. But he'd always been too streetwise to be caught, and he just kept on going up in the world. Now he'd made it all the way to the "posh" houses.

This far away from the town centre the money showed. The houses sat, big and solid, in large swathes of garden. The trees grew tall, mature and stately, and the drives all held ever bigger four-wheel drives. Each house made a big show of its burglar alarm, evidence that even here they were aware that not everybody was on the same side of the tracks as them. If they knew some of the things I knew about Jim Crawford they might not have been so willing to have him as a neighbour.

As I turned into the Crawford's drive, I thought it was a pity that his money hadn't bought more taste. The driveway to the front of the house had been lined in bright blue gravel around and between pink flagstones. Dotted here and there across a perfectly manicured lawn statues in the classical Grecian style lounged and posed; all women, all nude.

Just to the left of the gold-painted front door sat a bright red sports car with its hood down. It wasn't an MG or a Ferrari... no that would be too tasteful for Crawford. It was a modern Japanese version of what a sports car should be. Crawford had tried to tart it up by having the paint job redone with a sunburst finish on the bonnet, but all he'd done was make it look even cheaper. This must be the wife's car...Crawford always made a point of driving his gold "roller" when he was out and about.

To the back of the house, I could just see a long garden, dominated by a huge glass structure, a greenhouse or a conservatory, in mock-Victorian style. I couldn't make out the plants, but I knew they would be big, gaudy and too expensive...just like Jim Crawford himself.

The doorbell played Amazing Grace when I pressed it.

I stood there rehearsing what I would say in my head, but I still didn't know my lines when the door opened. It wouldn't have mattered. No amount of rehearsal would have prepared me. It wasn't Jim Crawford who answered. The door opened and revealed a small, pneumatic blonde.

I couldn't vouch for her number of brain cells...I was too busy looking elsewhere.

She wore a short red silk kimono slit at breast and thigh, leaving nothing to the imagination. Her skin looked smooth, her tan deep and luxurious. She moved slowly, sinuously, like a cat.

"It's just as well I'm not a priest," I said. "I'd be tempted to give up my vow of celibacy."

That went right over her head. I don't think she'd even started to register my presence. In her right hand she held a crystal glass with enough whisky in it to give you a hangover, and in her left, she had a thin cheroot that she puffed on with small, delicate movements of her mouth that made me look, then look away fast. Her eyes were glazed, and I guessed there was plenty more of that whisky already inside her.

"Mrs Crawford?"

She struggled to focus, and nearly managed it.

"You can call me Jill," she said, looking me up and down. She gave me a long, slow, smile. Suddenly I felt hot.

"I'm looking for Jim."

"Aren't we all sweet-heart," she said, and took a slug of whisky that would have had me gasping. "Aren't we all?"

"He's not in?"

"Obviously," she said. "He came in drunk last night and went out angry this morning. Nothing new there then."

She looked me up and down again.

"You can come in and wait if you'd like," she said. She puffed slowly on the cheroot and stood back, leaving a gap I might be able to squeeze through if we both breathed in. "He could be a while. Quite a long while."

I stood there, mouth flapping, no noise coming out.

"I like a man in a suit," she said. "And I don't like drinking alone."

I tried to keep my gaze on her eyes. I got hotter by the second, but I wasn't even remotely close to taking her up on the offer. I might be many things, but I'm not stupid. And messing with Crawford's wife would be a very bad idea.

"Sorry, I've got things to do."

"*Things* are exactly what I had in mind," she said. "I can think of many *things* we could do."

"So can I sweetheart," I thought, but didn't say. If I'd said it, I might have to act on it, and I wasn't sure my heart would take it.

"Tell him I'm after him. The name's Royle, John Royle. He knows where to find me."

She didn't even look disappointed. She knocked back another slug of whisky and her eyes started to look dead; dead, with nothing behind them but need. She looked me up and down and sneered. That was it. I was dismissed.

"Okay," she said, and shut the door in my face even before I'd turned away. I stood there for a long second, part of me wanting to knock on the door again, the other, bigger part, wanting to turn and run away.

I settled for walking down the driveway at what I thought was a dignified pace. Across the road net curtains twitched, and I waved cheerily at whoever was watching. That made me feel slightly better, but the image of the red silk kimono stayed with me all the way back into town.

CHAPTER
Eight

IT TURNED out that the kimono was to be the highlight of the afternoon; my only sighting of anything connected with the case.

I drew my second blank with Sandy.

I walked down to the caddy's hut by the Third green. The wind blew cold against the ears, and cries of <u>fore</u> rung out all over the course as visitors started to struggle. Far out to sea the fog bank had inched a bit closer, and white horses scudded over the sea.

The caddies' hut is where the workers of the course gather to moan about their lot in life and infuse their bodies with whisky and tobacco. If Sandy was free, that was where he'd be, telling stories and winding up the apprentices.

I couldn't immediately see him when I entered the hut, but that might have had something to do with the grey-blue fug that hung at head height in the small room.

"Has anybody seen Sandy Thomas?" I called out.

"Not since yesterday," one of them replied. "He was a wee bit the worse for wear. I think he'd had a heavy session on Saturday night."

"No, it wasn't the booze," I said. "He was up playing poker in the Halt."

"That's right. He said he'd won some money off a Yank," one of the green-keepers said. "And he was away to play the ponies."

That meant only one thing. He'd be sitting in a Dundee book-makers, far from anybody who might know him and far from the prying gaze of his wife, losing the money he'd earned over the weekend.

I wasn't going to find him today. Every couple of months Sandy felt the need of a blow out. He took a day or two off work and sat in smoky book-makers premises, always losing steadily, winning just enough times for him to always go back for more in the hope of the big score that was surely just around the corner. I understood the mindset; I'd watched my father for enough years, lost in a dream that was never going to come true. He got steadily bitter as the bookies got richer, taking him away a piece at a time until all that was left was rage and all that could assuage it was booze.

"Did any of you talk to the big Texan on Friday?" I asked.

Nobody replied for a couple of seconds. One of the other caddies finally spoke.

"Sorry John, I knew he was taking the Yank round. I saw them tee off. The two other guys playing carried their own bags."

"Did you know them?"

He shook his head, and even the offer of a twenty pound note couldn't sway him.

I DIDN'T FARE MUCH BETTER in my quest for a chat with Foulkes. I phoned his office from the call box outside the bus station.

"Can I speak to Mr Foulkes please?"

A prissy female voice answered.

"I'm afraid *Professor* Foulkes isn't in his office."

"Do you know where I can find him?"

"He is around the house somewhere," she said, "Or maybe in the garden."

"When will he be back?"

"I'm sure I don't know," she said.

"You *are* his secretary, aren't you?"

"I'm his personal assistant," she said haughtily.

"Well then, do some assisting. Please tell him I'll be right round to see him."

"I can't do that," she said. "He's got a very busy diary."

"That's all right," I said. "It's him I want to see, so his diary can be as busy as it likes."

That one went over her head.

"As I said. That's impossible I'm afraid. His next free slot is on Wednesday morning."

"You did say you were his <u>assistant,</u> didn't you?" I asked.

"Yes."

"And here was me thinking you were more like his mother. There was a tall Texan visited the Professor on Friday. There's twenty pounds in it for you if you'll tell me what they talked about."

"I'm afraid I couldn't divulge that kind of information...."

"What about if I made it fifty?"

"Not for a thousand pounds. I've been with the Professor for five years and his business is confidential."

"Five years, eh? I'd have thought by now you'd know where he was during the day."

"Are you trying to tell me my job sir?"

I dropped into Bogart again.

"No. Just having fun trying to guess what it is."

IT TURNED into four-for-four when I asked for Ms Courtney at the Excelsior reception.

The Excelsior lives on past glories from the days when the tweed and plus-four set filled it with upper class English accents during hunting shooting, fishing and golf weekends. Back in the twenties it had been the height of fashion, but now it exuded the faint whiff of decay. It is a rambling, Edwardian building, with thirty rooms and nearly as many corridors. The décor is all mock-Scottish—dark furniture, stuffed stag heads and heavy on the tartan for wallpaper and carpets. Staff are forced to wear tartan uniforms, a hideous red and yellow that clashes with everything else in the hotel, and the young receptionist looked embarrassed to be dressed in it.

"Could you ring 312 for me please," I said. "I need to speak to Ms Courtney."

"I'm afraid Ms Courtney isn't in sir," the girl said.

"You don't look afraid of anything," I said, but it didn't get a response.

"Did she say when she'd be back?"

I got a look that said, 'Do I look like her keeper?'

"No sir," she said, laying on the sarcasm on the 'sir'. "She went out earlier in the afternoon, and I couldn't possibly say when she'll be back."

"Was she alone?"

That got me the look again.

"I couldn't possibly say sir," she said. She was starting to get bored with me. I could tell by the relentless tapping of her pencil on the desk.

"And Mr Courtney? Is he around?"

She checked the key rack behind her.

"His key's here. He's out."

"You forgot the 'sir' that time." I said.

She stopped tapping the pencil and pointed it at me. I suspect she'd have preferred it to be a knife.

"Is there anything else ... sir?"

"No. You should talk to Professor Foulkes assistant over at

the Uni'," I said to her. "You could dumb up together ... it could be the beginning of a beautiful friendship."

That got me a blank stare. The number of people who understood the cultural references of a Bogart-obsessed PI was just getting smaller every year.

I wasn't quite finished with the Excelsior. With hotels there are better people to try than receptionists. The front desk people are trained in circumspection and client confidentiality. The other staff, who get paid a whole lot less, are much more amenable to approach, especially when you open your wallet.

First stop was the cleaning staff. I found them round the back in a small, dingy courtyard cluttered with food waste, bin bags and carpeted in cigarette butts. There were two of them there, a woman of around thirty and a boy, another student at my guess. Both of them jumped and ground their cigarettes underfoot when I pushed open the fire escape door and joined them in the courtyard.

"Christ," the woman said. "I thought you were the boss. I just threw away that fag, and it was just lit."

I passed my pack around and they both took one. Soon we were all three lit up. I was grateful for the smoke... it hid the rancid, greasy smell of old food.

"I'm after some info," I said.

The young fellow spoke first.

"I'm afraid we can't say anything," he began, but the woman shushed him.

"That depends," she said.

I knew exactly what it depended on. I took a twenty from my wallet.

"I need to know if there's been any sign of one of the guests. The big Texan."

"Which one?" she said, "The man or the woman?"

"The man."

Her eyes never left the money.

"Last time I saw him was Friday," she said, "But I did his room the last two mornings. His bed hadn't been slept in."

"Luggage?"

"Still there. His wash bag is still in the bathroom. I don't think he's done a runner."

"What about the woman?"

"Oh, she was here," she said, "She left just after breakfast, and came back around lunchtime. She might be in her room, but I wouldn't know."

I passed her the twenty.

"I'd like to get into the man's room." I said. "There's another twenty in it for you?"

She shook her head.

"Sorry son. My job's worth a lot more than that."

"How about you," I said to the boy, but he shook his head.

I left them another cigarette each and headed for the bar.

CHAPTER
Nine

I ORDERED A BEER.

"And one for yourself," I said to the barman. I didn't know him, which in itself was unusual. Time was when I knew every barman in town.

He was small, wiry, and immaculately dressed. His shirt was ironed smooth, his black bow tie was done just right and the crease in his trousers was razor sharp. Obviously, he had special dispensation ... he'd been excused the tartan waistcoat.

"Thank you, sir," he said. "I'll have a beer with you."

There was only one other patron in the bar, an elderly gentleman next to the fire, nursing a lager.

I passed a twenty to the barman. He was on his way to the till when I spoke.

"Keep the change," I said softly.

His right eyebrow rose.

"I need some info," I added.

"It's against hotel policy," he said.

"So is pocketing a twenty meant for the till," I said. "Let's see if we can start with that?"

He nodded, and the twenty disappeared.

He poured a beer for me and another for himself.

"What do you need to know?"

"You've seen the big Texan fellow?"

He nodded.

"He spent Thursday night, sitting where you are. Him and the lady. Good tippers too."

"When did you see him last?"

"Yesterday lunchtime. He came in, all excited."

"Did he say anything?"

"Something about fortune and glory," the barman said, "But I wasn't really paying attention. We had a coach load of Irish pensioners in, and I was on full time Guinness pouring duty. He left about twelve thirty."

"He went outside?"

"Yes. I saw him and his sister go out through reception."

"Did you see which way he went?"

He shook his head.

I couldn't get anything else out of him. A group of well-heeled women came in demanding chilled white wine and chocolate cake. I left him to it and sat quietly at the bar, smoking a cigarette and wondering where the Yank had got to.

All I knew was that he had won eight grand, gone back to the hotel, left the money with his sister and gone out again with her. She's gone for an ice-cream, and he said he was going for a beer. Nobody had seen him since.

I left my card with the barman, just in case.

"Private Investigator, eh?" he asked. "What's that like? Is there good money in it?"

"I'm not starving," I said, "But I couldn't afford to eat here every night either."

"You wouldn't want to," he said quietly, making sure he wouldn't be overheard. "The chef hates tourists. He pisses in the soup."

I SPENT the rest of the afternoon walking the town, asking if anyone had seen my Texan, and leaving messages with contacts in bars, restaurants and shops with instructions to contact me. That done, and with aching legs, I climbed the stairs to my office and slumped in the customer's armchair.

I smoked cigarettes and watched the fog roll up against the window. The sounds of the town deadened, and the Eighteenth green went quiet as the damp grey took hold and the townsfolk shut themselves in against the dampness.

I waited.

This too is part of the job. Prospective clients thought it was all about the legwork, facing down hardened criminals in a showdown, drinking cocktails with racy women. Actually, I'd come close to the last one today, but mostly the job was about waiting.

I had two approaches to it. Sometimes I did what I was doing; sit in the armchair and stare at the phone. Other times I'd head for the Halt and drink until coma took me. That appealed as well. In fact, over the past year, it had started to appeal more and more.

It had all been different, ten years back, when everything was fresh and interesting. It started, like most things in my life, with a conversation in the Halt.

I'd been unemployed and broke, spinning out a pint of Guinness that had already lasted the best part of an hour and would need to last an hour more if my budget wasn't going to be blown. Dave had just started work on the news desk, and Willie and Davy were telling us a story about a divorcee, a bishop and a professor of mathematics. Not the most promising threesome for a story, but the telling of it was so funny I almost missed the reference that would change my life.

"It was my cousin that caught them at it, all three of them" Willie said, "You know, the detective?"

"He's in the 'Polis?" Dave asked.

"No, a private detective," Willie said. "Like Jim Rockford."

"What? That fat bastard of a cousin? More like Frank Cannon," Davy replied.

There was more laughter at that, but I didn't hear it. The seed had been planted, and over the next week or two it took hold. I don't know if it would have been the same if I'd been employed at the time, but my non-working status meant I had plenty of time to consider...consider and dream. It wasn't a hard choice... not for a kid brought up on Spade and Marlowe, Hammer and Archer.

My granddad had been a ferocious reader of American crime novels, and when I managed to escape from the hell that was my own home I spent a lot of time at his feet, soaking up his cigarette smoke and reading his cast-offs, immersing myself in Mid-twentieth Century California. And on Sunday afternoons, some real treats, when the old movies were shown, sometimes back to back, on BBC2. It had been after one of those, a fourth or fifth viewing of "The Maltese Falcon", that he gave me his pocket watch.

"It's older than me," he said, "So treat it gentle. And don't let that bastard of a father of yours get at it."

I'd promised and been as good as my word. My father never knew I had it...if he'd found it, it would have gone on the booze or the horses. I found a variety of hiding places for it over the years and managed to keep it away from him.

The watch was my link to the good times, and I think that's what made me start to dream in the first place. After that it was just a question of making the decision.

I surprised myself with just how easy getting set up in business was, and selling my only other valuable possession, a five-year-old Ford Escort, made me enough money to get a lease on the flat for six months. George at the Halt put a couple of small muscle jobs my way to get me started and I was off and running. Hell, back then I'd even enjoyed the anticipation, the waiting; the thrill of a case ready to break.

Somewhere along the line I'd become jaded. Now all I

wanted was to get paid and make enough money to keep the flat and stop me having to get a real job. So why wasn't I down the Halt knocking back the double whiskies? In truth, I didn't know, but Elsa Courtney got to me. I didn't believe much of what she'd told me so far, but she brought back the dream of the Bogart case and for that, I was willing to put in a little waiting time.

CHAPTER
Ten

I STARTED WELL.

For the first hour I stood at the window. The street below me was just visible through the fog, and I watched the locals head home. Once fog like this came in there was little else to do but grin and bear it. Sometimes it lasted for days, sometimes for minutes, but it was always cold, grey and damp, seeping into your bones and making you think of moving permanently to somewhere sunny. After a while the street went quiet, and I turned back to my desk.

I put Bessie Smith on the stereo and let the old blues wash over me for a while, but something in the old girl's voice kept reminding me of that red kimono, those too-red lips wrapped around the cheroot. I turned to the radio instead but got only modern pop and talking heads too intent on making a noise to wonder whether it meant anything. I tried to read the newspaper, but it was all politics, show and tell, lies and deceit. There were just too many celebrities and not enough fame to go round.

And always my mind would turn back to that red kimono.

I started to seriously consider heading for the Halt. A combination of Willie and Davy and cribbage would be guaranteed to drive any thoughts of sex away. But then I remembered my client, and the crisp fifties she'd counted out for me.

I took a pad from the drawer and made notes, but that only made me realise how sloppy I'd been. I hadn't asked Dave what exactly my quarry had been looking for, I hadn't asked Willie and Davy whether anyone had left the game for any period of time, and I hadn't asked Mrs Crawford what time her husband had come home last night, nor what time he'd left this morning. I felt like a poor excuse for an investigator, and the whisky in my drawer started up its siren call again, but I managed to make do with another cigarette. I leaned back in the chair and tried to fit Hank's movements into a timeline, but every time I came up hard against Sunday lunchtime. He'd left the hotel and vanished. And no matter how hard I looked at it, I wasn't going to get anywhere further until I talked to Sandy, Foulkes and Crawford.

I got my laptop out of its bag for the first time in months and fired up the chess program. It beat me inside twenty minutes. I picked a game and watched as Fischer demolished Spassky, but my mind kept wandering and I couldn't appreciate the intricacies. I switched the chess off and spent a fruitless hour searching on Google for Courtney, Texas, poker, St Andrews, golf and combinations of the five. I got several hits for Courtney in Scotland, but none more recent than the 1930s. Over in Texas there was a record for a Mrs Courtney who made her own 'Deep South Dixie quilts', and a John Courtney who'd won the Amateur Medal at the Houston Open in 1966, but nothing for Hank or Elsa. I tried the genealogy sites, but if Hank had searched for ancestors, he hadn't left any traces on the 'net. I gave up when my head started to hurt, and at some point, I slipped into sleep.

I WOKE SUDDENLY, and at first, I didn't quite know where I was. Night had fallen, and darkness filled the room save for the red flashing light on my phone. And that's when I realised where the ringing was coming from. I snapped fully awake and answered the phone.

Elsa Courtney sounded distressed.

"Mr Royle…John. I got a call. Someone wants to meet me this evening, and if I don't, he says I'll never see Hank again. I need you to come….oh, please say you'll come…I don't know what I'll do if…"

"Slow down Ms Courtney," I said, but the steam train had been set in motion and it was difficult to stop.

"You must come. He said he'd meet me at the Seventeenth green and that I'd to bring the money. I think he means the eight grand… I can't imagine what other money he thinks there is. Meet me at seven. Please. Say you'll come. I need you."

"Ms Courtney," I said, but the line had gone dead. I hit redial. It was a mobile number. I noted it down while it rang in my ear, but nobody answered. I tried the Excelsior reception.

"Room 312 please," I said.

"The lady is out, sir" a very proper voice said.

"Try anyway," I said."

"But I saw her leave," the voice said. I recognised the voice. It as the girl I'd spoken to earlier.

"Listen, stop pointing your pencil and ring the number."

"How did you know…" she began. She stopped herself, and her training kicked in. "Just hold the line a second sir."

I got a five second blast of an out of tune string section playing 'The Girl from Ipo Nema'.

"I'm sorry sir. There's no reply."

"What time did she leave?"

"I'm afraid I can't say," she began.

I interrupted her.

"Listen. I think the lady is in trouble, and I have to find her."

"Are you a policeman?" she asked.

One of the cardinal rules of Private Investigation. If someone asks you that question, the answer is always <u>Yes</u>.

"I am," I said. "Do I need to get a warrant?"

Now I felt like a heel as she started to blub uncontrollably.

"Don't tell my boss," she said, "I'll get into trouble."

"That's all right," I said softly, "Just tell me when you last saw her."

"She left at two," she said.

"On her own?"

"I think so. She had a caller earlier, but he didn't leave a number."

"A man?"

"Yes. He called her Elsa, so I think she knew him."

It smelled funny. But could I afford to take the chance?

I thought about ringing the police, but they'd have ten junior constables barging into each other to organise and that would just take far too long. Besides, I'd got my biggest case for years; I wasn't about to let it go easily.

I rang George in the Halt.

"George. The game's afoot."

"You've found the Yank?"

"Not yet, but I think I'm getting close. I might well have to give the Polis a body-swerve. If any of them come looking for me tonight, I told you I going to Dundee to follow up a lead. I left at four o'clock."

"Four. Got it. When did you say you'd be getting back?"

"When they've stopped looking for me," I said.

"Always a good idea son," he replied, laughing. "I'll tell them you didn't know when you'd return. Is there anything you need?"

I knew what he was asking. George had provided me with plenty of help in the past; from muscle and money through to a handgun on one case that turned particularly hairy.

"No. I don't know enough yet to know what I need."

"Just another day in the life of a dick," he said sarcastically, and I laughed.

"It gets me out of the house."

"Be careful," he said.

"Touching," I relied. "I didn't know you cared."

"I was worrying about having to write off your tab."

I was about to hang up when I had another thought.

"George? You wouldn't know anybody who could do a trace on the owner of a mobile phone number?"

"I might do," he said cautiously. "Depends on whose phone it is."

"Ah, but if I knew that, I wouldn't have to ask, would I?"

He laughed again.

"I suppose not. It'll cost you fifty. And it won't be until tomorrow."

"If I'm still alive tomorrow, you can add it to the tab," I said. "At least by then you'll know it's still running."

"Aye. And it's still growing."

I gave him the number.

"I'll be able to get a name and address," he said, "But that's no guarantee of anything these days... every second phone out there seems to have been stolen."

"With my luck it'll belong to Prince William," I said.

"With your luck it'll belong to his granny," George replied.

I heard him laugh as he put the phone down.

It was only then that I checked my pocket-watch. It was already quarter to seven.

At this point in the movie the PI takes a gun from his drawer and heads out to meet the bad guys. But this wasn't the movies...this was St Andrews. Armed only with a pack of cigarettes and a Zippo I went out into the fog to help the damsel in distress. Okay, so she wasn't a damsel, and she might well not be in distress, but she was the client, this might turn out to be the case, and what else did I have to do on a damp night in March?

CHAPTER
Eleven

I MET Old Tom again in the hall. He waved a bottle of whisky in my face.

"Tamdhu, twenty-five years old," he said, "A present from a client. Want to come and get some inside of you?"

"I wish I could," I said. "I'm in a hurry. Duty calls."

"Working after dark? She must be paying you well."

The cash register in his brain was starting to crank. Next would be the call for payment of the rent. I pre-empted him.

"If the Polis come looking, you haven't seen me."

"It's like that then, is it?"

"Aye. It's like that."

"Well, I'll away and see how much whisky I can drink before they get here. I enjoy talking to them when I'm drunk. I can tell them any old nonsense and they believe it."

He waved the whisky bottle at me and went into his flat. I was half tempted to follow him. My conscience took over at the last minute and reminded me of Elsa Courtney's voice. I pushed open the front door and went out into the grey dampness that had engulfed the town.

The fog threatened to chill my lungs, so I lit a cigarette as I hurried to the sea wall once more. It had settled in for a long spell, and there was no traffic on the road. Locals hereabouts learn fast that it pays to be tucked up safe and warm when the North Sea fog rolls in. For one thing it's cold, and for another, tourists always seem surprised by it and lose their ability to drive. The local traffic cops hate the fog; it always leads to a spate of minor traffic calls, arguments and recriminations. Private Investigators love the stuff; it gives us a chance to snoop and look mysterious at the same time.

I kept walking down past the car parks to the shore. At this point I started heading off at ninety degrees to my eventual destination. The Seventeenth green is in easy reach by the path down the west side of the Eighteenth, the 'road' that gives the hole its name. But if this turned out to be a set up, I wasn't stupid enough to make it easy for them. I headed down to the sea road and across the burn to the bus park at the far end of the first hole.

There was no one around. I could have been alone in the whole world and things couldn't have been any quieter. I stood for a minute, smoking down the cigarette before stubbing it out on the gravel. I checked there was no one watching and clambered over the security fence and cut back through the rough, past the Second tee and across the Second fairway.

The fog brought the visibility down to ten yards, less in places. I wasn't worried. As teenagers we'd spent many an evening on the Old Course, sitting in the bunkers drinking, smoking and trying to persuade the local lassies to go all the way with us. No matter that we never managed the last bit; the memories of summer nights spent under starry skies were still with me. Back then I could probably have walked the course blindfold, so a bit of fog didn't bother me now.

It seemed I was the only one stupid enough to be out on a night like this. There wasn't even the screech of gulls to keep me company as I crossed onto the Seventeenth fairway.

I approached the green from the north. The noise of a vehicle cut through the fog, not too far away, but I couldn't tell from which direction, and the sound of the engine was soon lost in the night.

I stopped well short of the green and checked the time on my pocket-watch. The fog had just enough luminosity for me to read the face and see it was just short of the hour. If something was going down, it would happen soon. Adrenaline jolted through me, telling me to go charging off in the opposite direction. I focused on my client and kept going.

Feeling slightly foolish I paced forward, keeping to the short fairway, up the little incline towards the green. I moved slowly, straining for the slightest sound. But there was no noise; there was just the damp, grey, fog that enveloped me like a blanket. I walked up onto the green itself; the highest point at this part of the course and tried to peer through the gloom. All I could see was the darker patch in the fog where the ground fell away into the road hole bunker; a deep sand trap that had caught many professional golfers over the years.

I remembered the fuss during one of the Opens when some-one, a man worth many millions of pounds, had been humiliated when his ball had gone into this trap, and he'd been unable to play it out for stroke after stroke as he got redder and redder and his ball got plugged ever deeper in the sand. That was the image I had in my mind of this hole, but that image was about to be changed.

I'd been right about the set-up; the trap had caught another American. His sister had described him pretty accurately, although she hadn't mentioned that he might be a bit pale.

Hank Courtney lay there, face-up, in the bunker, dead eyes staring at me accusingly. The fine blonde hair above his left ear was matted with blood, but that wasn't what had killed him.

That would be the large knife sticking out of his chest.

I STOOD there for long seconds, my mind making busy work to keep me from thinking about what I was looking at. It was when I found myself trying to find a rhyme for "Bowie" that I realised I had to pull myself together.

"You're supposed to be an Investigator. Investigate!" I muttered.

I checked the perimeter of the bunker. There was no sign of any struggle, and the walls of the bunker itself were all intact. It looked like he'd been dropped in from a height. His feet were above the level of his body; his right foot at an angle, caught in one of the logs used to shore up the wall. His fists clenched, tight, and his mouth showed as a black hole open, as if ready to scream.

I let myself down into the sand gingerly, careful to leave foot-prints only where I'd be able to remove them easily. I checked his pulse, just in case. His skin felt warm to the touch, but no blood flowed in his veins... it looked like most of it was soaked up in his shirt.

That made checking his pockets a tricky job, but I did it as fast as I could. They were all empty, save for a single envelope in the inside pocket of his leather jacket. It felt like it contained some thick sheaves of paper. I transferred that to my own inside pocket and made to climb out of the bunker when I happened to look at his feet. A large lump of dark, wet, mud had been wedged up against the Cuban heel of the left foot of his snake-skin boots. If I was determined on playing detective, I might as well do the job properly. I transferred the last four of the Camels to my shirt pocket and used the empty packet to collect the mud. I cleaned my footprints up by smoothing them over. Once I had satisfied myself I had left no trace I climbed out of the bunker.

I looked back down. Something bothered me, and it took a while to register. A knife wound like that would have bled... bled a lot. Blood pooled in the Texan's shirt, sure. But not enough, and the sand around the body hadn't changed from its normal colour. The body showed all the signs of being killed elsewhere, moved, and later dumped here.

A car horn hooted over past the bus park, then another.

Suddenly I felt exposed, despite the fog. I'd hung around too long, giving anyone around a chance to spring their trap. I had to move, and I had to move now.

I made my decision just in time. Muffled voices reached me through the fog, coming in from the direction of the town. I crouched low and rolled away down towards the fairway, like a kid rolling down a grassy bank. Getting to my feet at the bottom of the incline, I moved away from the green, heading north back up the Seventeenth towards the tee. I knew at any minute that I might be noticed, and my back tickled, waiting for the torch beam that would find it.

"Watch out for the sand pits," a voice called out.

"Round about here they're known as bunkers," an older voice said sarcastically. "Just don't fall in one. I've got enough on my plate without having to fill in forms in triplicate for the Health and Safety."

"Hey, there's something in that hole," the young voice called out. I didn't recognise the owner, but I knew the second voice... it was Detective Inspector Joe Boyd.

"Get over here," Boyd shouted in the darkness. "We've got a body."

My heart sank... not because I didn't like the man. No. I now knew I would have a much harder job getting away. Joe Boyd took his job seriously, worked hard at being smart and, worst of all, he'd been my best friend since before Jim Crawford tried to beat him up in that school playground all those years ago.

"Shit," the young voice said. "Is that blood?"

"Well, it's not raspberry jam," Joe said dryly.

I walked faster. More shouts rang out in the darkness and, just as I got to the Seventeenth tee, the distinctive nee-naw of an ambulance rose above all other noise. Further away still, police car sirens started up. It looked like the whole force had just been mobilised.

"You can slow down boys," I whispered to myself. "There's no rush."

I stood on the tee for a second, listening for pursuit, but the only noise came from up around the green. Torches sent flashes in the fog, and a pair of headlights threatened to light me up. I headed west fast, making for the dim lights of the hotel that bounds the edge of the course at that point.

Part of me wanted to turn back and throw myself at Joe's mercy. Joe Boyd wouldn't believe me to be a murderer... and even if he did, he'd give me a fair crack at proving him wrong. But it wasn't as simple as that. Somebody tried to set me up for a fall, and if I threw myself on the mercy of the law, I'd be tied up in the system for so long that there would be no hope of ever getting to the bottom of it. My best hope was to stay active and find out what was going on before the police did.

I clambered over a security fence that wasn't really all that secure, nor much of a fence, and made my way fast to the rear of the hotel. I knew my way around here as well. As a kid Joe and I collected lost golf balls from around the courses in the area, and stood at the back door just here, selling the balls back at extortionate rates to the golfers and hotel patrons. It kept us in fags and cider through most of our teenage years until Joe saw the light and became a model citizen. Me, I never quite managed it.

I needed to get moving. If I remembered the back way in, then so would Joe.

The back door wasn't locked, and I let myself in to a long, empty, corridor. To my left was a changing room and locker space for patron's use while coming and going from the course.

I ignored that and headed, as fast as I dared, along the corridor. A door opened ahead of me, throwing a rectangle of light on the floor. Laughter and giggles echoed as a small group of people rolled drunkenly into the hallway. I took the first door on my left and got inside, hoping I hadn't been seen.

The room I ducked into was used as a cloakroom for people using the bars at the front of the building. There was no one around, and I had no trouble lifting a long overcoat and a scarf from one of the pegs. I put them both on, wrapping the scarf around my lower face. I stood at the door, ear pressed to the wood, but there was no sound from outside. Feeling as if I had a big target on my back I crept out.

The corridor was empty once more. I headed through the hotel, fast but not too fast, a man who knew where he was going but was in no way running away from anything.

Oh, no, not me officer.

I reached the main reception area before there was any sign of any people and headed out of the door before anyone even noticed I was there. Three taxis sat idling at the rank, and I took the first one, getting in the back and sitting in the far corner so the driver wouldn't be able to see my face in his rear-view mirror.

"Dundee pleez" I said in an outrageous French accent. "I 'av to be at ze Carnegie Hall in 'alf an 'our. Eet ees verry importaunt."

The driver sucked his teeth.

"That's a long haul, away over the other side of the river," he said, "I was just away to get my tea."

A police car entered the hotel driveway a hundred yards away.

I leaned forward and showed him a fifty.

"Ees this ample?" I said.

"Oh aye guvnor," he said, "Nae bother. It's always a pleasure to help our foreign pals."

He pulled away, and the police car slowed. My heart leapt in my throat, but the police pulled to one side and let us past. Joe would shout out the officer in that car later if he found out that that they'd allowed someone out of the hotel. What was more likely was that the officer in the car would 'forget' to report the cab he'd pulled over for.

I'd made it clear… for now anyway.

"Have you been in town long guvnor?" the cabbie asked.

"Ah aam zo zorrry," I said, "I not speak ze English much."

"That's all right guv," he said, "You're in Scotland now, the Auld Alliance and all that happy shit. We don't speak English all that well either. Just sit back. I'll have you over the Tay in no time."

I sat back in the corner again and, for the first time in twenty minutes, began to relax enough to start thinking properly.

I was in trouble. Whether my client's phone call had been a true one had become a mute point. Either she, or someone else, just tried to fit me up for her brother's murder.

What I needed was an alibi. George at the Halt would cover for me but that wouldn't be enough. I needed to build a cover story, and I needed to do it fast. I knew Joe Boyd. He'd be all over this case in minutes … and I didn't have a monopoly on the information that flowed in and out of the Halt Bar.

I tried to think, but all that came to mind was the image of the dead, staring, eyes looking up at me from the bunker. I leaned back, closed my eyes, but in the movie playing behind my eyelids the Texan moved, crawling up the trap walls towards me. I snapped my eyes open, lit a cigarette and stared at the blackness beyond the car window, trying for calm.

THE CAB DRIVER drove like a demon, taking the corners at over fifty and reaching ninety on the straights. I could have done something, but I didn't trust that dodgy French accent over any length of time. I squeezed myself tight in the corner and gripped the overhead hand support so hard that my palm ached.

"You're a French gentleman then," the cabbie said as we approached the Tay Road Bridge.

I didn't reply at first, but that doesn't stop cabbies. They're the same the world over; they spend so much time in the same little bubble that they have to constantly keep trying to break out of it, and they do this by making contact with their fares, even if its only to the extent of passing on some tidbit of information or remarking on the weather.

"I only ask because of the accent," he said. "I had that Sacha Distel in the cab once. Do you know him?"

I grunted in reply to stop myself laughing.

"A nice polite gentleman," he carried on, "And a good tipper. Not that I'm wangling for a tip from you sir. No, fifty pounds will come in very handy. It's the youngest bairn's birthday next week and he wants a skateboard. When I was his age I..."

I tuned him out. Cabbies don't expect to be listened to anyway, they need to hear themselves talk ... it reminds them that they're still alive in that bubble I was talking about.

We sped across the bridge, the suspension rattling as we passed a fifty sign while doing ninety. The cab overtook an aging saloon, its driver white faced in astonishment as we rushed by. Our progress was halted only by a queue of traffic at the north end of the span.

"Bloody old women," the driver said.

He waved his hand at the queue ahead of us crawling down to the off ramp. "Do you know what this is? This is the bingo queue. Would you believe it? There's three hundred old women head out of Fife every night, driving for miles, just for the chance to win a few bob. Have you ever been to a bingo hall? No, I suppose over in your place they've got casinos and flash croupiers and hostesses with big tits and gold lame dresses. Over here we get modified picture houses, sweaty Betty the bike of Ballochmyle and a wee baldy man who thinks it's funny to flirt with women twice his age. If I had my way, I'd...."

I tried to tune him out again, but it was getting harder. I was almost on the point of getting out and walking when the traffic finally started to move.

"About bloody time too," the driver said. He slipped down the outside on the hard shoulder the first chance he got and jumped out onto the main road only six inches in front of a bus. The bus driver flashed his lights at us, but in ten seconds he was no more than just another light in the distance.

Ten minutes later we screeched to a halt outside the Carnegie Hall. I hoped the driver wouldn't notice that the place was closed and quiet.

I needn't have bothered worrying. I got out of the car and stood at the driver's window, making sure I kept my face out of his sight. I passed him the fifty, and it disappeared into his wallet before he spoke.

"You're all right Mr Royle. Nobody followed us. I was checking," he said. He put his head out of the window and smiled at me, a grin that showed the gaps in his teeth. It was only then that I realised I knew him... his name was John, or maybe Jim ... and he was a regular in the Halt.

"You knew it was me all the time?"

"Oh aye," he said. "Here's a wee tip for you, Mr Royle. If you're going to travel incognito, you need to disguise your walk. There's only one man in these parts that walks like John Wayne, and everybody knows it. Auld Willie in the Halt told us it was because you had piles from sitting on the sea wall all the time."

I had to laugh.

"If I catch up with the old man it'll be him that's walking funny. John Wayne? I didn't know."

"You never do. The missus used to tell me I looked like a film star. There I was imagining myself as Clint Eastwood or Michael Douglas. It was years before she told me she meant King Kong."

We both laughed at that one.

"And what was all that about Sacha Distel?"

"Well, it was either him or Jean Van Der Velde, and I didn't think you'd know the golfer," he said.

"You'd have been right about that."

"What now?" he said. "I can take you back the long way round, no extra charge?"

I thought about it for a while.

"No. It'll be best if I get myself seen up here," I said. "I need an alibi."

"Well, if anybody asks me, I took a Frenchman to the airport," he said.

"I owe you a beer," I said.

"Make it two and I won't tell anybody who he walked like," he laughed again.

He was about to drive off when I remembered the packages in my pocket.

"Are you heading anywhere near the Halt?" I asked.

"Aye, I'll be popping in for a pint. My shift is finished, and there's a nice new fifty burning a hole in my pocket."

I gave him the envelope and the cigarette packet.

"Do me another favour. Give these to George to hold onto for me. Tell him I'll pick them up as soon as I can."

"Will do. That's another pint you owe me."

"Tell George to put them on my tab," I said.

"Aye, that'll be right," he said, mocking. "The day you pay that one will be the day you start walking like a Scotsman."

I didn't get a chance of a comeback line. He was off and away into the night. The last I saw of him he went through a red light, accelerating.

A row of cabs sat, engines idling, at the rank on the corner.

"Town Centre," I said to the first man.

"That's not much of a fare, is it?" he said. "It's less than a mile."

"I'll make it worth your while." I showed him a ten pound note. "You can keep the change."

He was right. The journey was over almost before it started.

"I need a receipt," I said. "And I need the time on it to say six-thirty."

He never even blinked.

"Righty-ho sir," he said.

Ten seconds later he dropped me off on the corner of Debenhams on the edge of Dundee's shopping centre. I pocketed the receipt and headed into town.

Dundee has changed a lot over the years, nowhere more so than here in the town centre. In my youth it had a life and texture all of its own, large Victorian shops, tram lines in the cobbled streets, and individual shops owned by local tradesmen. Now it was just like any other big town. Plastic chain stores vied for space with fast food outlets and mobile phone outlets. Without the shoppers to give the place life it was just a big shiny mausoleum to consumerism.

I took the coat off and carried it over my arm as I walked along the quiet High Street. The shoppers had long since gone, and the real drinkers were all inside the pubs by now. All that was left on the streets were teenagers with nothing better to do and students on their way to the pub.

I spent a while looking for a newsagent or tobacconist. Only the big supermarket at the east end of town was open. I deposited the coat in the store's charity skip for clothing... it made me feel slightly less guilty at stealing it. I needed a smoke badly, but the remaining loose cigarettes in my pocket were crumpled and unsalvageable. I went into the supermarket, and set about building my alibi.

CHAPTER

Twelve

I SPENT a while standing in the entrance to the store, pretending to check my pockets. I made sure I was in a well-lit spot, and made a point of looking straight at the CCTV camera... I only hoped today was one of the days they put a tape in. After that I wandered the aisles for a while, always stopping where a camera might be watching. After a while I drew the attention of a store detective.

"Can I help you sir?" he said. He had one of those officious little voices that I hated immediately. In another life he'd have made a perfect traffic warden.

"I hope not," I said. "I'm looking for a woman."

"Maybe I can help you sir," he said, but from his tone it was obvious that help was the last thing he would offer me. "What does this woman look like?"

"Oh, I don't know," I said. "Five-five, blonde, tits like Monroe, legs like Elle McPherson and the IQ of a gnat would be a start."

I didn't even get a smile.

"If sir would like to leave, we won't make a fuss," he said, taking my arm in a tight grip.

I slipped away from him easily.

"You mean this isn't singles night? I saw it on the telly. Some kind of special offer, wasn't it? Come to the store on a Monday might and meet the woman or man of your dreams it said. Well, here I am. Bring her on."

He tried to take my arm again.

"I appreciate the offer," I said, "But you're not my type. Just show me where all the women are, and I won't tell anybody."

He went red.

"I'm afraid I'll have to ask you to leave."

"And I'm afraid I'll have to go," I said. "I could have this shop under the Trades Descriptions Act, promising women and putting up homosexuals instead."

"I'm not homosexual," he spluttered.

I patted his arm and walked away.

"Just keep telling yourself that. I'm sure you'll do fine."

THE SECOND PERSON I spoke to was the teenage girl behind the counter at the cigarette section. I asked for two packs of Camels, which was enough in itself to get me remembered as they're seen as an exotic brand in Scotland. Then I set about making myself memorable.

"It's a tremendous place, isn't it?"

She gave up chewing gum long enough to look at me.

"What?"

"Whatever happened to grace and good manners?" I said.

"What?" she said again.

"Ah. I see I'm in the company of one of the world's great conversationalists," I said. "I was merely saying that the public library in town here is a tremendous place. I've been up there all day."

I spoke deliberately loudly, so that anyone else in earshot would be bound to hear me.

"It's full of books you know?" I said. By now the girl was convinced I was a madman and was looking around for help.

She passed me the Camels quickly, as if I might be contagious, and I've never seen anyone make change faster than she did. She didn't bother counting it back to me, merely dropped it into my palm and looked away fast, hoping there would be another customer waiting.

Unfortunately, luck wasn't on her side. She was stuck with me for a bit longer.

"Do you ever visit the library yourself?" I asked. "You should you know. It's very educational."

She looked around to make sure nobody was looking.

"Listen you pervert. You've got your fags. Now eff off or I'll call security."

An old lady turned up at the far end of the counter, and the assistant scuttled away along the counter as if I was contagious.

"Okay then. I'll be off," I shouted. "Don't forget what I told you about the library."

"Is this man bothering you hen?" the old woman said.

"No," she said, but she didn't look at me. She would remember me though, and I smiled as I left the store and lit up a Camel. I made sure I put the receipt in my wallet, finished off the cigarette and headed to the nearest fish and chip shop.

CHAPTER
Thirteen

THE WEST COAST OF SCOTLAND is generally thought to be the worst place in terms of diet, with huge swathes of the population falling to early death due to clogged arteries and congested hearts. Judging by the queue at the chip shop the denizens of Dundee were vying for the honour. The line of people stretched for nearly twenty yards. I considered walking on, but my stomach rebelled at that. I latched on to the end and we inched forward slowly.

A busker entertained the head of the queue ... if you could call the noise coming from his harmonica entertainment. He was small, slightly portly, aged around fifty, with one of those noses you see on people that drink too much too often. His hair, combed over a bald patch, flew in the wind for six inches above his ear, but he didn't notice. The effort of playing the tune had got him completely lost in concentration, eyes screwed up, cheeks puffed. He danced a jig, surprisingly light on his feet, in time with a truly awful rendition of the sailor's hornpipe.

"Haw Jim," a voice shouted, "Stop that shite and gie us <u>Blawin' in the Wind</u>."

The busker stopped abruptly. His face flared red, and his eyes looked too big for their sockets. I was afraid he was in danger of exploding.

"I dinnae ken that wan," he said. "But if anybody can whistle it, I'll pick it up."

There were no takers. He put the harmonica back in his mouth, blew three more bars of the hornpipe and picked up the flat cap that had been sitting at his feet. He walked along the queue, shaking the hat at anybody that might be interested. I figure he collected less than a pound in total, but it didn't seem to faze him. He went back to the head of the queue and started the hornpipe again.

By the time I got to the door of the chip shop he was on his third rendition. The law of diminishing returns kicked in, and when he went along the queue this time, he got no money at all.

"I don't think Larry Adler has got anything to worry about," I said as he came back beside me.

"I don't think Larry Adler's arse would have anything to worry about," the man said. "But I'm skint, and this is all I know."

He raised the harmonica to his mouth. Luckily, I wasn't to be subjected for a fourth time. The queue moved forward and finally I entered the chip shop.

A young woman stood at the front of the queue. She looked no more than eighteen, but she had a three-year old hanging at her coat and a baby in her arms. Her face showed all the signs of someone living too close to the edge; her eyes sunk back in her skull like lifeless black pits, her teeth already crooked and broken, and cheekbones sharp enough to cut paper across skin so thin it was almost translucent.

"So, two ten-inch pizzas at four pounds each, that's better than a sixteen-inch pizza at eight pounds, isn't it? Two tens is twenty... that's better than sixteen."

It was time to add another brick to that alibi.

"Excuse me," I said, loud enough so that everybody in the place could hear me. "You need to think about the surface area of the pizza. Area is Pi times r squared. So, two times five squared, times Pi, is fifty times pi square inches for the two ten-inch ones. Whereas eight squared is sixty-four times pi for the sixteen-inch. So, the sixteen is twenty-eight per cent better value for money."

The place went deathly quiet for two seconds, before the young woman turned back to the girl who was serving her.

"So, two ten-inch pizzas at four pounds each, that's better than a sixteen-inch pizza at eight pounds, isn't it?"

The serving girl agreed with her.

"It's no use trying to educate anybody round here," an older man said behind me. "They think that Pi is something you eat."

"Shut yer face, ye old bastard," the girl said,

"Bastard," the three-year-old echoed with a grin.

The old man shrugged and turned away. I got a glare from the three-year-old. I tried smiling back, but the kid looked like it didn't know the meaning of the gesture.

Ten minutes later the girl left with her two pizzas. She gave me a self-satisfied smirk as she left, as if she'd put one over on me.

"See," she said, showing me the pizza boxes. "Two tens... better than sixteen."

"Come and see me if you ever need a quote for getting your walls painted," I said. "I'll do you a good deal."

All that got me was another blank stare. She turned and left, but the three-year-old still had a parting shot. It kicked me in the shins, and ran away, giggling.

There were two kids ready to get served in front of me, small and rotund, rolls of fat hanging under tight sweatshirts. I couldn't tell what sex they were, but they were no more than eleven years old, and already the size of small elephants.

"A deep-fried Mars bar and chips," the one on the left said.

"Same for me," the other added, "But with curry sauce."

I looked over at the huge man manning the fryer. His belly was a warning to the kids of what was to come later for them.

"Tweedledee and Tweedledum, eh?" I said, pointing.

Once more I got a blank stare.

"No. That's Sean and Jason McGuire. I don't know any Tweedles."

I didn't bother with the cabaret act this time... I don't think he would have been able to keep up. I contented myself with collecting another receipt to add to my wallet.

The fish and chips left salt, vinegar and grease on my hands as I ate while I walked down towards the old docks. Eating fish and chips in the open air always reminded me of summer days as a kid, a magic that never quite left me no matter how old I got. Even in the centre of a run-down former industrial giant like Dundee I could almost hear the screams of people on the roller coaster, taste the candy floss and feel salt spray on my face. I let those thoughts wash the case away, just for a short while, as I strolled, not really caring where I was going.

When I finished, I wiped my hands on the scarf I'd stolen, dropped it on a litter bin, and made my way to the Unicorn.

IN ANY BIG city there are places the 'cognoscenti' go when they want something out of the ordinary. The Unicorn in Dundee is one of those places. It is a run-down bar on the edge of the docks, a dank, dingy, drinking hole with battered 1960's furniture, tattered linoleum flooring and a pervading smell of tobacco, stale beer and fresh urine. If you wandered in searching for a warm welcome and friendly discourse, you'd be sorely disappointed...this place served a different purpose.

Things that fell off the back of lorries ended up here, as did men who knew men that rigged horse races for big bookies. Anything was traded, from truckloads of booze and cigarettes to lion cubs. It was rumoured that the Ministry of Defence were short of a Chieftain tank, and that it 'passed' through this pub. I didn't disbelieve it. And the good thing for me tonight was that people remembered you if you turned up here… just in case you had something they might be able to use later.

This wasn't a bar for the faint hearted. It was a drinking establishment, pure and simple. There was no 'theme' here, no games consoles, no CD jukebox, just a solitary television above the bar, and even that had its volume turned right down. No, what we had here was a bar in the old style… a place where men came to drink in the company of other men and talk about anything except their work. I'd been in before, but it had been years before. I was pleased to see that the place hadn't changed at all.

Smoke hung heavy in the air over figures hunched across small wooden tables. Most of the patrons had both beer and whisky on the table in front of them, and more than a few looked like they'd been sitting in the bar since opening time that morning. Not that they were drunk, no, not yet. But the noise level in the bar rose as the drink started speaking. Over in the far-left corner menace hung in the air as voices were raised in anger and a chair got overturned, but the barman put a quick stop to any nonsense with a well-timed curse. I took up a stool at the bar and started to build another brick in the wall of that alibi.

I ordered a pint of Guinness and paid with a fifty, making sure that the patrons around me noticed. And as I'd suspected, a new friend found me less than two minutes later. I hadn't even started the Guinness when a small wiry man sidled onto the stool next to mine.

"You got a light, mate?" he said, the standard opening gambit in pubs the world over. A self-rolled cigarette hung in the corner of his mouth, so thin there could be hardly more than a thread of tobacco in it.

I countered by using the Zippo, putting as much flourish into it as I could muster. I lit myself a Camel at the same time, leaving the nearly full pack on the bar in front of me. His eyes kept straying to them.

"Nice lighter," he said. His breath smelled worse that the fish market down the road, and I took a quick gulp of Guinness and a long hit of smoke, hoping that would be enough to disguise it.

It wasn't.

I couldn't tell how old he might be, somewhere between fifty and eighty, and so thin to be almost skeletal. His face looked grey, thick with grime, and he wore a nylon tracksuit that might have been fashionable sometime round about 1980 but was now held together with safety pins and sellotape. He held a half-pint of lager that had gone flat... he'd probably been working on it for hours.

I knew what he'd say next.

"Can you lend me a fiver for a wee drink?" he said.

"Jimmy, leave the gent alone," the barman said. "I've told you before. There's to be nae mooching in the bar."

I waved the barman away.

"No, it's okay," I said. "I don't mind."

The barman looked astonished.

"You don't have to worry sir, I'll get rid of him," he said.

I shook my head and turned to the wee man who looked as surprised as the barman.

"Jimmy, is it?"

He nodded. With his mouth hanging open and his eyes wide he looked just like a puppy. My guess was he had about the same level of intelligence.

"Here," I said to the barman, handing him a fiver, "Give the man a couple of drinks."

Jimmy suddenly thought I was his best friend. He threw an arm around my shoulder, and I nearly gagged at the sudden whiff of his armpits.

"Ta pal," he said. "I've had a drooth all day, but this bunch of sad-asses in here wouldnae even gie me the time o' day. After all I did for this country as weel."

"You were in the Forces?" I asked, prising him off me, gently, so as not to disturb any other odours that might be looking for an opportunity to escape.

"Jimmy in the forces? Aye, that'll be right," the barman said. "The only thing he ever did for his country was getting himself arrested for nutting an Englishman after Scotland won at Wembley."

"He was asking for it," Jimmy said. "He called Jinky Johnston a wee ginger poof."

The barman moved over to the tall font.

Jimmy went quiet. Suddenly all his attention was focussed on the golden liquid coming out of the tap. I watched as the barman poured a pint of lager and Wee Jimmy drooled. As he took the drink his hands shook so badly that the foam of the head started spilling over the side, but the glass wasn't full for long ... half the pint disappeared in the first gulp. He smiled at me, his lower face a mask of foam.

I noticed that the area around me had gone quiet. The locals looked at me as if I was mad.

"You shouldn't encourage him," the barman said to me. "It only makes him worse."

"It's my good deed for the day," I said.

"We don't need any Boy Scouts," he said, "But I wouldnae turn down a couple of Girl Guides."

He turned back to Jimmy.

"You just get the one Jimmy," he said. "Just be glad I'm in a good mood. Mooch at the bar again and you'll get my boot up your arse."

Jimmy scuttled away to a corner.

"He saw you coming," the barman said as he handed me my change. "You're too soft."

"Aye. My missus is always telling me the same thing. I blame the beer."

That got a laugh. Noise filled in around me and the bar went back to normal. I was no longer a stranger. I was just someone else drinking in the bar. But once more I'd made sure I would be remembered.

Somebody stuck an elbow in my back, and I turned, giving a baseball-cap-wearing teenager behind me a hard glare.

He glared back.

"Whit's your friggin' problem?" he spat at me.

I turned away. Kids looking for a fight were ten-a-penny round here. The trick was not to give them an opening. Unfortunately, this one didn't need any second chances. He put a hand on my shoulder and pulled me towards him.

"I was talking tae you, bampot," he said.

My mouth took over before my brain had time to stop it.

"Is that what it was? I'm sorry, I don't understand ape-speak."

It took him a second to realize he'd been insulted...you could almost see each individual brain cell struggle for a synaptic connection. Eventually, realization came to his eyes, and he remembered to be outraged. He stepped around in front of me and stood, nose to nose.

"It's a square-go you're wantin' is it?" he said in that belligerent swagger that only a young Scotsman can muster.

"No. I just want to finish my pint."

"Aye. Well, you'll have to get to it through me."

"Okay," I said, and hit him as hard as I could manage. He didn't see it coming, and he went down in a heap at my feet, his eyes rolling in their sockets. I stepped over him, and lifted my beer, aware of the gaping customers staring at me. I smiled sweetly back, and they turned their gazes elsewhere. I was about to write the encounter off as just another hazard of the city at night when the kid got off the ground screaming.

"Friggin' bastard. I'll have you."

As he came forward, he took a carpet knife from his pocket.

"You're getting chibbed," he said, "I hope your mother can sew."

He got within three feet of me when my new friend wee dirty Jimmy smashed him over the head with a pint glass. The kid went down again and didn't get up. Two burly men carried him away, and the bar patrons went back to their drinks. I guessed they hadn't seen anything unusual.

Wee Jimmy held the bottom half of his smashed glass. He looked like he might cry.

"Bloody waste," he said. "I had half a pint left."

It looked like this stage of my alibi was just about secure.

CHAPTER
Fourteen

I STAYED in the bar for a couple of hours. Before I got settled, I tried to phone Ms Courtney, but the Excelsior still had no idea where she had got to.

"Ms Courtney went out for the day," the woman said at the other end of the line. She sounded strained. It wasn't the girl I'd spoken to earlier.

"Did she leave a contact telephone number?" I asked.

"No sir. But people rarely do. This is a hotel, not an answering service."

"Do they go out of their way to employ the unhelpful?" I asked, "Or do you get special training?"

"Is that the police again," I heard a voice say in the background in the hotel reception, just as she hung up on me.

It looked like I wasn't the only one looking for Elsa Courtney. I knew I needed to get back to St Andrews, get back to finding whether she was really in trouble, to finding out just how tangled this case had become. But first I had some final bricks to build in the wall.

Two men came in and stood at the bar beside me. They wore suits and carried briefcases; office types working late and in for a quick drink before home.

"Can I buy you a drink, gents?" I asked.

"He's the big spender tonight," the barman added, "I'd take him up on it quick before wee Jimmy comes back."

We passed the time about the state of the Scottish railway system which we all agreed was a) crap and b) too expensive. No deep thoughts, but that was two more bricks in the alibi.

I joined in a game of brag at a table near the bar, winning eight pounds and thirty pence. I made sure that everyone at the table knew that I'd spent the day in the City Library, bought them all a beer, then I went back to the stool at the bar. Once I'd got another Guinness, I told the barman my life story. Barmen are good at listening, and this one listened for nearly an hour. I was just about to leave, my job done, when someone shouted from behind me.

"Ho Jock, turn the telly up. There's something happening."

The television blared suddenly, and I looked up to see a reporter standing in front of the fog-shrouded clubhouse of the Old Course. Behind him you could see other reporters all vying for a spot from which to make their own reports. I suddenly realised how big the case had become. The story had gone global, and with an American dead, no, murdered, in a bunker on one of the most famous holes in golf, it wasn't going to go away for a while.

The reporter talked into the camera in that earnest sombre way they do, spoilt somewhat by the fact that his arms waved around like crazed windmills while he spoke.

"A major police operation is underway in St Andrews tonight after the discovery of a body in the famous road-hole bunker on the Old Course. I'm standing here, on this historic spot where the legends of golf have fought each other over the years.

"We often talk of sport in terms of metaphors or war or death. Losers get blasted, slaughtered, demolished. But it seems, tonight, one has been murdered. Details are still sketchy, but a local policeman has described the case as a particularly brutal slaying.

"The police are not releasing the details of the victim until his relatives have been notified, but I have been informed by sources in the club here that the dead man was a tourist. Of course, it's too early for speculation, but the ramifications for the summer season here are enormous."

The picture cut back to the studio and a leggy blonde perched on the edge of a desk trying to look both provocative and serious at the same time. She almost managed it.

"More details to follow ... And in another twist to the Beach-gate story, we'll be asking why the Prime Minister's wife found it necessary to go naked on a beach in the Caribbean."

The barman turned the volume down again.

"A body in the bunker eh," he said. "That'll stir up the brandy and cigars crowd."

"Aye," I said, "No doubt they'll be moaning about the incon-venience of it all in the morning."

"They'll probably just declare the Polis a hazard and allow players a free drop," the barman said. "It wouldnae surprise me if it was wan of their own that did it."

"Nor me," the man beside me said, "I remember the time I told one of them it was 'Only a game'. He told me if he had to choose between his wife and the golf, he'd choose the golf every time."

"Hell, John," the barman said, "If I had to choose between your wife and a night with only myself for company, my right hand would win every time."

Talk in the bar moved on to the size of the PM's wife's breasts and I finished my beer and left.

The fog had cleared, and the night was clear and bright, a new moon hanging over the Tay Bridge and shimmering in the estuary. I crossed the network of roads that separated the town from the riverside, stood at the wall and watched the river flow while I smoked another cigarette.

The news report had me spooked. I'd asked for the big case, now here it was, fallen in my lap whether I liked it or not. I was used to dealing with small local concerns among people I knew. I wasn't sure I was ready for newspapers, television and the steady, unblinking, stare of every golfer in the world.

The urge to run was growing in me. I still had plenty of fifties in my pocket … enough to get me a long way away. But I had nobody to run to, no family home to take me in.

Besides, I still had a client, one who might be in trouble. All I had to ask myself was one question.

What would Bogey do?

And there was only one answer to that.

I let the calm fill me for all of five minutes, then I headed for the bus station; back to St Andrews.

BY THE TIME the bus got me to the Old Course it was close to eleven o' clock. The Seventeenth hole had been lit up like a Christmas tree with police cars, ambulances, reporters and television units. A small army of people milled around, all across the fairway and on the green. The groundskeeper would be having kittens.

"There's something going on," the driver said, "The Polis have got the road closed ahead of us. I hope none of you are in a hurry."

"What is it son?" an old lady asked the driver. "Is it an accident?"

A police cordon had been thrown around the Old Course Hotel. The traffic on the main road inched past the roadblock, so I had plenty of time for a good look. A large crowd of disgruntled guests milled around in the front drive, and harassed traffic officers tried to stop people arriving or departing. As the bus stopped to get past the police roadblock, I saw Joe Boyd in animated conversation with the hotel manager. Neither of them looked particularly happy.

My heart rate went up a notch or two as the driver rolled his window down and spoke to the police, and I slumped in my seat, trying to look inconspicuous. I needn't have worried. The bus got waved through with no fuss... it looked like they were more concerned with checking people going out of the town than coming in.

"Did you see anything?" the old lady said to the driver. "Was there a body?"

"The Polis just asked what time I'd left town earlier tonight," he said.

I wanted to ask one more question but didn't want to draw attention to myself. Luckily the old lady was nosy enough for both of us.

"Did they say who they were after?"

"Nope," the driver said as he picked up speed away from the cordon. "But you know the Polis. They don't even tell you the time without consulting their bosses."

I waited till the bus pulled into the bus station and the old ladies disembarked before I got off, slowly, so that the driver would remember me... another brick in the wall.

I was dog tired. The earlier adrenaline rush had worn off, and all I wanted to do now was drag myself to bed and sleep. There was little chance of that. I had a feeling that sleep was a long way off yet.

CHAPTER
Fifteen

THE HALT WAS STILL busy when I looked in from outside. Willie and Davy were deep in conversation in their corner seat, and George stood in his usual place behind the bar. I rapped the window and George looked up. He saw me and raised a thumb up. The coast was clear.

By the time I went in and got to the bar he had a beer ready for me. He waited until the man beside me took his drinks from the bar. He leaned close so no one could hear our conversation.

"Joe Boyd was in earlier looking for you," he said. "I told him the story about you being in Dundee, but he didn't believe me."

"No. I guess he wouldn't. Somebody tipped him off that I would be out at the golf course at seven. I only just got away before the Polis turned up."

"Is this about the body in the bunker?"

"Aye," I said, "It was our poker playing Texan."

He sucked at his teeth. He never did like to lose a customer.

"They said on the news it was murder?" George said.

I nodded.

"It sure looked like it to me. They used his big knife. It was messy."

"You saw the body?" George asked.

I nodded again.

"Just for a minute. I had to get out of there fast. As I said, somebody tried to set me up."

"Do you know who?"

"Nope. But I'm going to find out."

I noticed with surprise that I'd already finished my beer. George nodded towards the empty glass.

"Another?"

I nodded.

"Has this got something to do with that mobile number?"

"It might. Did you have any joy there?"

"I'll know in the morning. There's a lad I know who's a genius with the technology. He'll have an answer for you."

George turned away. A second later he turned back.

"I just remembered. John, the cabbie, gave me these to hold for you."

He produced the envelope and cigarette packet from beneath the counter.

I lifted the envelope. The address showed it had been sent to Mr Hank Courtney, 17001 Abeline, Houston, Texas, from the UK, nearly nine months ago. On the back of the envelope a faded return address label said it was from the Scottish Antiquarian Society in Edinburgh. Inside I found an old, folded document, brown and liver-spotted with age like an old man's hands. I slid it out of the envelope and opened it gingerly.

It looked like some kind of legal contract, but it was written in a cramped, dense, hand. There wasn't anything immediate there for me; most of it was in Latin and I'd never got past Amo, Amas, Amat. There were only two things I could make out with any clarity: a name, John Courtney, and a date, 1689. I slid it back into the envelope. I couldn't see where it fitted in to the case, but then, I couldn't see how anything fitted in to the case. I passed it back across the counter to George.

"Hold on to this a wee while longer," I said. "The Polis will be lifting me at some point, and I might need a wee something to bargain with."

I lifted the cigarette packet and looked inside. The soil was beginning to dry out.

"What have you got there?" George asked.

I showed him.

"I thought you gave up collecting turds when you left school," he said, laughing.

I tapped the side of my nose.

"Evidence ... that's what I've got here," I said. "George, you're the font of all knowledge. Any geologists in? A student in need of some readies maybe?"

The barman looked around the room and called out.

"Fraser. Doug Fraser. Come over here for a minute."

A short fat youth left a crowd and came towards us.

"He's a botanist," George said to me, "I knew his father."

The lad staggered slightly as he approached, almost spilling his beer, and it took him a second or two to focus on me.

"What do you want," he slurred.

"How'd you like to make fifty quid," I said.

He sobered up fast. I handed him the cigarette packet.

"I need to know what this is."

"It's a fag packet," the kid said.

I took a fifty from my wallet and waved it in front of his nose.

"I do the gags son. I need an analysis done of the soil that's in there. Anything you can find... I'm especially interested in where it came from. Can you do that?"

He opened the packet and looked inside.

"Doesn't look like anything out of the ordinary at first glance. It's dark enough to be just a common garden soil."

He wiped his lips with the back of his hand.

"It'll take a wee while, but I can use the lab in the department at any time."

"Can you start now?" I asked.

He looked over at his friends, then back at the money.

"For fifty quid I'll also shove a broom up my arse and wipe the floor."

"Come back tomorrow morning," George said. "I might take you up on that."

Fraser took the cash and the cigarette packet.

"Just bring the results back to George here," I said. "I'll pick them up from him.

The lad took some abuse from his friends on the way out for leaving early, but he never looked back... the fifty was all the incentive he needed.

"So, what now?" George asked.

"Buggered if I know," I said, and I meant it. "I've got a body, a missing client, and nobody to talk to."

"What about this?" he said, tapping the envelope. "Is it a clue?"

"Maybe. I'll need to talk to that archivist, Foulkes. The Yank saw him on Friday. It might have been about that document. And I need to talk to Crawford, if the cops don't get to him first. Right now, he's the one with the motive."

A thought struck me.

"Do the Polis know about the poker game yet?"

"Not that I know of. Nobody's asked, and I'm not about to volunteer."

"Thanks George. Maybe if I can find Crawford first, I can get this sorted."

I left my second beer half-finished, waved at Willie and Davy and headed back out into the night.

"Hello John," Joe Boyd said from my left. "I thought I'd find you here eventually."

HE STOOD, just in the shadows.

"Hi Joe," I said, trying to be nonchalant. Inside my innards were tumbling. "I was on my way home, but I've got time for another pint."

He shook his head.

"After the night I've had you owe me better than that," he said. "I need to ask you a few questions."

"Down at the station?"

He laughed.

"No. I don't think you'd like your picture in every paper tomorrow, would you? The place is heaving with reporters. Hell, even Dave Turner is down there, playing at being 'King of the Hill' and trying to squeeze his local angle into the nationals. It's a madhouse."

He looked dog-tired. St Andrews doesn't get many murders, and certainly not a high profile one like this. Joe was a good local cop, but now he'd been thrown into something much bigger. I knew he'd be thinking whether he was up to it.

"Come along to the office," I said. "I've got a bottle of Highland Park in my desk that's got your name on it."

And that's when I knew he was tired. He didn't say no.

We didn't speak on our way back down the High Street until we got near the Excelsior. It was obvious from even two hundred yards away that the residents weren't going to get much sleep. Two police squad cars stood sentry out front trying to maintain a cordon, and a ring of photographers and television crews jostled on the other side of the narrow road. I knew there would be reporters crawling everywhere, some maybe even on the inside by now. They'd be offering bribes to the night porters, looking through the register, trying to get pictures of the dead man's room ... all the things I should be doing about now.

"Shit," Joe said. "Cut through here, quick, before they see us."

We took another of the town's narrow alleyways, cutting across the north-south main streets, and eventually came out on the shore road above the sea-life aquarium. The seal barked at us as we passed its pond, but apart from him we seemed to be the only ones around on this side of the town.

To the north arc-lights lit up the area around the Seventeenth green and judging by the lights and torch beams swinging around, plenty of policeman were still trampling on the hallowed turf.

"We chewed the Seventeenth fairway to bits," Joe said. "It's going to take them days to sort it out."

"They could ask old Tom back for the duration," I said. "He could work magic. Remember that time the Fifteenth flooded the night before the Open?"

"This is worse," Joe said. "My boys tramped everywhere in their size fifteens. It's not just the fairway either. The green looks like a rugby team's been practicing on it."

"The members aren't going to like it," I said.

"Tell me about it," Joe said, running his fingers through his hair. "I've had the club chairman in my office, demanding to know when the course will be cleared."

"What did you say to him?"

"I told him it would take as long as it takes. He's away talking to the Chief Constable now. No doubt I'll get called in and be told to take the case off course."

"The chief's an 'R and A' member, isn't he?"

"Of course, he is. What with the golf and the Masons he's got everything sewn up. You don't think there's any chance of us getting to actually preserve the crime scene, do you? Golf's more important than that," he said bitterly. "And that's why I need to talk to you. If I can get a break on this case before the papers, we might get it wrapped up quickly enough for the Chief, and I might avoid a bollocking."

"What do you think I can do?" I said.

He gave me a look that he'd been giving me for years; every time he knew I was trying to put something over on him.

"Come on," he said, leading the way to the door of my flat. "You've got some explaining to do."

CHAPTER

Sixteen

FIVE MINUTES later we were in the leather chairs on opposite sides of my desk, the bottle of malt between us and our glasses full. I took a long sip, feeling the warmth settle in my stomach, the peaty odour lingering in my throat, reminding me I should be having another one sometime soon.

"So, John," Joe said, a slight smile on his lips. "Tell me about the Texan."

He put a hand up before I started.

"And before we start, here's what I know … it'll save you some of the lies you're about to tell me."

"Come on Joe. When have I ever lied to you?"

He started to count on his fingers.

"Well, there was that time you told me that you could lose your virginity by masturbating…"

"Hey, I believed that one…"

He ticked off the second finger.

"Then there was Mary Dunlop. You told me that she fancied me and let me make a fool of myself in front of everybody at the school dance."

"Well, if it's any consolation," I said. "She wasn't worth your while anyway. She couldn't kiss for toffee."

He was already on to the third finger.

"There was that case with the old lady's will, when you had me running all over the country looking for it when you had it all time."

"Well, you'd put on a bit of weight. You needed the exercise," I said.

He smiled thinly, tapping his fourth finger.

"Do I need to go on?"

"No," I sighed, "You don't have enough fingers. What do you know?"

"The Texan arrived in town late last week. He's chasing up some family history and has been asking around about where he can find records. He's also a golfer and was out on the Old Course on Friday. His sister reported him missing this morning, but because it was only a day, we let it slip...and the Chief is less than happy about that."

He took a long sip from his whisky.

"I know you were hired to find him. I know that you spent most of the day asking around about him, and I know he turned up dead in a bunker. Now it's your turn. Just fill in the blanks for me."

I'd been thinking just how much to tell him. I decided on some of the truth.

"It started this morning, when she walked into the office..."

I told him about Elsa Courtney's visit. He sat quietly until I finished.

"When did she last see the brother?"

"Why don't you ask her?" I said.

He sighed.

"You see, that's just the kind of thing I've been getting from the Chief all evening. *Why didn't you do this, why don't you do that?* It's like being back at school all over again."

He ran his fingers through his hair again and slouched deeper into the chair.

"We've been trying to find your client all day. She left the hotel earlier, and she's not come back yet. There's been no sign since lunchtime."

"I phoned her earlier," I said. "She hung up when there was a knock on the door."

"What time?"

"Just after twelve I think, though I can't be sure."

"And you haven't spoken to her since?"

I shook my head. I neglected to mention the call I'd taken at twenty to seven.

"But I might have something for you," I said.

He sat up straighter and put the whisky down for the first time since I'd poured it.

"The Yank was into more than golf. He was in the Halt most of the weekend, playing poker in the back room."

"I'll not be telling the Chief about that," Joe said. "What he doesn't know can't hurt him. Who was he playing against?"

"Willie Brown, Davy Clark, Sandy Thomas and ... you'll like this ... Jim Crawford."

His ears pricked up when I got to the part concerning Jim Crawford. Joe had been after him for years. It wasn't a vendetta...Joe wasn't the vindictive kind. But given a chance, he'd take great pleasure in finally putting the big man away for a spell.

"Was there much money changing hands?" he asked.

"Hank was a Texan. What do you think? Rumour has it there was eight grand left Crawford's wallet and made its way into the Texan's."

"Eight grand? That could be a motive."

"That's what I've been thinking," I said, and started to lie to my best friend. I left out everything about trying to meet Foulkes and Sandy Thomas, and went straight for the jugular.

"I went to see Crawford. He wasn't in, but his wife said he was up in Dundee. I went looking for him."

Joe's right eyebrow rose.

"Really? What time was this?"

"Just after four. Surely George in the Halt told you?"

"I never believe George on principle," Joe said.

"Generally, a good idea," I said, "But this time he'd have been telling the truth."

The eyebrow rose again.

"And did you find Crawford?" he asked.

"No. He wasn't where his missus said he'd be. After that I spent some time in the City Library. I got a taxi back into town, then..."

"Slow down," Joe said. "Back up. Where were you round about seven o'clock?"

I'd been thinking about the alibi most of the night. The lie came slick and easy.

"I left the library about half six and got a cab into the Town Centre, bought some fags and chips then went to ' the Unicorn...."

He raised his hand again.

"Whoa cowboy. Too fast again."

He got up to pour himself more of my malt and sat back in the chair.

"You're saying you were in Dundee all afternoon?"

"Yep," I said, and poured myself a smaller glass than the one he'd taken. "I just got back about ten minutes before we met."

I tried to let the next question out as if I didn't care about the answer.

"Why? Did you expect me to be somewhere else?"

He looked over the top of his glass and shook his head.

"Come on John. We both know you were out on the Old Course at seven."

I was in too deep to back out now.

"Nope. I was in Dundee." I took my receipts from my wallet and laid them on the desk. "Taxi, fags and chips. Like I told you."

He didn't look at them.

"Since when do you keep receipts?" he asked.

"Since my client agreed to an expense account," I said.

Joe downed the whisky in one and poured another. He'd already drunk more than I'd seen him drink in total over the past year. He sighed loudly.

"Listen. You know I don't think you killed him. It's not your style. But if you and Crawford are in something together, I'll make sure you both…"

"What gave you that idea?" I asked, astonished. "Me and Crawford? You know what I think of him. You of all people should know better."

It never hurts to remind cops of favours you once did for them, although this one hurt as soon as it left my mouth and I felt soiled and dirty. He looked at me, as if trying to read something in my eyes and finally he came to a decision.

"We got a phone call, at six forty-five. It said you and the Yank argued, out near the Seventeenth green, and there was a knife being flashed around."

"And what else did they say? 'Come quick or someone's going to get hurt?' Come on Joe, you and I were trying that one on the cops ourselves when we were fourteen."

"That was then," Joe said. "Were you out on that green tonight? Come on John, this is me asking."

"I told you. I was in Dundee. The caller? Was it a man or a woman?"

"A man. One of the policewomen took it. She said it sounded like a Scotsman, but she said he was near hysterical and got off the line fast. And it was called in from a phone box, so we can't trace the caller."

"Convenient."

"Aye. And bad for you," he said. He rose from the chair. "Are you sticking to the Dundee story?" he asked.

I nodded.

He swept the receipts from the desk and put them in his pocket.

"We've been pals for a long time," he said. "But that'll not stop me arresting you if you're involved."

"I never thought anything else." I said. "But I promise you Joe, I had nothing to do with the Yank's death. Crawford is my main suspect at the moment."

"Mine too," he said, "But I know you. There's something you're not telling me."

"Nothing important," I said.

"I should be the judge of that."

I let that one lie and took a sip of whisky.

He took a long look at the bottle before turning to leave. He turned back at the door.

"I'll be checking your story out. Don't go anywhere; we'll need to talk tomorrow."

He slammed the door behind him, and the room shook as he made his way down the stairs.

I sat at my desk for a long time, cradling another whisky. If it *had* been a man that phoned the police, it meant there was someone else involved. So, either my client was in partnership with someone, or someone had used her to get me out on the course.

Using my own logic, that someone could conceivably be Jim Crawford. It didn't sit right with me. Not for the first time I realised there were just far too many missing pieces in the case. Now I had the police on my back, and an uphill struggle to stay one step ahead of them.

I'd asked for the Bogart case. I'd got my wish. Now I had to live with the consequences.

CHAPTER
Seventeen

I WOKE in the morning still sitting in the chair. It didn't want to let me go, and I had to fight to get my legs to realise they were needed. My back cracked and popped as I pushed myself upright and my shoulders felt like a weightlifter had been using them while I slept.

I warmed up some of yesterday's coffee, lit a cigarette and stood at the window to see what the day would bring.

The first light started to paint the sky outside, a watery sun coming up out of the sea so calm it looked like someone had laid a film of water over a sheet of glass. The high clouds were shot with flecks of pink and streaks of deeper red and the gulls prepared for their first raucous cries of the day.

Although the clock hadn't yet reached seven o'clock, a small bunch of golfers warmed up on the first tee, wrapped up like Michelin men against the spring chill. Out on the sands the first of the runners ploughed their furrows on the beach and cyclists tracked each other along the promontory. It was the usual scene for a St Andrews spring morning.

Closer into town things were different. The car parks near the sea wall were full, and people strode between the parked traffic, all looking purposeful...a thing mostly unknown here at that time in the morning. Almost below me four large trucks had been illegally parked opposite the war memorial. They carried logos of national broadcast companies. Thick wires ran from the trucks into the hotel next door. Alex Dunlop, the owner, would be making a small fortune, selling electricity, renting rooms at extortionate rates and selling gossip for a tenner a time. He'd be loving this... it'd be like an Open Championship come early.

I opened the window and stuck my head outside. By craning as far out as possible without falling out I could see down to the Seventeenth green. The road near the green held a long queue of vehicles, but the playing surface itself had been cleared, and there didn't seem to be any police tape cordoning off any of the area... it looked like the club chairman and the Chief Constable had come to an agreement. What they wouldn't be able to do much about was the hordes of journalists and television people already making their way down the road by the side of the course. Two policemen guarded the Seventeenth green, but they were about to be swamped any minute now. I guessed the Chief Constable would be getting another call soon.

A chill breeze from the sea forced me back inside. I put the whisky back in the desk drawer. Joe and I had made a big dent in it last night. I hoped he was feeling better than I was.

I showered, shaved and changed and finally felt almost human. I was about to start my second cigarette when the phone rang.

"John? It's George here."

"Christ man, don't you ever sleep?"

"Sleep? I haven't been to bed yet," the old man said. "We had a wee game of brag going on in the back room, and the boys kept buying whisky all night. I made nearly two hundred pounds."

"Just as well the tax man doesn't know about your room out the back," I said.

George laughed.

"Who do you think I was playing against? We had two guys from the Revenue Office in East Kilbride in. They're supposed to be playing golf today, but I doubt they'll be surfacing any time soon."

"So why are you calling at this godforsaken hour?"

"I got your name and address for the mobile, but you're not going to be happy."

"Nothing on this case is making me happy," I said.

"The phone was registered to a Mrs Helen Smith, 14 Gloucester Terrace, in Edinburgh. I got somebody to check it. She reported it stolen on Saturday afternoon, here in the town."

"I don't suppose there's any connection between her and Jim Crawford," I said.

"How would I know?" George replied laughing. "You're the detective. I'm just a barman."

I thanked him and hung up. Dead ends and nobody talking…this kept getting better. The newspaper thudded to the floor behind me as I refilled my coffee cup.

"Tourist brutally slain," the headline screamed. "Road-hole bunker claims a new victim." I read the article that followed, but the reporter knew even less than I did. It didn't mention a murder weapon. Nor, I was glad to notice, had anybody mentioned the possible theft of a coat from the hotel. Somebody had found a nice picture of the coal-hole bunker, but not of the body. Joe ran a tight ship and knew better than to give much away. The reporter had managed to find out that there was a sister somewhere. The report offered some speculation as to her whereabouts, and also as to the motive, but nobody had turned up the card game yet, or my own involvement. It would only be a matter of time though. A reporter would splash cash in the Halt sometime today, and a thirsty regular, or maybe George himself, would spill the beans.

I expected it would happen sooner rather than later, and I had to stay ahead of the game. I got my jacket and went in search of Jim Crawford.

THE SUN STARTED to warm the air as I walked up Scotlandwell Road again. The school run was under-way, and large SUVs, big enough to traverse sand dunes in the Sahara or glaciers in Canada, left to take the dangerous and challenging two-mile round trip to the High School. Large cars edged gingerly out of driveways as captains of industry started their commute, and the air filled with "cheerio's" and "byes". Until I got to the Crawford house.

All was quiet. The curtains, both upstairs and downstairs were closed. The red sports car sat in the drive, but there was no sign of Crawford's gold roller. The door played Amazing Grace at me, again and again as I leaned on the bell.

"Piss off. I told you everything last night," a female voice shouted from deep in the house.

I peered through the letterbox.

"Mrs Crawford, It's John Royle. I was here yesterday?"

Something heavy bumped its way down the stairs in the hall beyond. The door finally opened ten seconds later.

I had to look twice. She was still petite and with a body to die for, but she was no longer blonde. Her hair had been turned jet-black, and had been cut in a short, boyish bob. Her face was scraped of makeup, and she wore a baggy jumper five sizes too big for her along with a pair of denims. If anything, she looked sexier than before.

She looked me up and down.

"You said you were here yesterday? I don't remember you."

"You were a wee bit under the weather," I said, "It was yesterday afternoon."

She nodded, still no recognition in her eyes.

"I had a wee bit too much to drink," she said. "I hope I didn't make a fool of myself?"

"No, you were fine. And the kimono was very nice."

She almost smiled.

"We didn't... did we?"

"No, I'm sure at least one of us would have remembered."

"Oh, I'm sure of that," she said. "Nobody ever forgets me."

It was time to turn the conversation around. She was making me recall that red kimono again, and my heart was telling me things my head didn't want to think about.

"Listen, can I come in?" I asked. "I need to talk to you about Jim. I think he's in trouble."

"Oh, you think so, do you?" she said sarcastically. "That makes you *and* the polis."

"They've been here already?"

"Oh yes. Half past one in the morning, and not a word of apology. It was all *'Where is he?'* and *'When did you last see him?'*"

"And what did you tell them?"

She looked at me as if I was stupid.

"What do you take me for? I told them nothing. Jim would kill me if I spoke to the Polis."

It was only then I saw the suitcases in the hall.

"You're going away then?"

I got that look again.

"Hello!" she said, rapping me on the forehead with her knuckles. "The Polis are after Jim. That means the game's up and there's nothing here for me anymore."

"Are you going to meet him?"

"Am I hell," she said. "If you ask me, he's done a runner already."

"What makes you say that?"

"I've had no word since yesterday morning. And this is the man that likes to know where I am every minute of the day. No, whatever happened, he's long gone."

"Aye, him and the eight grand," I said.

That brought her up short.

"What eight grand?"

I told her about the poker game and the Texan.

She shook her head.

"Nope. If he killed the Yank, it wasn't because of the money."

"How do you know that?"

She bent to the floor and lifted a briefcase. She motioned me closer and flipped it open. It was packed tight with fifty-pound notes.

"There's near two hundred grand here," she said, "He kept it under the bed...his *'fuck-off'* money he called it. And he hasn't been back for it."

Suddenly she had tears in her eyes. She brushed them away angrily.

"He's probably hiding out somewhere, waiting for a chance to come back for it. Well, I'm not waiting. Here," she said, pointing at her suitcases. "Make yourself useful and put these in the boot."

By the time I put the cases in the boot of the car she was in the driver's seat. She'd left the front door of the house lying open.

"Aren't you going to lock up?"

"Why?" she said.

She looked me up and down again.

"I'm heading for Amsterdam," she said, patting the briefcase. "It'll be a hell of a party if you want to come."

I laughed.

"No thanks. Jim wouldn't like it."

"Jim can go fuck <u>himself</u> for a change."

The last I saw of her was as the car backed away down the driveway. She blew me a kiss then she was gone.

CHAPTER
Eighteen

I STOOD and looked at the open doorway. For all of a second I considered closing it and walking away, but I couldn't let the opportunity go by. I stepped inside and shut the door gently behind me.

The inside of the house was no more tasteful than the garden —all mock-antique and thick flock wallpaper in garish flowers. I went upstairs first. She'd already done a good job of clearing out anything of interest in the main bedroom... there were drawers open everywhere, and men's clothes strewn about on the floor. In the adjoining en-suite a towel had been thrown carelessly on the floor, black dye streaked through the pink cotton.

The main bedroom was the only one in use...the only one that had been used since they'd bought the house. I walked thorough empty room after empty room, all sterile and clean like a new hotel.

Downstairs was little better. It felt like no one had lived there for years. Apart from the kitchen. Mrs Crawford was obviously no cook...all available surfaces were strewn with takeaway cartons and the remains of TV dinners interspersed with empty liquor bottles. The kitchen held a carton of yoghurt, unopened, a bottle of milk, curdled, and twelve cans of strong continental lager. That proved it; Jim hadn't been home...the lager wouldn't have survived his visit.

The main living area was dominated by a plasma television as wide as I was tall, and a huge state of the art stereo system that made me drool. There were no books, and no desk space. That didn't surprise me much... the big man was never much for reading or writing. The only thing I found of interest was a notepad beside the phone. In amongst the numbers and addresses were several in St Andrews, two of which I recognised as being just on the edge of the old town. I put the notebook in my pocket and went through the rest of the house, but found nothing else...well, nothing that would help me with the case; there was enough hard-core European porn in boxes in the garage to keep someone aroused for years.

I went back through the house, wiping off anything I'd touched, and left.

THE NET CURTAINS of the house across the road twitched as I reached the pavement. I waved again, and the curtains opened. A little old lady beckoned me towards her.

"Come here," she mouthed at the window, looking like a goldfish perpetually surprised by its surroundings. By the time I got to the front door she had it open, and ushered me in, looking around furtively, worried that the neighbours might see.

"Has she gone? Has she left him? About time too, after all the trouble he's given her. I'm surprised she lasted so long. It was only last week that he threatened to batter her all over the town. And he's always drunk...Come in son, don't just stand there gawping."

She was tiny. She only came up to my chest, but was wider than I was, and twice as nervous. She pulled at a thread of her cardigan, fiddled with her horn-rimmed glasses, patted her hair and straightened a picture, all in the time it took me to enter the narrow hallway and close the front door behind me.

She showed me into a living room straight out of the nineteen fifties, all dark heavy wood and floral patterns that hurt the eye to look at them. On the wall hung faded black and white pictures of family, but none of them were recent. No school pictures of grandchildren, no family reunions. The place was clean, but there was a certain mustiness that told me the animals might rule the roost here. She had at least four cats, two budgerigars and a very old dog, and that was just in the living room. The dog lay by the fire. It lifted its head when I walked in, then went back to sleep. I hoped it didn't dream of chasing rabbits; the shock might be too much for it.

"Have a seat son, but mind the new carpet, and try not to sit on the Siamese. She might look dead, but she'll give you a nasty scratch. I keep meaning to get her claws clipped, but just keeping an eye on that house across the road takes up all my time. You're that detective chap, aren't you? I saw you the other day and I…"

She had to stop for breath, her hand held tight to her chest. She was flushed, as if she was having palpitations.

I put up a hand.

"Slow down missus," I said, "Just take your time. Do you have something to tell me?"

She nodded. She waved me to a seat.

"It's about that man Crawford," she said.

She sat opposite me, and a black cat, so fat it looked stuffed, climbed slowly into her lap and glared at me balefully.

"You've been keeping an eye on him?" I asked, noticing for the first time the binoculars and tripod at the window, and the small notebook and pencil on the table beside it.

She saw me looking.

"I'm keeping records," she said. "That's what the police do on stakeouts, isn't it. I've seen it on the telly."

I nodded, having to stifle a laugh at the sudden image I had of the old lady at the window, eating donuts and drinking coffee out of polystyrene cups.

"He's up to something dodgy," she said. "He gets deliveries at all hours of the day. I've been having to sleep down here just to try to catch him at it."

"What kind of deliveries?"

"Big boxes. Hundreds of them."

Her voice dropped to a whisper.

"I think it's fags and booze…smuggled in on that wee boat of his. I've got records of every delivery for the past six months."

"Let me see," I said.

A cat tried to climb up my leg. I brushed it away and it sauntered off, showing me that it was above anything I might have to offer.

The old lady scuttled over and retrieved the notebook. She opened it and showed me the tiny, neat handwriting, but she drew it away when I tried to take it from her.

"How do I know you're not working for him?" she asked. She backed away from me, eyes wide. Her hand went to her chest again, as if trying to keep her heart in. "You could be a double agent. How do I know you're not in on it?"

I suddenly got inspiration.

"If I was, you'd have seen me here before yesterday, wouldn't you?"

She checked the notebook, rifling through pages, mumbling dates to herself. She sounded like a buzz-saw on a go-slow. When she finally looked up at me, she had her smile back.

"You're not here," she said. "Apart from yesterday that is. That kimono was awfy short, wasn't it? Was there anything underneath it? I couldn't quite get a close enough look."

"That's all right. I was close enough for both of us," I said.

"She looked like she was looking for a man," the old lady said. "Do you think she was trying to make Crawford jealous. I'll bet that's what it was. I've seen her try that trick on the milkman, but the poor boy took fright. You've never seen anybody run faster. The kimono's new though. I haven't seen that before. Was it real silk?"

I was having a hard enough time forgetting about the kimono without her asking more questions. I tried to change tack.

"Did they have any other visitors? Say from Sunday lunchtime onwards?

She consulted the book again.

"Sunday, 1:30 am. White van, four boxes in, three boxes out. Sunday, 5:00 a.m. White van, twelve boxes in. Sunday, 6:50 p.m. JC...That's him...arrives home. Drunk. Monday, 3:30 a.m. White van, ten boxes in, three out. Monday, 6:30 a.m. JC...him again... leaves on foot. Monday, 8:00 a.m. Postman, letters, no parcels. Monday, 2:30 p.m. Dick gives MC...that's her...the eye. Monday, 8:00 p.m. White van..."

"I get the idea," I interrupted. Did Jim ever come back?"

She checked, muttering times under her breath. Eventually she looked up.

"No. Not since Monday morning."

"Did the police ask you anything?"

"Last night you mean? No...they were over there for a while, but they never came to talk to me. You'd have thought they'd have been more efficient than that. That's the trouble with policemen these days. They're all too young and too busy with their own lives. You see it on the telly ... they're always talking about their family or their sex lives, or they're down the pub drinking. And they never get the real criminal first time. I know that."

I realised she was more than a bit confused about the difference between television and reality. Then again, it wasn't an uncommon occurrence in this day and age.

"And how long have you been collecting this information?"

"Since they moved in," she said. "I had to go and buy the binoculars specially... my eyesight isn't what it used to be. Since last month they've had five hundred boxes delivered, and they've sent out nearly four hundred. If it is booze and fags that's an awful lot of money. I always wondered how a man like that managed to afford a house here. It used to be such a nice street, but now anybody can get in. The man three doors down is a homosexual. Did you know that? If my Jimmy was still alive, he'd be spinning in his grave.

"So, you see why I can't tell the Police?" she said. "They might be in on it. You hear stories about police corruption. And I've seen that on the telly as well. All sorts of stuff gets let go by the cops when there's a brown envelope stuffed with fifties involved. And even I know there's a lot of money in this town. I'd be surprised if the cops don't take some of it. I know what I'm going to do. I'm going to send my wee notebook to the Prime Minister. He'll know what to do with it."

"You do that," I said, rising. "But be careful. I hear he's a closet smoker. He might be part of the conspiracy."

She thought about that for a bit.

"Then I'll have to get Interpol involved, won't I? Or maybe the CIA? Do you think they'd be impartial?"

I kept a straight face as I left.

"Just keep gathering evidence missus," I said. "That's what they like. Lot's and lots of evidence."

The old dog lifted its head and watched me go, then went back to sleep.

The old lady showed me to the door.

"I'll keep watching," she said. "One of them might be back. And there's still all those boxes in the garage."

I nodded.

"And the police will be back sometime."

"You know that?"

"I know. I have my own way of keeping an eye on what's going on."

"Well, if you like, I can be one of your 'snitches'."

"You're already there," I said. "Just keep an eye on the house. You never know what'll come in useful later."

When I got outside and looked back the curtains twitched,

but I couldn't see through them. She'd be at the binoculars though. She'd always be at the binoculars.

I checked my watch as I walked back to town. It was eight-thirty; still too early to approach Foulkes at the University. I decided to try to catch up with Sandy Thomas at the Old Course.

CHAPTER
Nineteen

QUEUES SNAKED BACK from the first tee. They were being held up from teeing off by groups of reporters, all shoving microphones at people in search of 'opinion' pieces. One of the reporters, a face I recognised from a national television news programme, had cornered a golfer, a stocky, ruddy man in hairy tweeds with an exuberant moustache that almost reached his ears.

"Do you think the club has acted too hastily in reopening the course? Do you think it is insensitive?" the newsman said breathlessly.

The golfer was very well spoken, if not exactly polite.

"Would you think it insensitive if I took that microphone and shoved it up your arse?"

The reporter looked shocked for all of a second, but within a heartbeat he was on to the next person in the queue.

"How does it feel to be playing golf so soon after such a terrible tragedy?" he asked a short swarthy man.

"Terrific," the man said, "I've been looking forward to this all year."

I felt like telling the reporter to quit while he could; he wasn't about to get any joy out of people who'd paid a small fortune for the privilege of playing on the hallowed turf. But he persevered, moving down the queue away from me.

Behind the queue Joe Boyd did a piece to a group of journalists. He looked uptight and uncomfortable. I didn't wave to him ... it wouldn't do for the cop in charge of the case to throw a wobbly on air. I headed down to the practice green. Another group of golfers queued there, waiting to warm up. There were plenty of local caddies around as well, but no sign of Sandy Thomas.

"Hey Bob," I shouted over, annoying a man who was bent over a short putt. His caddie, Bob, came over to speak to me while the golfer missed the putt and glared at me as if I'd just insulted his wife.

"Mr Royle," the young caddie said. "What can I do for you?"

"I'm looking for Sandy," I said.

"He's up at the driving range," Bob said, "With a group of businessmen. He'll be glad to see you ... they're a bunch of tossers. What with them, and the Polis trampling all over the course, he's not in the best of moods."

"I've got twenty reasons to make him happy," I said.

"Anything I can help you with?"

I shook my head.

"I'd forgotten Rule 1 of the golf-course."

"What's that Mr Royle?"

"Never let a caddie get a smell of your money," I said. That got me a laugh all round.

The driving range was further along the shore. I smoked another cigarette as I walked round the bay. The tide was in, forcing the users of the beach into tighter groups above the ribbon of seaweed that marked high tide. Runners had to dodge Frisbee throwers, dog-walkers and kite flyers. The sand was softer up above the water line, and the runners were forced to trudge rather than their usual fluid jog. The scene was more like rush-hour than restful, and I had no qualms about staying off the sand and on the road.

The small café just past the car park was open for the first time that year, but as yet there were no customers, and the sign outside advertising whipped ice-cream looked far too optimistic this early in the season.

There were plenty of cars in the car park though; BMWs, Mercedes and Jaguars aplenty. I guessed a large bulk of them belonged to the businessmen Sandy Thomas was babysitting on the driving range. They weren't doing too well, judging by the cursing coming from my left.

There were fifteen of them, launching themselves at the ball as if their life depended on it, and some of them even managing to make contact. None of them moved the ball more than a hundred yards, and Sandy had the same look on his face that he'd have had if a wasp stung his tongue.

"Caddie!" one of them shouted. "I need more balls."

"You're right about that," one of his friends shouted, laughing. I noticed half of the men were swigging deeply from hip-flasks, and some already had the flushed red glow of the morning drunkard.

"Just keep practicing gentlemen," Sandy said as he saw me, "We'll make golfers of you yet."

Sandy was small and wiry, with an exaggerated waddle in his walk developed over his years in the Merchant Navy. He'd travelled the world as an engineer for Shell, playing golf every-where he went. He retired to St Andrews, but he was far too rest-less to settle. Five years ago he'd taken up caddying, and his organisational ability, coupled with his linguistic skills and knowledge of the game, meant he'd risen to Head Caddie on the retirement of the previous incumbent. He looked like he'd been here forever.

He came over and took the cigarette I offered him.

"Advertising salesmen up from Glasgow," he said, shaking

his head. "They think that with two hours of practice they'll be able to play round the Old Course."

"Any of them capable?" I asked.

He laughed loudly.

"A sorry bunch of piss-artist amateurs the lot of them," he replied. "Some days I don't know why I bother."

"Well, it's better than working for a living," I said, waving my hand at the Old Course, the beach, the sea.

He grunted in agreement.

"What brings you out here anyway? As if I didn't know... it's the Yank, isn't it?"

"Aye. Is it true you caddied him round on Friday?"

"That's right. And he was a good tipper ... he gave me fifty quid and bought me a skin-full of whisky ... then won most of it back in the back room of the Halt later."

"I heard he took Jim Crawford to the cleaners?"

Sandy nodded.

"And then some. That was the biggest hand of cards I've ever seen. Crawford couldn't believe he'd lost. He just sat there with his head in his hands for the longest time. The Yank didn't hang about though. He collected his money and was out of there like a shot."

"Did you see him again?"

"No. It was strange that. I would have expected him to be back on the links sometime, even after the poker. He was mad for this place... couldn't keep away."

"Was he a good golfer?"

"Not too bad at all," he said. "He said he was playing off eight, but it looked more like four or five to me. And he had respect for the course. On the first tee he stood there for at least a minute, tears rolling down his cheeks. 'This is the place,' he kept saying, 'This is the place'."

"A wee bit over the top then?" I said.

Sandy shook his head.

"Its obvious you're not a golfer. This place gets to some folk like that. I've seen many a man reduced to a mess on the first tee. It's the history, the tradition, the thought that they're standing where all the giants of the game have been before them. Some days you can almost feel it in the air."

"Have the Polis asked you about him?"

"Aye. I had Joe Boyd at my door first thing this morning ... he didn't even give me time to put my trousers on. I told him all about it. He seemed to know about the big pot of money ... I suppose somebody in the Halt told him."

I said nothing. Everybody knew I was close with Joe; they didn't have to know how much I'd told him.

"What about his playing partners on Friday? Anything useful there?

Sandy chewed the filter off his cigarette and spat it out before sucking a long draw from what was left.

"That's better," he said. "You need a poultice on your neck to get a draw out of these things. We'll need to wean you on real cigarettes. When I was a lad…"

Sandy was nearly as bad as Willie and Davy when it came to story telling. It was best not to encourage him.

"The other players on Friday?" I said.

"Oh aye. I remember them fine."

A golf ball whizzed between us and flew off into the car park where it bounced once on the bonnet of a Jaguar before disappearing off into the dunes beyond.

"Hey. That was my car," a voice shouted.

"At least it wasn't mine," another voice replied.

I looked over in time to see two men, beer bellies quivering, start to push each other around like a pair of three-year-olds. Voices got raised, and words used that I was sure were not included in the Advertising Sales manual.

Sandy sighed heavily.

"Give me a minute," he said.

And that was all it took. He didn't say a word. He walked between them and looked each in the eye. Although Sandy was a good six inches shorter than either of them, they backed down immediately.

"Come on gentlemen," Sandy said to all fifteen. "Another ten minutes and we'll start on the chip shots."

The group went back to flaying in the air and Sandy came back to join me.

"You were asking about Friday. As I said, there were three of them, the Yank and two others. One of them I knew from before ... he's big in Glasgow. He says he's in property, but everybody knows he's bent."

"Bent? As in a villain?"

"One of the biggest. They say he's got fingers in lots of pies; drugs, porn, illegal immigrants and cheap booze."

"I wonder what the Yank was doing with him."

"I wouldn't ask too much," Sandy said. "I hear they're building a new bridge over the Clyde. That means there's loads of wet cement about that you could have a wee '<u>accident</u>' in."

"Do you know his name?"

"Johnson. Brian Johnson. He's about six foot two and two hundred and fifty pounds, all of it ugly. I'd never seen the other chap before, but I think he was a lawyer or something. He was a good golfer though. He hit this one shot, on the fourth and..."

"<u>Sandy</u>. The Yank? Remember?"

"I remember. Just give me time to get there. At first, he wasn't in the best of moods. He'd had some meeting in the morning that had gone sour. But he perked up when he took a phone call about three o'clock. After that all three of the gents were yakking away all the time. Their mind wasn't on their golf, I'll tell you that. Johnson took a ten at the twelfth. A ten! He was hacking away in the long grass so much that we'll not need to cut it again this year."

He laughed loudly.

I passed him another cigarette. He bit the filter off, spat it out, and lit up from the butt of his old one.

"What were they talking about?" I asked.

"Some property deal or other I think," Sandy said. "They were shy about giving away particulars, but they were talking astronomical amounts of money."

"The Yank was trying to buy property?"

"No. He was trying to sell it."

That gave me plenty to think about.

"And what about Sunday? Did you see him on the course then?"

"No. I left the Halt at eleven in the morning and came straight to work. I was knackered; I can tell you that for nothing. I'm getting too old for these all-nighters. I remember the time ..."

"*Sandy,*" I said again.

He sighed loudly.

"No. I didn't see him on Sunday. And Joe Boyd already asked me that as well. His name isn't in the visitor's book, and none of the lads remember seeing him."

"That visitor's book? It wouldn't have the names and addresses of Hank's partners on Friday, would it?"

I took a twenty from my pocket, but his eyes never left mine. Sandy was old school.

"You know, it just might. I'm heading that way after I get rid of this lot. I'll have a look. I might bring the gen up to the Halt at lunchtime," he said. "I'll need a drink after a morning with these guys. If I can't get away, I'll phone the info to George."

I passed him the twenty pound note which disappeared so quickly into his shirt pocket that even I was unsure it had ever been there.

"You can buy me a beer," I said.

"I'll just put it on your tab," he replied, and laughed.

He smoked the cigarette down until all that was left was a quarter inch of stub. He rubbed that out between his fingers and dispersed the remains to the wind by rubbing it to a fine powder between his hands.

"An old Navy trick," he said. "Never leave a butt behind... that way nobody will ever know when you've had a fly smoke."

The last I heard was him shouting at one of the businessmen.

"No sir. *That's* a putter."

CHAPTER
Twenty

I'D COME TO A CROSSROADS, and one with more than
two choices. I could pursue Jim Crawford through the contacts
in his notebook, chase up Foulkes at the University about his
meeting with the American, or try to find my client. Sandy's
news about Hank settled it for me. I needed to know why the
Texan had been in such a bad mood after his meeting in the
morning...and what had changed it. I worried about Elsa, but as
I didn't have the first idea where to start looking for her, I
headed for the University.

The Royal and Ancient might think it is the *raison d'etre* for
the town's existence, but the University has been around far
longer. Founded in 1413 it is Scotland's oldest school of learning
... and it knows it. It clings to its traditions like a limpet. Even
now in the Twenty-first Century students walk around in long
capes and stewards patrol the old quadrangles looking for
people who might be abusing some obscure Eighteenth Century
by-law. A while back a story had gone round the town that a
student had refused to sit his Finals unless he got a free pint of
ale, as stipulated in a bylaw of 1654. The beer had been brought
and the student sat the exam. Then was failed because he'd

walked across the quadrangle while improperly dressed; he wasn't wearing his sword.

Foulkes' office wasn't actually part of the main group of university buildings. The post of Archivist came with an office and flat in one of the most sought-after properties in town; a tall detached Victorian sandstone extravaganza perched on the cliffs to the north of St Andrews Castle. If it ever came on the market local estate agents would be climbing over each other for a share of the millions it would fetch. But the chances of that were slim. Tradition again, the cement that holds the town together, wouldn't let it happen.

The office was downstairs. I could see a woman working at a computer in the huge bay window that dominated the frontage. To the right a large expanse of well tended garden ran for thirty yards and more past an impressive greenhouse and pond to a massive stone wall that bounded the property. To the left was a garage big enough to house a small bus, and in front of me was the main door, a solid piece of oak as wide as it was tall. I hoped somebody would open it from the inside; I wasn't sure I had the strength to push it open by myself.

The door-knocker was a black iron lion's head with a brass ring on its mouth. It thudded when I used it, metal on wood, loud in the suddenly quiet morning. The woman from the window answered.

"Mr Foulkes please," I said. I flashed my wallet, quickly, my false ID foremost. "Tell him it's Detective Sergeant Adams from CID to see him."

She looked me over.

"Don't they give you a clothes allowance anymore?"

I tried to look sheepish.

"I'm on secondment from Edinburgh due to the murder," I said. "I didn't have time to change."

She still wasn't convinced. She had a no-nonsense look to her that would brook little discussion and certainly no argument. I decided to try charm first.

"Listen," I said, leaning forward conspiratorially. "I'm sure you can help. You must know everything that goes on around here. You know there was a man killed over at the golf course last night?"

She nodded.

"A terrible thing."

I nodded and inched forward a bit closer to her. She smelled of lavender and soap. This close I could see she was fastidious about her appearance. Her nails were buffed just so, and her clothes looked as if they'd been washed and ironed that morning. Her hair was tied back tightly, a ponytail without a hair out of place draped straight down her back almost to her waist.

"Well, the victim was an American tourist," I said, keeping my voice low. "We have reason to believe he met with Mr Foulkes on Friday morning. We just need to know what they talked about, so we can fill in some holes in our enquiries."

Charm hadn't worked. She stood up to her full height.

"I'm sure Professor Foulkes knows nothing at all of this carry-on."

"If I could only see him..."

"I'm afraid that's out of the question. He's working and has asked not to be disturbed."

I sighed. If Joe Boyd ever found out what I was about to do I was going to be in even more trouble than I was already.

"I'm afraid you don't get a say in the matter," I said, and pushed my way past her.

"Don't you need a warrant?" she said and grabbed my sleeve.

"You've been watching too much television missus," I said in my best cop voice, and pulled away from her.

There were three doors off the hallway, but finding the Professor was easy...his name was on his door in big, gold, gothic, lettering three inches high.

I didn't bother to knock.

A grey-haired man sat behind a huge desk, but I almost

didn't notice him. I was too busy looking at the window that ran the length of the room. The window split in two at the middle, a sliding door opening at the right-hand side onto a small balcony. That wasn't what caught the eye. The whole of St Andrews bay lay spread out, framed in the window like a perfect picture postcard.

"If I was you, I'd sit facing the view," I said.

The man spoke without lifting his head as he put something into his desk drawer.

"I don't need to. All I need to know is that it is there," he said. "Eternal and unchanging."

The woman from the door finally caught up with me.

"Professor, I'm so sorry. This policeman just barged his way in here without a by your leave. Shall I call campus security?"

The man raised his head.

"And what use would that do Margaret? Security would only call the police. And they're already here."

He dismissed the woman and waved me over to a chair in front of the desk. My eyes were irresistibly drawn to the view, so it was several seconds before I looked at him and found him looking me in the eye.

I realised he was younger than I'd thought. He might affect the persona, and look to be about sixty, but in reality, he was no more than his early forties. But he was trying hard. He wore the archetypal professor's uniform of tweed suit, checked shirt and bowtie, in this case a vivid bright red one, and his hair was tousled and uncombed. He was going grey on top, but his goatee beard and moustache were still shot with black, and his eye had a youthful twinkle behind his horn-rimmed bifocals,

"You might have fooled Margaret," he said, "But I know you. You're the one that comes close to beating Davy Clark at chess. You're no more a policeman than I am."

I felt my confidence draining away.

"How do you know?"

"Oh, I know Davy well," he said. "We play a couple of times

a month. He keeps telling me that you're getting better. But I understand you've not won a game yet?"

"No. He's too wily."

"I've never beaten him either. Did you know he was Scottish Schools Champion in 1950?"

I laughed despite my situation.

"The old bastard never told me that. I'll have to get him to spot me a pawn from now on."

"It's never helped me," Foulkes said.

He sat back in his chair and put his hands together, steepling his fingers.

"So, I know you're no policeman, but why have you come here? Are you 'on a case'? How exciting."

"It's about the murdered American," I said, "I'm working for his sister. She told me he came to see you on Friday."

"That he did," Foulkes said. "He has, or had, I should say, a deed that he wanted me to look at. It was a legal document from the late Eighteenth Century. He thought it would prove he was due a plot of land near Pitlochry. I'm afraid I had to disappoint him."

"The deed was faked?"

He looked astonished.

"Oh no, it was nothing like that. It was just that the Latin was particularly dense and obscure; not unusual in a Scottish document of that age. It had been mistranslated, that was all. All the deed proved was the gentleman's ancestor had sold the land, not bought it. I'm afraid our American friend had got things the wrong way round. I sent him in the direction of Cupar records office for more information but warned him not to hold out much hope."

"And that's it?"

Foulkes retrieved a pipe and bag of tobacco from his jacket pocket and took a long time to get it going. I got out my cigarettes and lit up a Camel while he was occupied with it.

"Yes," he said finally, sending out a puff of smoke so dense it almost obscured the view beyond. "And he didn't take it well. He called me all kind of names. But that's our colonial cousins for you...no sense of etiquette or tradition."

"That was all?" I asked. "He didn't come back; you didn't call him?"

He gave me the astonished look again.

"I found the man both uncouth and unreasonable," he said, sending out another puff of smoke. The air in the room was getting thick with it. "He left saying he would get a second opinion. That was the last I saw of him."

"And have you told the police any of this?"

"They haven't asked me," he said, "And I didn't equate my visitor with the dead man until this morning. I suppose it's too late to be of any help now."

"It's never too late to help the police," I said.

"It's too late for our American friend, that's for sure," he replied. The smoke from his pipe started to make my eyes water. I stood, trying to get above the smoke line. It worked to a degree. I now had a clearer view out of the window.

"You must be the envy of everybody in the University, having a view like this," I said.

"I have much more than that to provoke the envy of my peers," he said. "A view is just a view, but a brilliant mind is a thing of ephemeral beauty."

"If you say so Prof," I said. "But given the choice, I'll take the view."

"You know," he said, smiling, "I think I would too. Especially this one."

He turned in his chair and looked out.

"Eternal and unchanging. All is well with the world."

He turned back and took a book out of his desk drawer.

"Now if you'll excuse me, I have some work to do. Let yourself out."

I was dismissed. I guessed professors were used to getting

their own way. He didn't look up, even when I stopped in the doorway for a last look at the view. A squally shower was coming in, and rain hit the window like rifle-shot, but still he didn't look up as I closed the door behind me.

CHAPTER
Twenty-One

THE RAIN CAME ON HEAVIER as I left. It spattered against the back of my head in intricate rhythms and a cold breeze ran up my back inside my jacket. A gust of wind swirled an empty fast-food carton away up the road towards the abbey, and the flags on top of the arts faculty building stiffened to attention. I hurried across the road and up the alley to the Halt, hunched against the late reminder of winter.

I gave George the Indian sign on the window again and he let me in. It wasn't long before opening time, and once more the young student was slowly clearing up the bar in preparation for the day. If anything, she looked more bored than yesterday. George was already in position behind the bar, a cigarette clamped between his teeth.

"Well, at least you're not locked up. I was worried when I saw Joe lifting you last night. Did he give you a hard time?" he said.

"Not particularly. But he warned me to stay quiet."

"So where have you been?"

"Off making a noise," I said, smiling.

He lifted a beer glass.

"The usual?"

"Nope," I said, "I'm still working. Let me see that envelope I left with you, would you?"

He passed the packet over, and once more I pored over the contents.

"What is it?" George asked.

"An old legal document. I got it out of the Yank's pocket."

"Does Joe Boyd know?"

"What do you think?"

He smiled. He liked secrets, and I'd just told him a big one.

"How's your Latin, George?"

"Rusty," he said, laughing, "There's not much call for it behind the bar."

I showed him the document.

"I've just been to see Andrew Foulkes about this."

"The archivist? The one with the cape and the stick?"

"That's the one. He says this is worthless. I'm not so sure, but I've no way of proving him wrong."

"Well, for my part, I've never heard a bad word said about the man. He's a stickler for tradition, and some of the students find him too unbending. But apart from that, he keeps himself to himself. He wouldn't even buy the cheap baccy when I offered it to him. He said he didn't want anything tainted with even a hint of criminality. So, I think he's just about as straight as they come."

"Aye, he seemed harmless enough," I said.

I went back to studying the document. I wasn't an expert; I couldn't make out anything that would prove Foulkes a liar, but the man hadn't convinced me. Or maybe I just didn't like the professorial indifference he'd shown. Whatever it was, my bull-shit detector started buzzing loudly when I was with him, and I've found over the years that it pays to take heed of it.

I put the document in the envelope and put it away in my inside pocket.

"Any further on the case?" George asked.

I shook my head.

"Crawford still looks like the best bet," I said, "And that's what the Polis think as well, but my client has gone AWOL, and I'm beginning to get the idea that the Yank was up to something bigger than the poker game."

"The old 'spider sense' working overtime, is it?"

I tapped my nose.

"Never fails me," I said.

"Except when it doesn't work," he said. "Remember that lad who hired you last year to find his girlfriend?"

"Don't remind me," I said, and a shiver ran up my spine. I'd thought he was up to no good, but I took the case anyway as I needed the money. I found his girlfriend for him, but it turned out I'd got it wrong...she was already married, and my client was found hanging by his tie in his bedroom, the floor strewn with red rose petals.

"Nobody can be right all the time," I said.

"Right enough," he replied. "But some people's average is better than fifty-fifty. And here's more bad news—young Fraser hasn't been able to start on that soil analysis yet. He couldn't get into the lab last night. He says he'll get to it this morning."

"I've come to expect it on this case," I said. "Nobody seems to be talking; nothing much seems to be happening."

"Apart from the body in the bunker I suppose?" George said dryly.

"Aye. We mustn't forget about that. If it wasn't for Joe Boyd, I'd have been fitted up for that one by now."

"On the plus side, Sandy Thomas sent you a message," George said. He passed me a small card. There were two names and addresses on it...one a legal firm in Edinburgh, the other for Johnson, listed as a property developer in Glasgow. I put that away in my pocket as well. It was getting busy in there; I had the envelope, the card, and Crawford's notebook, and once more it was time for a decision. The trouble was, all three made my 'spider sense' tingle.

"I'd better be going," I said. I didn't know where to start, and the beer started looking awfully tempting.

George waved an empty glass at me.

"On the house? One more on your tab won't make a difference."

Willie Brown and Davy Clark made my mind up for me. The girl left the bar to officially open the doors, and the two oldsters were already waiting on the pavement outside. Willie insisted on buying me a drink.

"I won some money at crib yesterday," he said, "I'm feeling flush."

"You never beat Davy?" I said, astonished.

They both laughed.

"Naw. We took yon reporter pal of yours to the cleaners; nearly thirty quid. He disnae have the sense of a sparrow when he's had a couple of drinks in him."

"In that case, if it's Dave's money you're spending, I'll definitely have a pint."

I joined the old men at their corner table and George brought the drinks over. They already had the day's argument under way, and it sounded like it had been going for some time.

"It was Philip Marlowe. I'm telling you. Raymond Chandler did the screenplay. He adapted it from one of his short stories," Willie said vehemently.

"No, it wasn't Marlowe," Davy said. "Marlowe was never as nasty as that fellow. And Marlowe would never have driven anything as flash as yon sport's car. I've told you already. It was Mike Hammer."

"It can't have been Hammer, you daft bugger," Willie said, "It was far too early."

"What! 1956! You're definitely going senile." Davy said, "Marlowe was much earlier than that. If anything, '56 is far too late."

He turned to me and smiled.

"This one's all your fault John," he said. "And you can answer it. 'Kiss Me Deadly.'" Tell the auld man here who wrote it."

"Spillane," I said. "And it was definitely Hammer ... don't you remember his secretary, Velma, with yon pyramid bra under the tight jumper? *Va-va-voom, Mikey!*"

Davy laughed, but Willie looked puzzled.

"Was that not the one with Lauren Bacall in the tweed suit?"

Both Davy and I said it at the same time.

"No. That was 'The Big Sleep'."

All three of us laughed.

"Anyway, how is it my fault?" I asked.

"Och, Willie said you were daft, walking about in Scotland dressed like Mike Hammer," Davy said.

Willie at least had the good grace to look embarrassed as Davy continued.

"I told him it wasn't Hammer; it was Marlowe. From there we got on to the films and the auld man here tried to tell me that 'Kiss Me Deadly' was a Marlowe movie. As if I didn't know it was Spillane. I took Carol MacGuigan to the pictures to see it in '57."

"Ah, Carol McGuigan. She was a wee stoater," Willie said, and he did the most disgusting thing you've ever seen with his false teeth and upper lip. "I remember the time ..."

"Stop changing the subject and pay up," Davy said. "You owe me a fiver."

Willie moved to get his wallet out when I stopped him.

"Actually, you're both wrong. It's Sam Spade."

"What, the film?" Willie said.

"No, you idiot," Davy replied. "He means the clothes ... the suit, the braces, that smelly hair gel he wears."

"Oh. Sam Spade. Was that Alan Ladd? He was good in that one about the wee eagle."

I started to interrupt when I realised Davy was barely containing fits of laughter. When I looked at Willie, he winked at me and smiled.

I'd been had, big time.

It was my round, again.

CHAPTER
Twenty-Two

GEORGE HAD LEFT his position at the bar, and when I made the circular motion with my hands the young student looked at me as if I was demented. I sighed and went to get the drinks. By the time I got back they were arguing, golf again, about whether Nicklaus or Woods would hit the ball further if both were in their prime. As ever, it was one that neither would win, but that wasn't the point.

I sat, half listening to them talk of yardages and four-woods, remembering all the times I'd spent in the company of the old men over the years. I wouldn't have given up a minute of them; this was my part in the town's tradition, as Foulkes had said, eternal and unchanging. The way I liked it.

"What do you think John?" Davy asked, but I had no idea what I'd been asked so I made a guess at an answer.

"You know me Mr Clark. What I understand about golf could be written on the back of my fag packet."

"No," Willie replied, "We were asking about the Yank. Who do you think did it?"

"And are you still on the case?" Davy asked. "We saw D.I. Boyd take you away last night."

"Well, Joe thinks I'm off the case," I said, "But my client is missing, and I'm still on it till I get paid. As for big Hank...the general idea among the Polis is that Jim Crawford did him for the poker money. I'm surprised Joe hasn't been to talk to you two yet."

"I'll get round to it sooner or later," a voice said behind me, and Joe Boyd put his hand on my shoulder.

I must have stiffened.

"Relax Johnny boy," he said, "I've come to talk to Mr Brown and Mr Clark."

"Will you have a beer Inspector Boyd?" Willie Brown asked. He surprised me with the offer, but I should have expected the next remark. "John's in the chair."

Joe smiled, but he looked even more tired than he had in front of the clubhouse earlier.

"I've just come off a twenty-hour shift during which I've been dealing with reporters, television crews, chief constables and Old Course officials; Jim Crawford has done a runner, and my pal John here is refusing to do as he's told. Yes, I think a beer is in order."

George nodded towards Joe as I got to the bar.

"I can stall him if you want to slip out the back door?" he said.

I shook my head.

"No, he's just chasing his tail. Give him a beer. He looks like he needs it."

When I got back from the bar again, Joe was already asking them the same questions I'd asked them yesterday. I listened carefully, but Joe got the same story as I did ... not a common occurrence when these two were involved.

"And you've no idea where Crawford went after he left here?"

"No sir," Willie said. "We left before he did."

It was strange to see the deference the old men paid to Joe, who they'd known since he was in the cradle. But that was the way they'd been brought up. Police and doctors got respect, at least until they showed they weren't worthy of it. Joe was still worthy of it.

"And you've no clues as to where Crawford's gone?" I interrupted.

Joe turned to the old men.

"If you'll excuse us," he said to Willie and Davy, "My sergeant here and I have police matters to discuss."

My heart went pitter-patter.

He knows I've been to see Foulkes, I thought. And even after Willie and Davy laughed, and Joe and I made our way to a quiet corner I still wasn't sure. I lit a cigarette to cover my confusion and sat opposite him.

He leaned forward, his voice just above a whisper.

"I've just been round at Crawford's house," he said, "It looks like the wee blonde has gone to join him. She's cleared out."

"Did you find..." I said. I had to bite my tongue. I faked a cough to disguise the fact that I'd almost mentioned I knew about the porn.

I started again.

"Did you find any clues as to where they've gone?"

"Not a sausage," he said. "And that's why I need a favour."

He leaned even closer.

"You know this town as well as anybody. Is there anywhere he could be holed up that I don't know about?"

Rule one of the Private Detectives handbook; never turn down a chance to do a cop a favour. Ten minutes later we were on our way to the first address in Jim Crawford's notebook. I didn't tell him how I knew about the addresses; I wasn't that stupid.

HE WASN'T keen on me tagging along with him, but if there was anything at those addresses pertaining to the case, I wanted to see it.

Outside in the daylight he looked more tired, and far older than his years.

"Rough night?" I asked.

"You don't know the half of it. There were a couple of times when all I could think about was that bottle of whisky on your desk. And I'm still nowhere nearer the killer."

"Do you really think it was Crawford?"

He nodded.

"Forensics are going over everything now, but I'll bet you a tenner that the big man's prints are on the knife. I can feel it in my water."

"Did they find anything else?"

"No," Joe said, shaking his head. "I spent a bad hour in the morgue watching the autopsy. Whoever killed him did a good job. Whoever did it bashed his head in, and the knife smashed two ribs before it got to his heart. The lab boys are going over the knife and the clothes now, but it'll be a while before I get any results. Meanwhile, the Chief wants action. And if he finds you and me together, I'll be in deep trouble."

"Not if we find Crawford. He'll give you a medal."

"I'll settle for things going back to normal," he said.

The rain settled into a constant drizzle and the sky turned slate grey. That drove most of the shoppers inside and we were able to walk down North Street unimpeded by pedestrians. We turned left at the Whey Pat Tavern and down the hill away from the old town.

"Remember Granny Martha's sweetie shop?" Joe asked out of the blue. I realised we had just walked past the spot where most of our pocket money got spent in our youth. It had been turned into a flat many years ago when the old woman died, and I hadn't thought about it for a long time. But the mention of the old woman's name brought back the smells and tastes of the shop, with its tall glass jars full of many different things to rot young teeth.

"Four chews for a penny," I said.

"Aye, and sherbet dips with a stick of liquorice for tuppence. Happy days."

"Maybe for you," I said. "I'm just glad that I finally made it into long trousers. Come on. The first address is just at the foot of the hill."

It turned out to be a closed and boarded up hairdressing salon. The last time I'd noticed it, it had been a video rental shop. And before that, an ironmonger's. It was on a corner spot away from the centre of town...I guess passing trade wasn't enough to sustain a business.

Joe turned the handle on the front door. It was locked tight. He tried to peer through the windows.

"I can't see anything in there. It's too dark."

"Stay here. I'll look round the back," I said.

"Don't do anything illegal," he said.

"As if I would."

The back yard was like back yards everywhere. It smelled, of Chinese take-away, chips and something worse. Black bin bags lay strewn everywhere, like bloated maggots. Some of them were burst, their guts spilling on the concrete to be pecked over and examined by the herring gulls that struggled, screeching, onto the roof as I passed. Something small and furry dived out of my way. It may have been a rat, but I didn't like to look too closely, and it didn't stop to examine me.

Even in this squalor, someone had tried to make a place to live. A cardboard box on end in the corner had an old carpet on its floor and a small forest of empty fortified wine bottles guarding its entrance.

I tiptoed through the remains of a Chinese meal and tried the door handle which spun loosely in my hand. The lock was bust but there was a window next to the door that was badly cracked, and I only had to lean hard on it for it to fall in with a muffled crash. I turned to call Joe, but he was already by my side.

"It broke in my hand. Honest," I said.

"Aye. You tried that one on me when we were twelve," he said. "I didn't believe you then either."

It didn't stop him being first inside though. I followed him through.

"Careful," he said. "Some idiot has got broken glass all over the place."

We were in a dim back room. It smelled musty and old, like a wet book. The dust we disturbed on entering still floated in the air, tickling my sinuses. A sink in the corner seemed to be filled with something oily, black and best avoided. Piled high along all available wall space were huge cardboard cartons.

"What do you think is in them?" I asked. In truth I had a good idea. The boxes looked to have come from the same batch I found in Crawford's garage. I was proved right when Joe kicked one of the boxes over and a pile of hard-core magazines spilled on the floor.

He picked one of them up and flicked through it.

"Christ. Would you look at that," he said. There was both wonder and disgust in his voice. He held the magazine out to me. It fell open at the centrefold picture. It was all in the sharpest possible focus and shot so close you could be in no doubt as to the reality of it. Two women were doing something unspeakable with a great Dane. The dog at least looked to be enjoying it.

Joe dropped the magazine to the floor in disgust.

"We found a garage full of that rubbish up at the house," he said.

I bent down and picked up the magazine again, studying the picture closer.

"I didn't know you were into that kind of stuff," Joe said, laughing when he saw me hold the magazine to the light in order to see it better.

"I'm not. But Mrs Crawford is," I said. I pointed at the blonde under the animal. "She wasn't doing that when I met her."

Joe had a closer look.

"Did she look as bored as that?"

"Worse," I said. "At least she looks sober in the picture."

Joe had another look.

"I meant to ask you about her. I remembered you saying you'd met her. She didn't say anything about going away?"

I chose to ignore that, covering my refusal to answer by dropping the magazine to the floor and kicking the spilled pile out of my way.

"Now we know what he was bringing in off the boat."

"Aye," Joe said, "We've been trying to catch him for years. We thought it was drugs."

"There a wee woman lives across the road from him. She thinks its fags and booze," I said. "But she's been keeping an eye on Crawford for months. She's got records of all his shipments. You'll probably need to talk to her."

"The old biddy with the twitching curtains and the cats?"

"That's the one. But play it easy with her. She thinks the Polis are part of the conspiracy."

Joe laughed hollowly.

"Her and half the rest of the country. I'll send a policewoman round this afternoon. Tea and sympathy should work."

I nodded.

"And whatever happens now, you've got a case against him," I said.

"Maybe," he replied. "But we've got to catch him first. And if he did the Texan, the porn will be the least of his worries."

There were more boxes in the front room, piled against the walls, filling the sinks, stacked in precarious piles on the chairs, but there was no sign that anyone had been there for a while. Our footprints left tracks in the dust, the only ones to disturb it.

"Over here," Joe said. "Give me a hand."

There was a door off to our left. We shifted three heavy boxes to get to it, but it opened out onto a cupboard, empty except for an ancient kettle and six cups.

"I don't think he's here," Joe said dryly.

"Don't worry," I said. "I've got a couple of other places to try yet."

We headed back through to the room at the rear.

"I should phone this in," Joe said as we climbed back out of the window.

"It's not going anywhere," I said. "Let's check out the next place first, then you can come back here if it's another blank."

He agreed reluctantly, and I led him away from the yard and out onto the road.

CHAPTER
Twenty-Three

I COULD STILL SMELL the stink of that back yard and the taste had inveigled itself into the back of my throat. I lit a cigarette and let the smoke wipe away the lingering memory.

"Give me one of them will you," Joe said.

"I thought you quit," I said.

"I just started again." He took a cigarette, and I lit him up.

He sucked smoke gratefully, taking it deep and letting it out slow.

"Careful," I said. "It'll go straight to your head...or your stomach."

"If I can survive watching a body getting cut up without losing my supper, I'm sure I can handle one fag," he said.

He took another long draw.

"First one since the autumn before last," he said.

"And only a hundred yards from the first one ever," I said.

"Aye. I remember. What age were we?"

"Thirteen. Nearly fourteen," I said. "It was summer, remember; just after the school broke up for the holidays."

"I remember. You stole ten Regal from your father."

"And got beat black and blue later. I'm not going to forget that in a hurry."

"I remember it like yesterday," Joe said. "We hid ourselves at the back of an old shed in the dye-works with the fags and a packet of safety matches."

"And you were sick that time," I said.

"Well, we did smoke five each in less than an hour. We deserved all we got."

Surprisingly the habit took with both of us.

"The old shed is long gone," Joe said sadly. "We had some good times playing there."

I nodded. The factory was supposed to be off limits to kids, but we always found ourselves drawn to it. The factory had been torn down long ago, replaced by the square, featureless concrete block of flats that we were walking alongside. By the look of them the flats themselves would be gone soon.

Meanwhile, I was still a smoker. Joe had given up frequently over the years, the last time for over eighteen months, but once a smoker, always a smoker. I wasn't surprised that the case had knocked him off the wagon.

We smoked in silence as we went past several car showrooms to a large row of small business units built into the structure of an old warehouse that had been part of the dye-works. They'd been built in the early nineties, part of an initiative to try to keep work in the town after the factory closed down. It had nearly worked. For a while mechanics, plumbers and electricians had rented the units and small businesses thrived. Then the local council put the rent up by sixty per cent. In the past two years the units had fallen quiet. Some were still used as storage, but more than half were empty, and the tradesmen had all moved on to ply their trades elsewhere.

The address I had was the nearest one to the road. It didn't look promising; the large roll up door was dented and bashed, and the bottom half of it was studded with rust. I went up to it and tried to pull the door up, but it was locked tight. I gave it a kick; the echo vibrated around us.

I hit the jackpot when I went round and looked in the

window at the side of the unit. Grease and dust coated the window with a thick film. I used my handkerchief to clear a spot and peered inside.

Crawford's gold "roller" had been parked in the centre of the confined space. He'd bought it five years ago when he felt he'd finally made it. He never used it much, but when he did, he made sure as many people in town saw it as possible. He took great delight in telling everyone in the Halt that he'd bought it from a famous television personality, and he'd found a pair of her knickers and a condom in the glove compartment.

He wouldn't be telling that story again. I'd been so excited about finding the car that I almost didn't notice the body slumped in the driver's seat.

YOU'D BETTER CALL YOUR BOYS," I said as I stepped away from the window. "We've found Crawford."

Joe had a look through the window, then immediately pulled out his mobile. He talked fast for about a minute. When he'd finished, he took me by the arm. He no longer looked tired, he looked excited; pumped up.

"Get out of here John," he said. "You don't want to be here when the troops arrive."

"Like hell I will," I said. "I want to see him."

"And I'm saying you can't. Not this time."

He held my arm tighter.

"Go back to the Halt," he said. "Drink beer; play pool; lose to Davy at chess. But stay away from here and stay away from that hairdressers. I'll get a message to you later."

I looked him in the eyes.

"Is that a promise?"

He looked back at me, and his stare didn't waver.

"One blood brother to another," he said smiling, and showed

me the scar in his palm. I showed him the match of it on my own right hand, and we shook on it.

I got away just in time. I moved away from the warehouses and turned against the wind to light a cigarette, just as the first of the boys in blue's cars sped past me, followed by an ambulance, and the first intrepid journalist; one who had obviously been paying attention. I took a quick left and cut through the council estate.

Joe and I were brought up here. As council estates go it wasn't a bad one to grow up in. It was clean and well kept, free of the graffiti and dereliction so obvious just twenty miles away in Dundee. Joe's mother still lived about two streets from where I was standing. Back then they'd been on the edge of town, with a small area of woodland immediately behind their back garden.

Joe and I spent a large amount of our summer holidays in that wood, alternately playing a cowboy or an Indian, or chasing down Edward's army at Bannockburn with home-made swords and spears. It was there, in a spot which was now in the middle of a modern estate of commuter villas, where Joe and I had pledged to be blood brothers.

We cut our palms with a bit of broken glass and clasped hands. I don't remember where we got the words, but we both knew them off by heart.

"Do you swear to be true," Joe said.

"I so swear it," I replied.

The blood ran from between our hands and dripped to the ground to be soaked up in the dry, cracked, mud.

"Do you swear that we are brothers, through fire, water, pain and even unto death?"

"I so swear it."

"Then brothers let us be," we said in unison.

I remember it as if it was yesterday. Twenty-five years ago, and we each still had the scars; and the bond. We'd stuck together through our school years, had our first beer together, our first dates were as a foursome; we were almost inseparable.

All that changed when we hit eighteen. I went to University in St Andrews, and Joe went to College in Aberdeen. Slowly, over the next five years, we drifted apart. He came home from college less often. I dropped out and went to work for the Council as a clerk and started drinking too much and sleeping too little.

By the time Joe became a Detective Sergeant and got posted back to St Andrews a lot of time had passed and we were tentative around each other. After all, detectives with a career in mind couldn't be seen socialising with the local drunk. Things stayed that way for a while, until the day I punched my supervisor, got sacked, and nearly got arrested. Joe made the charge go away, and I went to the Halt to hear Old Willie talk about his cousin, the fat detective.

We finally renewed our friendship when I got my act together and started the business. Now we were almost like brothers again; maybe not till death, but I still felt bad at lying to him. Walking the street of our youth didn't help in making the guilt any lighter.

As I walked through the estate, I noticed signs that urban decay was beginning to spread here. Some of the houses had boarded up windows; unkempt gardens and rusting hulks of cars in weed-infested yards. Others had front doors daubed with graffiti and curtains grey with grime. Here and there were dotted oases of gardens packed full with colour, recently trimmed hedges and clean shiny door and windows, but they were few, and far between. Groups of young children ran in the roads.

"Hey mister," one of them said to me. "Have you got a fag?" He was no more than ten. I walked on, ignoring him.

"Wanker," he shouted after me, and the rest of his 'gang', some as young as five, took up the chant. An old woman was out clearing her driveway with an old wooden brush. She shook her head sadly, but wouldn't look me in the eye, and scuttled away before I said anything she might have to respond to.

I realised my feet had taken me down a well-known path. I'd turned off the main road without even thinking and found myself in a street I hadn't seen in years. In my youth I'd walked this way home from school. After Joe left me to go into his own home, I'd get steadily slower the closer I got to home, delaying the inevitable. I knew every crack in the pavement along here.

The house where I grew up was one of the less well-kept ones in the street. Black bin bags sat like maggots, grouped around the door. Discarded kid's toys lay across a rough lawn, and there was dog crap everywhere, fresh and old, interspersed by some yellowed patches of grass. The front door was half open and I could see, just inside, discarded piles of clothes. A child, no more than two years old, sat in the garden and smiled at me, oblivious to the squalor. It wore a disposable nappy, and nothing else.

I walked past fast … too many memories, not all of them good. Mum lived in this house until she died, five years ago, cancer eating her away slowly until the last spark went out as I held her hand in Ninewells Hospital. Dad? He left when I was fifteen. I barely noticed, save for the fact that I collected less bruising, and I was able to walk home without fear or trepidation.

The sun came out as I walked round out of the estate onto the Anstruther Road. I crossed over and took the public footpath round the West Harbour. A small armada of yachts bobbed in the tide. One of them was Crawford's, but I had no idea which one. I sat on a bench and watched them for a while. My mind raced, wondering about the implications of finding the body.

If Crawford committed suicide, I knew that the Chief Constable would say 'Thank you very much,' and wrap the case up quick. But suicide or not, I couldn't get the image of the case of fifties out of my mind. The Jim Crawford I knew would not leave, alive or dead, without a hand on that briefcase. Something else was going down, someone else had to be involved. But I might not get a chance to find out who that might be.

I sat and smoked another cigarette, my head full of poker games, old documents, missing clients and dead bodies. Sometime in the five minutes I came to a decision. Joe had told me to stay away from Crawford's body, but he hadn't actually warned me off the case.

I did something I should have done last night. I headed once more for the Excelsior Hotel.

CHAPTER
Twenty-Four

THE PRESS PACK had got whiff that something was going on, and they'd nearly all moved away from the front of the hotel. Only the hard core were left; including Dave Turner. He scribbled frantically in a small notebook as I approached.

"I thought you'd be off ambulance chasing," I said.

He looked surprised to see me.

"I heard Joe Boyd lifted you," he said. "I was just writing the headline: 'Local PI arrested in murder hunt'."

"Much as I'd like to see myself on your little wall of front pages, I'm going to have to disappoint you. You've made the wrong choice staying here. All the action is down on the Kirkaldy Road."

I lowered my voice so the few remaining reporters wouldn't hear me.

"So, here's your scoop. Joe Boyd and I found Crawford. He's dead. Propped up at the wheel of that big roller of his."

His eyes went big, and he started scribbling even more frantically.

"Murdered?" he asked.

"I don't know. Joe wouldn't let me near the body," I said.

"But keep me out of it, and you can get one over on the big boys. Joe won't be bringing them up to speed for a while yet."

He clapped me on the arm.

"Thanks John. You're a pal."

"Not really," I said. "I'll be expecting a favour in return someday."

"Just say when," he replied. He was anxious to be off now; he'd started twitching.

"Away you go and file your copy," I said. "I'll see you in the Halt later."

He scurried off. The few remaining reporters looked at me.

"Do you know something we don't?" one asked.

I thought I might as well give Dave a head start on the others by putting them off the scent.

"Aye. There's been another murder. A bad one at that... blood everywhere they say."

"And that's where your pal is off to?"

"Aye. Down on the Kirkaldy Road. There's an army of Polis down there already."

In less than a minute I was on my own in the road.

I DUCKED under the makeshift cordon at the front of the hotel and walked straight into the reception area with nobody to stop me.

The pasty-faced black-haired youth behind the desk picked at his left nostril. He studied the result before popping it into his mouth.

"Where's the scary girl with the sharp pencil?" I asked.

"It's Carol's day off," he said. "And I agree with you, she is pretty scary. You should see her with a bread knife."

Then he remembered his job.

"Can I help you sir?"

"Ah, that's better," I said. "I don't know you. Are you new here?"

He nodded.

"Just for the summer. It keeps me in beer money. I thought it would be a cushy number, but today has been a nightmare."

"You must be glad to get rid of the rat pack," I said.

"You don't know the half of it. They've been trying to bribe the staff ever since they got here," he said. "One of them even managed to get into the dead gentleman's room."

"Terrible, really terrible..." I said. "I don't suppose they found anything."

He looked askance at me.

"You're not from the papers?"

"No," I flashed the false ID again. "D.S. Adams, CID. I'm just going over the ground again, making sure our lads didn't miss anything."

"Oh, they were very thorough," the receptionist said. "They talked to all the cleaning staff, and even to some of the guests."

"Has anybody questioned you yet?" I asked.

He shook his head.

"They never got round to it. Not that I could be of any help," he said. "The only time I saw the American gentleman was when he accessed his safety deposit box."

My heart skipped a beat.

"When was this?"

"Friday morning, just after breakfast," he said.

"And was he putting something in or taking something out?"

"I have no idea, but we could have a look?"

I let my heart calm down before I replied.

"Let's do that."

It was ridiculously easy. Five minutes later I was in a small room behind reception.

The receptionist took out a key.

"This will open it," he said. "Maybe I should stay while you have a look."

"And maybe it's just a wee bit too late for you to be getting concerned about your customer's privacy. Just go back to reception and stop anybody coming through here. Where's the box?"

"Down here."

He showed me a metal cupboard under the desk, with a set of twenty drawers, each with a small keyhole.

"You want number 18," he said. He handed me the key and left me to it.

My heartbeat was up again as I turned the key in the lock and opened the drawer. I don't know what I was expecting, but I was disappointed. Inside was a single piece of paper, a letter, to Hank Courtney, from the Scottish Antiquarian Society, dating back nine months.

Dear Mr Courtney,

During a wind up of the estate of Mr George Roberts of Crail a letter has been unearthed that never saw delivery. This correspondence was discovered in a box of family letters that seems to have been hidden inside a chimney of the Roberts family home and has only recently come to light due to refurbishment in the house.

The executor of the estate has requested that, as a document of historical importance, and, relating as it does to the Courtney family, this should be delivered to the appropriate surviving family members if at all possible.

We have established, through a search of records, that your grandfather, George Courtney, was himself the great grandson of the proposed recipient of the letter.

We hope that the letter may shed some light on your own family history, and if you ever need any help in this regard, do not hesitate to get in touch with us.

Yours Sincerely
Joyce Grant
Curator of Documents and Maps
Scottish Antiquarian Society

I could only guess that the 'letter' had concerned the deed I already had in my pocket. I took out the envelope and checked the postmark; the dates matched. But in that case, where was the 'letter' itself? I filed that away as something to think about later. I closed the box and put the letter inside the envelope with the deed.

"Was it any help?" the receptionist asked as I left.

"No. It was empty."

"I hope I won't get anybody into trouble," he said. "For not mentioning it earlier I mean."

"Just don't tell the D.I.," I said, smiling. "He'll have my guts for garters."

"D.I. Boyd you mean?" he said.

"I nodded."

"I talked to him earlier," he said. "He was checking up on Ms Courtney."

"Still no news?" I asked.

"Nothing since she phoned in to check out," he said.

I was struck dumb again for all of five seconds.

"For somebody that claims to know nothing, you're a mine of interesting information. When was this?"

"I told D.I. Boyd already," he said, the first trace of petulance showing. It was time for the 'cop' voice again.

"Well, you can tell me sonny," I said, "Or would you rather come down to the station?"

He looked like he might burst into tears.

"It was this morning," he said, "Just after I came on shift, about eight o'clock. She called and said she was checking out."

"Did she come back for her bags?"

"No," he said," She asked that we send them on to the airport. She said she'd pick them up from there. She was distraught. Poor woman, losing her brother like that."

His brain finally caught up with what he was saying.

"Does that make her a suspect?"

I tapped my nose.

"Police business," I said. "I'm sure D.I. Boyd has already checked it out."

CHAPTER
Twenty-Five

I WASN'T any further forward, and I wasn't going to be until Joe came back to me with news about Crawford. I yielded to the inevitable and headed for the Halt.

There are times on every case when you just have to leave things alone, let them stew. And the only way I could get my brain to switch off for long enough was to sit in a bar and throw alcohol at it.

George had already poured my first pint as I crossed from the door to the bar.

"I hear there's a bit of a flap on," George said as he handed me the beer, "Down at the old dye-works."

"Aye. The Polis are all over the place," I said. I didn't elaborate. This was Joe's gig now.

Willie and Davy were in their seats, but they were playing backgammon. I knew better than to intrude. I took my beer to a quiet seat, lit up a cigarette, and started switching off my critical faculties.

In cities you have young folks' bars, business men's bars, working men's bars, gay bars, each with their own clientele, each nicely segregated. But in a small town there isn't room for that. In bars like the Halt the rich and poor, labourer and landowner, elderly and youthful, they all rub shoulders together. And one of the things about pubs with regulars was that you got to know their habits, like old friends you saw every week.

Jessie and Jock Martin, over near the window, looked like they were onto their fourth round of double vodkas. At some point in the next half hour, Jessie would start crying and hit Jock. She'd storm out, he'd go after her, and they'd have their fifth round while making up. It happened every week...you could set your clock by them.

Over to my left a huddle of old men surrounded an open fire, although they produced more smoke than it did. Every fifteen minutes they all got up and left, only to come back in, some smiling, some scowling. They too were as regular as the sweep of the minute hand, slaves to the racing timetables and the bookmakers around the corner.

Nearer the bar five youths, scarcely old enough to be out of school, were laying attack to a fruit machine, excited that it had given them a payout that was in all likelihood a tenth of what they've put in. In about an hour they'd be getting louder, fueled by foreign lager and bravado. One of them would swear at George, and they'd all get marched out, only to come back later, sheepish and quiet.

Three middle-aged women sat at a table surrounded by plastic shopping bags, smoking menthol cigarettes and throwing vodka down their throats as if they were in a rush. I knew one of them, the mother of another schoolmate. They too were regular. By four o'clock, they'd all leave to head home and microwave their husband's dinner.

A very old man, Alisdair MacLean, sat at his corner table, a half-pint of beer and a whisky in front of him. He was fast asleep, and at his feet his equally old dog lifted its head and rooted for fleas. Mac was rumoured to be ninety-six, but even he couldn't remember any more. At six o'clock George would wake him and George's wife would take him home and see him to bed. He'd be back tomorrow, at one-thirty. His drinks had been on the house since he turned ninety, but he never drank more than a half of beer and a whisky, and most days he hardly touched either. Sometimes he'd join Willie and Davy at the cribbage board, but mostly he just sat, watching life go by.

That's what I was trying to do, but my brain kept rebelling, showing me pictures, of Hank the Yank, staring up from the bunker, or of Jim Crawford, slumped over his steering wheel. Drastic measures were called for. I finished off the beer and headed for the bar. I drew up a stool and ordered the first of what I hoped would be many whiskies.

"That's a nice line of malts," I said to George, pointing at the bottles lined along the gantry. I put a fifty pound note on the counter.

"I'll start at the left-hand side," I said. "Give me one of each. If the money runs out before I fall off the stool, let me know."

He gave me a look.

"Are you sure?"

"Never surer," I said. "Just keep them coming."

I was on the Bruichladich when Fraser the botanist came in and caused the first minor sensation of the day.

He ordered a beer and drank most of it in one gulp.

"The Polis have found another body down at the new warehouses," he said loudly. "Rumour has it that it's Jim Crawford."

The conversation level in the bar went up a notch. Speculation was rife, but I kept out of it. Fraser tried to make conversation, but he saw the look in my eye and left me to it.

For the next hour I sought oblivion in a succession of whisky glasses. I was somewhere around my eighth, a smooth fifteen-year-old Knockando, when the phone rang.

George answered.

"John. It's for you." He called out.

"Tell them I'm too pissed to talk," I said. In fact, I felt anything but. The whisky was having little effect, and I was considering moving up to doubles.

"Its Joe Boyd," George said, and I suddenly felt completely sober.

I DON'T HAVE MUCH TIME," he said. "I've got to report to the Chief. But just to let you know. It was Crawford all right. And he had the eight grand on him. There wasn't a note, but it looks like suicide. He had hooked a hose from the exhaust into the passenger side."

"That's not his style," I said.

"Neither is murder," he said, "But what else could it be? The money's all here, and we're getting the big knife tested as we speak. I'm still willing to bet that Crawford's prints are on it. Case closed."

"Aye," I said, "Case closed."

I went back to the whisky and tried not to think of missing women, old title deeds, and two hundred thousand pounds in a briefcase.

"Loose ends," I tried to tell myself, "Just loose ends. Case closed."

My brain still didn't believe me, so I set about trying to prove it wrong with a vengeance.

CHAPTER
Twenty-Six

DAVE TURNER CAME in about twenty minutes later.

He slapped a paper on the desk in front of me.

'Local business found dead in garage,' it said in big bold type. And smaller, underneath that, a sub-heading; 'Possible link to bunker murder.'

He clapped me on the back.

"The big papers in Edinburgh have been on the phone wanted to syndicate my story," he said. "My by-line will be on the Scotsman's front page in the morning. I owe you a drink."

"I'm on the whiskies. What's next up George?"

"Lagavulin. The twenty-year-old."

"Make it a double then," I said. "Dave's paying."

"I'll have the same," he said.

George poured the drinks, and Dave sat down on the stool beside me.

"I'm not in the best of moods," I warned him.

"Aye, he means it," George said. "He's on the whisky trail."

"Oh," Dave replied. He stepped off the stool. "I'll leave you to it. I remember the last time."

So, did I. We'd made it as far as the Powers before we'd got into an argument about whether Irish malts counted. It had got a bit heated, and George had thrown us out.

"Let me know if you get past the Powers this time," Dave said. "I might have another one with you then."

Things start to get a bit blurred from then on.

Afternoon flowed into evening. At some point I talked to Willie and Davy.

"What is it son," Willie said as I sat down, too heavily, next to him, "Woman trouble?"

"I should be so lucky," I said, "I haven't seen any action for months. And the last woman I saw in her bedclothes doesn't even remember me being there."

"I had a time like that with Carol McGuigan," Davy said. "I remember…"

"Would you shut up about Carol bloody McGuigan," Willie said. "Since you remembered her earlier you've talked about nothing else."

"She was well worth remembering," Davy said. "I spent most of '56 and '57 trying to get into her breeks."

"You and half the town," Willie said. "Anyway, Young Royle here never answered my question. Why are you back on the hard stuff? You know what it does to you."

"It's this case," I said. "It's been going nowhere from the start."

"What's your problem?" Willie said. "You're getting paid, aren't you?"

"That's my worry. The client has done a runner and her brother is in the morgue. I don't think there's any more cash forthcoming."

"Well let's see if you can change that. Three card brag okay for you?"

That's when I knew the drink was starting to take effect. I agreed to play. When sober, I knew better.

"Now are we gonnae play cards or are you gonnae sit there drooling over Carol McGuigan?" Willie said to Davy.

Over the next hour they happily took ten pounds off me. It was Davy who stopped me from playing any more.

"You're finished gambling for the night lad," he said, taking the cards off me as I made an abortive attempt at shuffling. "Willie and I have had enough of taking sweeties away from babies."

I returned to the bar for more whisky. At some point later a lad brought in the evening newspaper. It was one of the Edinburgh papers. "Local man found dead in garage," was the unimaginative headline. But Dave Turner was going to be ecstatic. He had his name on the front page. I couldn't check the quality of the rest of the story...the print wobbled and swam in front of my eyes when I tried to focus.

"Another whisky George," I said. "I can nearly read this paper."

George poured me a MacAllan.

"That one is six quid on its own," he said.

"Am I in danger of running out of money?"

"You mean apart from your two hundred quid tab?"

I wasn't quite drunk enough to rise to that one.

George sighed.

"No. You'll be well gone before the fifty is used up. Just don't spew on the bar... the bits get into the fonts and the regulars don't like it."

THE WHISKIES KEPT COMING FAST.

"It's the Powers next," George said at one point.

"Well get Dave Turner over here. He's paying for this one."

Dave turned up at my shoulder.

"Make that two doubles," he said to George. "I'm a happy man."

Dave and I sipped the Powers together.

"You know something," Dave said. "If this one isn't included on the trail, it bloody-well should be."

I agreed. It went down so smoothly you almost didn't notice you were drinking it.

"Thanks again pal," Dave said as we finished. "You've helped me to a lifetime's ambition today. Maybe someday I can do the same for you."

"Not unless you can get me Lauren Bacall and a time machine," I said.

He laughed.

"I'll see what I can do. Maybe somebody at the Scotsman has a contact."

Things got fuzzy quickly soon after that, and I'd almost attained the oblivion I sought when the chubby student Fraser approached me. He handed me a sheaf of papers.

"It's all there," he said, "Acidity tests, organic matter percentages, soil pedometer readings, nitrogen balance ratios and pollen analysis."

I took the papers from him and tried to focus. I could just about make out the charts and tables, but the text was even smaller than that in the newspaper.

"Just give me the management summary," I said. "I'll read the rest later."

He started as if giving a presentation.

"The tests started at eight-thirty a.m.," he said. "The soil proved to be pH 5.7, a slightly alkaline, friable garden soil mixed with large quantities of organic matter and straw."

I put up a hand, nearly spilling my drink in the process. I placed the glass carefully on the bar and tried to light a cigarette. It took three goes, but I managed it without burning myself or my clothes, which in itself was quite an achievement.

"Organic matter? What's that when it's at home?"

"Dung," George said as he passed along the bar.

"Horseshit," somebody replied.

"Aye, that as well," Fraser said. "Basically, it was garden soil that somebody has mixed a lot of manure in. Not much to go on. But I was able to get something."

"Don't get too smug son," I said. "I'm not that easily impressed."

"A gas spectrograph showed the soil to have unusually high nitrogen content," he continued. "But the really cool thing was the pollen analysis. I used the Schrieber-Turing technique and separated the pollen out from the organic matrix. Pollen is interesting. Did you know that all plants have different pollen types, and you can identify them separately under the microscope? You should see them under the electron microscope … like tiny planets with symmetrical ridges and mountains. I've got a blown-up poster of one on my bedroom wall…"

"Well, it certainly beats Farrah Fawcett-Majors," I said.

That got me a blank stare, and I suddenly felt really old. I could see that the kid was ready to start again but I stopped him.

"Good work lad," I said, patting the paper. "I'll read it later."

I turned my back on him.

"But the important bit, about the pollen…" he started to say.

"There's no important bit," I said. "The Polis have got their man. Away you go and enjoy the fifty quid."

"Oh, I already spent that on Doom 4," he said. "It's got some really cool new levels and…"

"Enough!" I said. "Take your technology elsewhere. Tonight, I am a Luddite. I don't suppose students still play pool?"

I soon found another activity I was too drunk to do. Fraser took a tenner off me, and it might have been more if somebody else hadn't challenged him. I left him to it and once more went back to the whisky. The papers the student had left were still sitting at the bar. Another regular read from the front sheet.

"Gibberelic Acid. What's that? Some kind of monkey juice?"

Fraser shouted out from the pool table.

"It's a plant hormone."

"I know how to make a hormone," the guy at the bar said, and four people gave him the punch line at the same time.

"There's a job lot of biologists in tonight," George said in explanation.

I gave him the soil analysis.

"Put this under the counter for me," I said. "I paid fifty quid for it, so I may as well read it sometime."

He put the papers away, and poured me a whisky, a 'Talisker'. I swayed slightly on the stool as I took it, but my grip on the glass was strong enough to get it to my mouth.

"A toast," I shouted. The bar went quiet, and everybody looked at me." God bless the fine people at the Talisker distillery, the Black Cuillins, the Red Cuillins and the Fairy Flag of Dunvegan Castle. Here's wishing long life to the Laird of the McLouds and to wee Dougie Ross, the barman at the Portree Hotel."

"*Slainte*," I said, and downed the dark liquid in one. It burned its way into my brain so quickly that the next thing I knew Dave Turner was holding me up to stop me from falling off the seat.

Somewhere somebody talked about me, but I was past caring.

"Can you see him to his bed Dave? His keys are in his pocket."

That was the last thing I heard. The world went dark, and all thoughts of the case finally went with it.

CHAPTER
Twenty-Seven

I WOKE IN DARKNESS. I lay, fully clothed, on top of my bed. My eyes felt gummed together, and a small family of small furry animals had slept in my mouth. The clock told me it was ten-thirty p.m., but that didn't mean much to me as I had no idea when I'd got back from the bar.

My bladder cried for relief, sending me struggling to my feet and staggering to the small toilet. I was still more than half-drunk, but as I stood at the sink washing my hands, I realised I wasn't quite drunk enough. My brain started up on me again: *missing client, title deeds, briefcase of fifties*. I remembered the bottle of Highland Park in my desk and headed through to my office.

Somebody was already there, sitting in my armchair, feet up on my desk, with a large measure of malt in a tumbler in his hand. Sandy Thomas had been right; he weighed about 220 pounds, all of it ugly. His chest made him look like a barrel, with a weightlifter's upper body, a small round, bald, head on top and dark, piggy eyes peering out from under a heavy brow. The fact he wore a very expensive Italian suit with a crisp white cotton shirt and a pale blue silk tie only made his bad teeth look more yellow and stained.

"Mr Johnson, I presume," I said.

He raised the whisky glass and toasted me. He looked me up and down.

"They told me you were a movie buff," he said, "But I didn't know you wore the props. You'll have to tell me where you get your clothes...I've been after a suit like that myself."

"I don't think Oxfam is on your list of preferred retailers," I said. "You look more like an Armani man to me."

He rubbed his lapel between two fingers.

"Finest Italian silk," he said. "But I'd swap it for a genuine thirties suit any day."

I sat down opposite him and poured myself a whisky.

"Cigarette?" I asked, pulling a crumpled packet from my top pocket.

He shook his head.

"I'll stick to my own," he said, and took a stick of gum from his pocket. "Nico-gum, doctor's orders. He said my lungs needed time to recover."

"Recover from what?"

"About fifty a day for the last ten years," he said.

He raised his glass and waved it round the room.

"So, it was PI's for you," he said. "Are you a shamus or a gumshoe?"

He didn't wait for an answer.

"For me it was the gangsters ... Capone, Little Ceasar, all the way up to Don Corleone. I was making other kids in the playground offers they couldn't refuse before I even knew what it meant."

He paused, chewed on the gum, and sipped my booze.

"I went through your record collection earlier," he said. "I was waiting for you to wake up, and I didn't want to put anything on. Do you mind?"

He rose to his feet and went over by the stereo before I could answer. He lifted an album and showed me the cover, 'The Cotton Club'.

"Is this okay?"

"Oh, it's better than that," I said.

A minute later the horn section started up and Cab Calloway began busking his way through *Minnie the Moocha*. Johnson sang along, miming Calloway's arm-down, loping, sashay across the stage. I had to applaud as he stayed in time during the fast scat section, and I responded to the call-back section. When the song finished, he fell into the armchair, a wide grin on his face.

"My party piece," he said. He motioned with his glass at the whisky bottle.

"Can I have another?"

"Help yourself whenever you feel like it," I said. "You're the most pleasant burglar I've ever had."

"Oh, I'm no burglar," he said, pouring himself a large one. "You left your keys in the door."

He looked steadily at me across the top of his glass. His 'performance' had charmed me, sure, but I remembered what Sandy Thomas told me. This man was a shark, and it wouldn't do for me to show a weakness.

I stood, managing to keep myself steady, and went to the stereo, turning King Oliver down.

"And what brings you to see me at this time of night?" I said. I sat back down…my legs weren't feeling too strong.

"I'm looking for a woman," he said.

"Aren't we all?"

He chewed gum for a while before replying.

"Where is she?" he asked.

"I haven't seen her since yesterday morning," I said.

He sat forward, and suddenly the congenial jazz buff was gone and he was all smiles and teeth.

"Now, now Mr Royle…we were getting on so well. A wee birdie saw you, seeing her off this morning, and having a wee look around the house after she left."

My befuddled brain finally caught up.

"You mean Jill Crawford, don't you?"

He nodded.

"Who do you think I meant?"

I let that one go.

"I saw the lady you're after this morning. She took off," I said. "She thought Crawford was going to do a runner..."

"And she beat him to it," he finished. "Now Crawford turns up dead, and she's nowhere to be found. All very convenient."

"You think she did it?"

"She was more than capable," he said. He sat back in the chair and sang along to the chorus with Fats Waller as he swung through *Ain't Misbehavin'*.

"What's your interest?" I asked. "I would have though St Andrews was too much of a backwater for a big city man like you?"

"Crawford was in my employ," he said. "He has some stuff belonging to me. I've paid him for it, and I want it, or my money, back."

"This stuff? It wouldn't be glossy, and come in big brown cardboard boxes?"

He nodded.

"Then I've got some bad news for you," I said. "The Polis found it earlier, in the Crawford's garage, and more in a locked-up hairdressers down the road from here."

I took a small sip from my whisky. Johnson's eyes had suddenly gone hard and flinty, and the room felt several degrees colder.

"Well now," he said. "That's not good news."

"Hold on to your hat," I said, "There's worse. Mrs Crawford had a case full of fifties with her when she left ... two hundred grand she said."

He nodded again. I could see the fury, the tension in his shoulders. He was fighting it though.

"Throw us one of your fags," he said. "This gum is giving me jaw-ache."

I passed him the packet and the lighter. He looked at both and grinned.

"The devil is in the detail, eh?" he said.

"Even down to the genuine 1940's underpants."

"Well, I hope you wash them," he said.

"Every year, on my birthday," I said.

He laughed, and the tension broke.

"I suppose she's away to Amsterdam for a party," he said.

"That's what she told me," I said.

He laughed again.

"She's nothing if not predictable. And I suppose she asked you to go with her?"

I nodded.

This time he didn't just laugh, he bellowed.

"You've got more sense than me," he said when he'd calmed down. "I went."

"You? In Amsterdam?"

"Aye. A big mouse with clogs on," he said. "This was nearly ten years ago. I wasn't so smart...I let my trousers lead me."

"Well, they're big enough," I said.

The smile left his face, only for the briefest of moments, but enough to remind me to be careful.

"Was it worth it?" I asked.

He smiled lasciviously.

"I'll leave that to your imagination," he said. "You've seen her. And she was even fitter when she was younger."

We sat and smoked, both lost in memories. That red kimono started to push its way to the front.

"I don't mean to be a bad host Mr Johnson," I said. "But it is past eleven o'clock, and I've had a long day. Is there anything else I can help you with?"

He thought for a while, his eyes closed, lips pursed. He was so still I was convinced he'd fallen asleep.

"So, about Crawford?" he said finally. "Do the Polis know who did him?"

So, there we came to it; the real reason he was here. I saw it in the way he paid full attention while pretending not to.

"Crawford did it to himself," I said. "A Yank took eight grand of him at poker, and the big man wanted it back. He was the one that put the Yank in the bunker."

"Then he had a fit of remorse and did himself in? I didn't have him down for the type that would be feeling guilt."

"Nor me. Especially when he had eight grand in his pocket. That would have bought him a lot of lager."

"Did the Polis find anything on him?"

It was my turn to pay attention. A slip now and I could be wearing some of those concrete boots that Sandy Thomas warned me about.

"Apart from the eight grand you mean? My contact didn't say."

He leaned forward, and there were no more smiles. He jabbed the cigarette at me as he made his point, the loose ash falling off onto my desk.

"Your contact is the man in charge," he said. "I've been checking. You and him go way back."

"Aye," I said, my mouth running away with my brain. "And that's why he doesn't tell me anything. He knows the kind of company I keep."

I thought I'd gone too far. He stubbed his cigarette out on my desk and stood, knocking the armchair backwards. It was all I could do to sit there, trying for calm. I blew a smoke ring and smiled at him.

"Is that any way for the Don to be acting," I said.

He stopped short. He threw his head back and bellowed with laughter.

"I'm working down to my Capone mood," he said. "It would be best if you didn't see that one."

He righted the chair.

"Sorry about that," he said. "Losing two hundred grand does that to me sometimes."

He poured himself another whisky, emptying the bottle.

"I'll send you another in the morning," he said. "You can keep it for when I'm next here?"

"You'll be back?" I said.

"Oh yes," he replied, and I saw the shark again.

He sat back and hummed along to St Louis Blues.

"I met the Yank. But you know that already," he said.

I nodded, not knowing how to reply.

"If the Polis knew that I might get into a wee bit of trouble. Do you understand?"

I understood all right.

"They won't hear it from me," I said.

He nodded, looking me in the eye.

"Then we're finished...for now. But if Crawford had anything in his pockets, I want to know. There's a couple of hundred in it for you. Savvy?"

I nodded again. There it was. The offer I couldn't refuse.

He rose, and the smile was back.

"You should come to my club in Glasgow," he said, "I have a trad night every Wednesday. I get muzo's from all over coming to play."

He handed me a card.

"Jazzers, 131 Union St, Glasgow. The Hip Joint."

There was a telephone number on the other side.

"Call me if you hear anything," he said. "I spend most of my time there."

He started to leave. I should have let him go, but old habits die hard.

"Your meeting with the Yank? What did you talk about?" I said as he was almost at the door.

The smile didn't fade.

"Business," he said.

He shut the door quietly behind him. The room suddenly felt empty.

CHAPTER
Twenty-Eight

THERE'S no law against liking a hardened Glasgow criminal. At least I hoped there wasn't. I'd met many worse over the years; and any meeting you get out of with all your teeth still in your mouth is a good one.

I moved to my own chair, settled my back into its well-worn contour, and put my feet up.

Trying to run away from the case hadn't worked very well, and I now regretted my earlier excesses. I poured what little remained of my own drink back into the bottle and put it back in the desk drawer. Sometime in the past ten minutes I had made the decision; the case wasn't over; not for me, not for Johnson, not for Elsa Courtney.

Joe had told me that it was a Scotsman that rang them to set me up. That could have been Johnson, but then why was he so pleasant now? And what was he looking for?

I took Crawford's notebook, the Yank's letter, and the title deed from my pocket and looked through them all again, but my brain wasn't giving me any new ideas; it felt like it was padded with cotton wool.

The whisky wanted me to shut down for a while. I took its

advice and dragged myself off to bed once more. This time I remembered to undress.

The sun woke me up nearly ten hours later, its rays spearing into my brain like daggers. They didn't bring any enlightenment.

I showered, shaved and dressed in a hung-over fug. Even a double-strong coffee failed to kick start the engine. There was a bright and breezy day outside the window, full of fresh air and vitality.

I took my cigarettes out to meet it.

THE FLAGS atop the Old Course club house fluttered, almost horizontal, in the wind. It came at a rush from the North-East, howling down the beach, blowing ever-shifting patterns on the sands. Only the hardiest locals were out in the open. Old men walked protesting dogs along the shore path, but even they kept off the beach as the white horses danced offshore and the rough grass of the dunes bent over in submission.

Even in the teeth of this gale golfers queued up at the first tee. I stood, slightly sheltered by the clubhouse, fired up the first cigarette of the day, and watched.

A tall lanky youngster, smartly turned out in spanking clean waterproofs stood up to the first tee and hit a one iron that, on his home course somewhere warm and still, would have got him two hundred yards down the middle. It flew high and handsome … and the wind took it fifty yards left, almost hitting a pair coming down the Eighteenth.

Next up came a short stocky local, aged about sixty, wearing a faded anorak, his club tie showing where he'd unzipped the top. He took out a four wood and spanked the ball, low, into the wind. It bounced, hit a down slope, and ended up in the middle of the fairway, a good hundred yards nearer the pin than his partner. I hoped the kid hadn't put any money on himself beating the older man.

"Feeling better John?" a voice said behind me. "I didn't think we'd see you before tea-time."

Willie and Davy stood behind me, coats buttoned up to their necks, flat caps clamped tight to their heads.

"Morning gents," I said. "I'm just blowing away the cobwebs."

"Cobwebs, is it?" Willie said, "And here was me thinking it was a bucketful of whisky."

"We're off up the far end," Davy said, "Are you coming? Willie's promised to show me the rabbit farms."

"Rabbit farms? Come on, you're pulling my leg, aren't you? Who do they get to do the milking ... Jemima Puddleduck?"

"No, it's legit." Willie said. "You must have noticed that the critters like the links course? The locals have got wee areas where they keep them under control, wee farms. There used to be dozens of them. Hell, the council even gave the farmers the whole course at one time. My grandfather told me about it. It was back in the early eighteen hundreds as far as I know. No' that there's that much trace left now. I remember when ..."

I held up my hand.

"Please Mr Brown. It's too early. Far too early."

"What's the matter," Willie said, "Did you kill too many brain cells last night?"

"Either that or not enough," I said.

"So, are you coming or not?" Davy said.

I shook my head.

"I need some breakfast," I said. "All I had yesterday was the booze."

"Making his excuses already," Willie said.

"Aye," Davy agreed. "He probably fell off yon stool due to starvation."

"Maybe it was the altitude," Willie said. "Did you get a nosebleed John?"

They left, laughing.

I realised I'd eaten nothing since the fish and chips in Dundee on Monday night. Whisky might be the water of life, but too many days like yesterday and I'd be heading for an early grave. I turned away from the first tee, but not before seeing the lad in the waterproofs try to cut a low hook against the wind into the flag. He learned fast, but his ball still ended up well short and left. The older man took his putter from well off the green and hit his ball hard. It ran, and ran, as if on a roller coaster, up onto the green coming softly to a halt ten feet from the pin. The kid's shoulders dropped. He was in for a long day. I left him to it and headed for something to eat.

I stopped for a newspaper. I might have one waiting for me when I got back to the flat, but I couldn't guarantee it. Of late the delivery boy had got lazy and had taken to leaving the papers, both mine and Tom's, on the doorstep. That would be fine in a Californian climate, but over here we were often left with the start of a papier-mâché sculpture.

"Bunker murderer found dead in garage," one read. "Gangland connection? Two dead," said another. The red-tops were having a field day. "Porn Baron comes to a sticky end," was the one that made me laugh the most, but the purists would like "Double bogey ruins St Andrews card."

I bought one of the broadsheets and headed for 'The Old Town Café'.

Jessie Beattie had run the small-town coffee shop for nearly as long as Willie and Davy had been frequenting the Halt, and she was older than either of them. She knew everybody in town, and everybody in town knew never to tell her any secrets...not unless the whole point was to get them out in the open. The place was little more than four tables, twelve chairs and a never-ending supply of coffee, hand-made sandwiches, biscuits and scones. Over the years I'd developed a habit of sitting in the window seat, reading my paper or, more often, just watching the town go by.

When I opened the door Jessie and another old lady stopped talking for a second, noticed it was me, and went back to their conversation. I beat a strategic retreat and headed for my usual seat.

"She never did!" I heard Jessie exclaim.

"She did," the other woman said. "And I'll tell you something else for nothing…" They both looked over at me, and I made a point of staring out of the window. The woman dropped her voice, but when a Scots woman of a certain age drops her voice all it means is that half the town can hear it rather than the whole town.

"She's only had that fishmonger in for coffee. That's twice this week. And it was nearly for an hour the second time."

"Maybe he's giving her the benefit of his experience," Jessie said, laughing.

"He's giving her something, that's for sure."

They both laughed; that peculiar dirty laugh that only women seem able to manage.

"I'd better go," the other woman said. "I need to get something for Frank's dinner."

"You could always get him some fish?" Jessie said.

There was that laugh again. The older woman's smile didn't fade until she was out of the door.

Jessie gave the table nearest her a cursory wipe then turned towards me. She had changed little in all the years I'd known her. Her bosom was still big enough to engulf a small army. Her make-up had got progressively heavier over the years, but she managed to keep it the right side of gaudy. She had shrunk a bit recently, seeming to fall in on herself, but she had a twinkle in her blue eyes and was always ready for mischief.

When my mother had her last spell in hospital, she was one of the few that took the time to visit her, and the night mum passed on Jessie found me, wandering, lost and forlorn, in the hospital car park, weeping like a baby. She'd got me home and, for weeks afterwards, made sure I ate something between the drinking.

"Morning Johnny boy," she said as she approached. "The usual, is it?"

She opened her arms.

"Come to Auntie Jessie. You look like you could do with a hug."

"Not today darling," I said, "I'll have a cup of black coffee, and two of your cheese rolls."

"Ah," she said, tapping the side of her nose. "Feeding the hangover, eh? I heard you had a wee accident in the Halt last night."

"News travels fast," I said.

"Only when it's either bad or funny," she said. "And yours was both."

She left me to get my order and I read the main article in the paper.

"Porn baron found dead in the saddle," one sub-headline said.

"The sleepy seaside town of St Andrews was rocked again last night with the death of James Aloysius Crawford (38). The local businessman was found dead at the wheel of his 1985 Rolls Royce Silver Shadow. On the same premises police found what was described by one source as 'The biggest haul of hard-core pornography to be found on the mainland since the Seventies'.

"Speculation is growing that the apparent suicide is linked with the death of Hank Courtney, an American tourist who was sensationally discovered stabbed to death in the famous Road Hole Bunker on the Old Course.

"Police have not so far released a press statement, but inside sources have revealed that the murder weapon used on the golf course is being tested for Crawford's fingerprints. An announcement is due imminently."

Again, there was little I didn't know already. And try as they might, nobody could hook the Texan up with the porn story. Then again, neither could I. The paper ended up following the police line, 'Suicide due to guilt'. I still didn't believe it.

Jessie came back with my coffee. She was about to turn away when I had an idea.

"Sit down Jessie. I've got a question."

"If it's about your Texan, I've been asking around. Nobody saw him after Sunday morning," she said. "It was a damn shame, him being on holiday and getting murdered like that. I don't know what this town's coming to. I remember when I was a lassie ..."

The opening gambit had to be dealt with the same way whether it came from Willie or Jessie. I spoke up quickly.

"No. It's about Mrs Crawford," I said.

Her eyebrow went up.

"The Scarlet woman?" She laughed loudly. "You were seen you know?"

"Me?"

"Don't put the innocent look on for my benefit John. You've been trying that one on me since you used to steal my biscuits on your way to school."

"It used to work then," I said.

She shook her head. "I just took pity on you," she said, "Your father ..."

She drifted off, suddenly quiet.

"It's an old story Jessie," I said. "I've forgotten him. About Mrs Crawford?"

"Aye," she said, perking up. "News is you were seen. Both times."

"Don't tell me. It must have been the mad curtain-twitcher across the road?"

She nodded.

"Meg Curran. When she's not watching Cop shows she's watching Crawford's house. She's always been that nosy. Back in the sixties she ..."

"Jessie. Please? Mrs Crawford?"

"I don't know what I can tell you. She's done a runner, but you know that. And she was no better than she needed to be. But you knew that as well. Did you get an eyeful under that red kimono?"

She laughed loudly when I blushed.

"There's no real gossip," Jessie continued. "She wasn't too happy here ... too quiet for her tastes. And she drank too much. But there are plenty of women in that situation all over the country. No. If it is information that you're after, you'd be better asking me about Ms Courtney."

She smiled; the cat had finally got the cream. She rose from the chair.

"Jessie. Please, tell me."

"After you've had something to eat," she said.

I sat, going through permutations, wondering just what piece of gossip I was about to hear. But nothing approached the story Jessie told me when she returned. I ate the cheese rolls, but I didn't taste any of it. She had my full attention.

"I got this from Mary, the cleaner at the Excelsior," she said, "And she got it from Alex, the night porter. You know Alex? Wee baldy man, hook nose, gammy leg and a hunch; a good looker... like the wreck o' the Hesperus." She laughed loudly and leaned over to take one of my cigarettes. Officially this was a no-smoking café, but I was the only customer. Jessie usually went out the back door for her hit, but made an exception when I was in.

"Alex has been the night watchman over there since '92. He used to be a porter in the community hospital in Cupar but got early retirement with a bad back. Bad back my hin' end! Mair like chronic laziness I'd say."

She stopped talking long enough to light the cigarette.

"Anyway, he was doing his rounds on Friday night. And that's a wee bit of a novelty for him. Mary, the cleaner, says she finds him sleeping in the kitchen most mornings, and the chef thinks that somebody's been drinking the sherry and topping it up with water. You don't need to be a genius to add two and two together."

She tapped the side of her nose.

"But he says he was doing his rounds on Friday. Actually, it was Saturday morning, after one o'clock. He was up on the third floor, checking the fire doors, when he heard a thump and a scream from one of the rooms. He says it sounded like a call for help. So, he opened the door. And guess what?"

"Come on Jessie, just tell me."

She took a long draw of her cigarette, prolonging the moment

"He couldn't see too well at first, and he had to use his torch. The noise was coming from the bed. And there was your Ms Courtney, buck naked, sitting on top of a man and using him like a bouncy castle."

Now there was an image I could live without.

"What did Alex do?" I asked, incredulous.

"He *says* he made his apologies and left, fast. But I think he stayed and watched through the keyhole...he's got a reputation."

She made an obscene gesture, a few flicks of the wrist with her free hand. It was so incongruous coming from her that I had to laugh. She blushed, suddenly looking like the schoolgirl she'd once been.

"And who was the man."

"Alex didnae recognise him. So, he says anyway. He was probably too busy watching the woman."

"At least it wasn't her brother," I said. "Now that would have been a story."

"Does it help you any?" she asked.

"I don't see how yet, but it might," I said.

I got one of her best smiles as she got up.

"See, your Auntie Jessie always comes up trumps. Can I get you a biscuit?" she said.

"Only if I don't have to pay for it."

I sat and finished my coffee. The image of Ms Courtney naked had replaced the red kimono in the part of my brain that dealt with such things. It wasn't a happy thought. I paid Jessie and headed out, looking for something else to think about.

CHAPTER
Twenty-Nine

FIRST STEP WAS to go back to the office. There were things to do that I should have done before now…long before now.

I'd been lazy, out of the game for too long and spending too much time daydreaming. Meanwhile the case was going to pieces around me. I couldn't find my client. Hank had a knife in him. And my suspect had been found dead. I was doing well so far.

But first, I had a couple of things to do. I walked down South Street and went into the local pet shop. It was my first time in the place…I'm not a pet person, never have been, and I didn't understand the mentality involved.

I must have shown it. A short man, jowly and red eyed, bounced towards me like a puppy.

"Are you after anything in particular—no, don't tell me— you're after a parrot. Or a cockatoo?"

I resisted the obvious joke about any bird being okay by me.

"No. I'm after a kitten…for a friend."

He looked me up and down and winked.

"A special friend? Male or female?"

"She's female. And about eighty," I said.

He laughed loudly and somewhere at the rear of the shop three small dogs barked excitedly.

"I meant, what sex of cat are you after?"

"Does it matter?"

"It does to the cat," he said, and laughed again.

"It's for old Mrs Malcolm," I said. "She lost her cat recently."

"Don't I know it? She's in here most mornings billing and cooing over the kittens."

"Does she have a favourite?"

"Funny you should ask," he said. "There's a wee ginger tom she's had her eye on."

"Well, do me a favour," I said, and took a fifty from my pocket and passed it to him. "Give it to her the next time she's in. Just don't tell her it's from me."

I might not be able to find her missing one, but I could ensure that Mrs Malcolm had a cat. It also helped me focus. I felt like I had solved a case, and if I could solve one, I could solve two.

CHAPTER
Thirty

FIVE MINUTES later I climbed the stairs to the news desk of the Fife Free Press. Dave Turner sat at his desk; a broad grin plastered all over his face.

He fanned three papers across his desk.

"I'm in The Scotsman, the Herald and the Independent. Not bad for a wee reporter from a 'regional backwater'."

"Don't get too smug yet," I said. "I'm calling in the favour."

"Want to discuss it over a beer?" he said, checking his watch. "The sun will be over the yardarm soon."

"No thanks. I had way too much last night."

"Tell me about it," he said. "I was the one that dragged you home. If I hear you singing 'My Way' one more time it'll be one too many."

"I didn't...Did I?"

His smile grew broader.

"Not just that, you told me I was your best pal."

"I must have been drunk then. No. No booze for me today. I need that favour."

"Ask away," he said. "But make it quick. The Polis are going to be calling a press conference anytime now, and I need to be there."

"My guess is they'll be telling you that the prints on the big knife were Crawford's."

"Inside information?"

"No. I just know how cops' mind's work. I need you to do some background digging for me. And I need you to be discreet. If he finds out I'm checking up on him, you can measure me up for a spot in the cemetery next to Jim Crawford."

"Who do you mean?"

"Brian Johnson," I said.

"The Glesca wide boy?" he said, frowning. "Where does he fit in?"

"That's what I'm trying to find out."

"I'll see what's known," he said. "I've got a few contacts in the radio and papers over there."

"Aye," I said, smiling. "It shouldn't be too difficult for a hotshot front-pager like you."

He grinned broadly.

"Do you want me to flash my credentials?"

"No way. Then I really would need a drink."

THE WALK back to the office gave me a chance to clear my head. The wind was still brisk, if not quite so strong as before, nor as cold. There was no sign of any reporters or television crew anywhere...the news had already moved on to the next sensation. The trucks were gone from outside the office, and the only thing in the carpark next to the sea wall was a battered mini-bus. As I entered the close Old Tom came out.

"Oh, it's you John, I thought it was a customer."

"Quiet day?"

Tom nodded.

"All the excitement has died down. Have you got time for a coffee?" he said. "I might have some news about the Yank's murder."

"You've heard something?"

He nodded. "Are you coming in?"

"No, sorry. You'd better just tell me. I've got things to be getting on with."

"Well, it was a customer this morning who told me. He was out for a drink in the Old Course Hotel on Monday night round about the time the Yank got killed. He left his coat in the cloak-room and..."

"And somebody stole it," I finished.

He was crestfallen.

"You knew already. I should have known."

"It's part of the case," I said. "I'll bring you up to speed sometime."

"How about now? The kettle's boiling."

"No," I said. "Maybe a wee bit later. I had a late start."

He chuckled.

"Aye. I heard."

"This town," I said, shaking my head. "Sometimes I wish I lived somewhere where everybody minded their own business."

"No, you don't," Tom said. "You'd be out of business in a week."

He turned before going back to his own door.

"I've got a wee bottle of Lagavulin in the back," he said, "If you fancy a hair of the dog."

"Get thee behind me Satan," I said.

He was still laughing as he closed the door.

CHAPTER
Thirty-One

THE FIRST THING I did when I got upstairs was fire up the laptop and put some coffee on while it was booting. While the coffee was brewing, I laid out my findings on the table; the notebook from Jim Crawford, the title deed, the letter, and the addresses of Brian Johnson and the solicitor in Edinburgh, David Taylor. On separate pieces of paper, I put the names of the players, and started to jot down what I knew. It didn't take long…all it did was make me realise how many pieces of the jigsaw were missing.

I fetched some coffee, lit a cigarette, and went in search of answers.

The Courtney's were first up. I hooked up to the internet and called up the PIs Anonymous site. The site owner, Chuck, had done some work for me in the past, and I'd reciprocated by tracing a rich Scottish aunt for a Florida college boy down on his luck. Chuck and I had never met, never talked on the phone; all our transactions were handled in cyberspace. Electronic data was his domain, and if the information was in the ether somewhere, he could find it, no questions asked. His site didn't give away where he was based. He had a dot.com domain name, but that didn't mean anything these days. If I was more net savvy, I could trace him through his IP address … but that was exactly the kind of stuff I paid him to do for me.

I noticed as I entered the site that he now accepted credit cards. Usually at that point I would have shied away, untrusting soul that I am, but Chuck had proved himself to me in the past, and I had no qualms about using his services again. I drilled down to the link that said 'Leave your MacGuffin here' and got into his message board. There were already four messages today asking for his services, and I added mine to the bottom.

"I need what you can find on Hank and Elsa Courtney, possibly of 17001 Abeline 35, Houston, Texas. Hank is recently deceased, Elsa is my client, now inconveniently disappeared. Anything you can find will be appreciated. Can you also check flight schedules … I need to know if Elsa has fled the country."

I had almost signed off when I had another thought.

"Please also cross reference anything you find with both Crail and St Andrews, especially if it's got a golfing connection. If you need anything, just whistle. You do know how to whistle don't you? … JR"

When I signed out a little animated icon of James Garner as Jim Rockford winked at me, over and over until I closed him down.

I sat and looked at the title deed for a while, trying to decipher the tiny, cramped, letters, but all I got was a headache. I could take it back to Foulkes of course, but I'd had as much of his supercilious manner as I could take. Once more I turned to the web. I googled for 'Latin translation' and Fife, and came up trumps first time, with the site of a retired teacher in Falkland. He was smart enough not to have his telephone number on his site. I emailed him and asked for a quote, telling him about the deed and its possible provenance.

Next, I spent a frustrating ten minutes trying to contact the Scottish Antiquarian Society online. They at least had a website, but it hadn't been updated in more than six months, and all the email links led to the dreaded 'Page not Found' message.

I rang the only phone number listed on the page.

"Hello," a gruff male Scottish voice said.

"Is this the Scottish Antiquarian Society?"

"Do I sound like an effin' Antiquarian," the voice said.

"Actually, now that you mention it…"

"Don't bother with the jokes, son. I don't have time. I've been taking phone calls for the effin' Antiquarians for six months now and it's getting on my tits. If you ever get through to them, tell them that Johnnie Davis is pissed off and gunning for them."

He hung up before I had time to thank him for his time.

I HAD to resort to directory enquiries. They kept me waiting for nearly five minutes. The girl tried her best to be helpful, but she didn't sound like the smartest pencil in the box. She attempted to be businesslike, but the South London girl inside kept showing through in her accent.

"You did say Edinburgh, Scotland?" she said when she finally got back to me. "We don't have a listing for anywhere of that name in this country. There's one in the USA though. Would that be the one you're after?"

I tried to be patient.

"It's the capital city of Scotland, with a big Castle, a big festival and a wee parliament. Is any of this ringing a bell?"

"It's not on the computer," she said petulantly.

I sighed. I'd been here before.

"How are you spelling Edinburgh," I said.

"E-D-I-N-B-O-R-O," she said.

I almost hung up but steeled myself and corrected her gently.

"U-R-G-H. Write it down quick in case your brain cell forgets it."

"Urgh…what's that supposed to mean?"

"It's the last four letters of Edinburgh."

"That doesn't look right," she said. She sounded like a

teenager having a sulk.

"Trust me darling, just trust me."

"Oh," she said, surprised two minutes later. Then she went all businesslike and gave me the number. It was one digit out from the number that I'd rang earlier.

Luckily for me the Antiquarian Society proved to be more on the ball when it came to telephones, and it was answered on the second ring.

The Scottish Antiquarian Society, how can I help you?"

It was time for role-playing again.

"Joyce Grant please," I said.

"Who's calling?"

"Detective Sergeant Adams, CID," I said in my gruffest voice. "It's in connection with a murder enquiry."

I got put through straight away.

"Joyce Grant here," a voice said. She sounded young, and more than a bit apprehensive.

I raised my voice to a more friendly tone.

"Miss Grant, I'm ringing about a Mr Hank Courtney ... you may have seen the news?"

"No, I don't think so," then it clicked. "Oh God! The man in St Andrews... the man in the bunker."

"Yes, I'm afraid so. I have in front of me a letter that you sent to him last year."

"Yes, I remember sending it," she said.

She had relaxed now, but there was still a slight tremor in her voice.

"In the letter, it mentions another document," I said.

"Yes. I remember that too," she said.

"Good," I said, believing I was getting somewhere. "It wasn't found with him, and we think it might be important. Can you tell me what it was?"

I hoped for confirmation that I was right about the deed. I even had that little tingle of anticipation that I get when a case is about to break. I got ready to light up a celebratory cigarette, and even felt up to finishing off the Highland Park in the drawer, but the cigarette stayed, unlit, dangling from my lower lip.

"Not over the phone, no," she said.

"Ms. Adams. This is a murder enquiry."

"Yes, you said."

And I am a policeman."

"Yes, you said."

"So, what else was in the envelope?"

"I can't tell you. Not over the phone."

I sighed loudly.

"Listen. You can call my superior officer and get my credentials if you like?"

She called my bluff.

"Okay," she said. "Give me the number."

I was forced to dissemble.

"He's giving a Press Conference at the moment," I said. "I'll get him to call you back."

"I'm not trying to be obstructive," she said. "It's just we have rules about divulging information. I'm sure you understand."

"Oh yes," I said, "I understand completely."

I put the phone down and cursed loudly.

I called the number back.

"The Scottish Antiquarian Society, how can I help you?"

"It's Detective Adams again. I phoned to tell you that the phone number on your website is wrong. I suggest you call the number and make sure you're not affecting anybody."

"I'll get right onto it. Thank you, officer."

"Don't mention it," I said. "All part of the service."

I felt a lot better when I put the phone down.

WHEN I LOOKED BACK at the laptop the retired teacher had got back to me by e-mail.

"Do you have a scanner?" he asked.

I cursed again. I have a scanner.

It hates me. Consequently, I keep it locked away above my wardrobe.

Half an hour later I finally had the damn thing connected and operating. I scanned the file and the dial-up modem on the laptop took another twenty minutes to send it down the line.

I got a reply two minutes after that.

"Got it, thanks. I'll get back to you later. Isn't broadband wonderful?"

I held off from telling him what I *really* thought about technology and went back to the jigsaw.

I picked up Crawford's notebook and looked closely at the entries. The derelict hairdressers where Joe and I found the porn had a small 's' next to the address in the left-hand margin. There were four other addresses marked the same way: three in Edinburgh and one in Glasgow. I rang the numbers beneath each but got no answer from any of them. My theory was that 'S' denoted a 'store'. Tenuous I know, but as a working hypothesis it gave me something to go on. And if there were stores, there were also possibly delivery points. I rang the number under an address in Stirling.

"The Dragon in the Basement, how can we help you?" a voice said.

"I have a delivery to make," I said. "A van load of boxes from Mr Crawford in St Andrews."

Only silence came from the other end of the line.

"I heard that there are distribution problems at the Fife end," he said quietly.

"You could call it that," I said. "Mr Crawford died suddenly, if you get my meaning. Mr Johnson has passed responsibility onto me."

Once more all fell silent for a while.

"I'm not sure," he said. "You might be the Polis."

"Aye, and you might be Mickey Mouse, but Mr Johnson is Mr Johnson, and I'm not going to go against him just because you're a wee bit feert. I'll ring him at Jazzer's and get him to phone you."

That worked.

"No, I'm sure everything is okay," he said quickly. The prospect of talking to the big man direct ensured his full attention.

"I'll drop the goods off later tonight," I said. "Is about nine, okay?"

"Make it ten. It'll be quieter."

"Okay. I've got a few more drop-offs to do. Keep the lights on. I'll be with you when I can."

We both won out of the deal. I'd found out just what the addresses were in the notebook, and the man at 'The Dragon in the Basement' didn't have to talk to Johnson.

I tried the routine at three more numbers; they all proved to be delivery points for the porn, all small independent bookstores with second handbooks and magazines in the front and a porn business through the back. One of them even placed an order with me.

"We'll take ten more boxes," the woman at the other end said. "I'll have the money ready when you get here."

I wasn't stupid enough to ask how much that might be. Besides, the back cover of the notebook had numerous sums worked out in pencil, and none of the figures in them was less than four figures. I realised just how much money Johnson stood to lose ... especially if Joe Boyd found out about the other stores.

I sat and smoked a cigarette for a while, letting my civic duty fight with my curiosity.

Curiosity won. I rang the number for Jazzer's night club.

I got a flunky first.

"Mr Johnson please," I said.

"He's not here."

"When will he be back?"

"Dunno."

"Where has he gone?"

"Dunno."

"Will he be in tonight?"

"Dunno."

I sighed loudly.

"Listen son. This is important, so don't give me the dumb act. The big man gave me this number last night and told me to call the minute I had the gen he wanted. Well, fifty seconds ago I got the gen. That gives you ten seconds to get him before I hang up and you can tell him you let me go. What's it to be?"

"Well, I dunno..." he said.

"Nine...eight...seven..." I said.

"I'll see if he's in."

Johnson came on the line twenty seconds later.

"Johnson here," he said cagily.

"It's Royle," I replied. "I've got a proposition for you."

His laugh boomed down the line.

"I haven't been propositioned since Annie Lauder took her breeks off at the Savoy in ninety-six. What's the deal?"

I took a deep breath.

"I'll give you what was in Crawford's pocket if you tell me what you were talking to the Yank about on Friday."

He didn't laugh, but he wasn't angry either, which I took as a good sign.

"Sounds like I get the best of that deal," he said. "As long as you're offering me what I think you're offering me?"

I crossed my fingers.

"It's something you don't want my mate Joe to see, that's for sure."

"I like you Royle," he said. "Come on over to Glasgow tonight and we'll do a deal."

"That'll take a while," I said. "I don't have a car and ..."

"Don't worry about that," he said. "There'll be somebody outside your door at seven. That'll get you here in time for the first set."

I was about to reply, but he'd already hung up.

CHAPTER
Thirty-Two

THE PHONE RANG JUST after I put it down.

"John. It's Dave Turner. I've got some stuff for you."

"That was quick," I replied.

"Aye, well, so were the phone calls I had with the lads in Glesca. There's only one thing to say about Johnson. Nobody wants to talk about him."

"Nobody?"

"Not a soul. Johnson is bad news. Stay away. Far away. That's the gist of it. I can dig further?"

"No. That's all right. I'm seeing the man tonight anyway."

I heard the sharp intake of breath at the other end of the line.

"Are you sure that's wise?"

"Probably not," I said. "But he's got some information I need, and I've got some he needs. I'll do the trade and get out fast. It shouldn't be too difficult."

"I've heard that before. Be careful John," he said. "The guys in Glesca were all scared. And these are hardened reporters. They don't scare easily."

"Neither do I," I said with more bravado than I felt.

When I put the phone down, I went to the kitchen for another coffee. It was just after one o' clock; too early to take Tom up on his offer of a whisky. My stomach wasn't quite up to it anyway... the cheese rolls, meant to settle me, had the opposite effect and my insides felt like an eruption might be imminent. I poured some more coffee down to join the mess and stood at the window smoking until I was sure everything was going to stay down.

Last night I'd let myself go, much further that at any time for years. I wasn't ashamed of myself; if all I'd done was fall off a stool then I'd got off lightly compared to others. For example, Dave Turner had, just last year, danced on the bar in his underpants. And George had the pictures.

I took the remains of my coffee and went back to the laptop. My Latin teacher had been busy; I had a response from him in my inbox.

"I've done half of the document," his email began. "And thought you'd like to see it. It's very boring I'm afraid, even to an amateur historian like me."

I won't bore you with the detail. The deed was a sale of property, from one William Macadam to one John Courtney: a plot of ten acres of arable farmland in Pitlochry, Perthshire in 1689. That was the gist of it. The rest of what the teacher had deciphered was all just legal clauses, as obtuse then as they are now. I stopped before I got to the sanity clause.

I still couldn't see where it fitted in to the case. Nor could I see why it would be important enough to be sent from the Antiquarian Society to the States. Maybe Johnson would throw some light on the subject, but I wasn't holding my breath. It felt like a dead end.

I also got an email reply from PIs Anonymous, but it was only Chuck,

"I'm on the job," he said. "I'll get back to you when I have something concrete. I heard about Hank on the news over here. I see you've managed to keep yourself out of it so far. You're learning fast. You'll get your gold star from the PI school of deportment and diplomacy yet."

My last job was to phone Derek Taylor. I should have known better to phone a lawyer in the afternoon. His secretary sounded just like I'd expect a lawyer's secretary to sound; prim, proper, and just ever-so-slightly disdainful.

"I'm afraid Mr Taylor is having a long lunch with a client".

I imagined him as fat, almost corpulent, brandy in one hand, cigar in the other, guffawing over his 'clients' jokes while the cash register in his heart rung up the bill.

"Can you ask him to call me when he gets back, please?"

"I'm afraid he's likely to be out all day," the secretary said.

"Must be a good lunch," I said.

She didn't rise to the bait. She hung up after promising me that Taylor would reply 'when he had a moment'. I wasn't going to bother holding my breath.

It looked like it was waiting time again. There was something lurking at the back of my mind; something that I should be remembering. It was determined to stay away, so I let it be. I knew from experience that it would be back...I just hoped I didn't need the information quickly.

I went back to Google and tried variations of Courtney, MacAdam and Pitlochry, but nothing came up.

Time started to slow down.

I spent a while drooling over first edition Chandlers and Hammetts on ABE, knowing all the time that, even if I had the money, I'd never buy one...I wouldn't trust myself with a twenty-dollar book, never mind one that cost a thousand.

But just looking at them had put me in the mood. For maybe the fifteenth time I took my battered paperback of 'The Long Goodbye' from the shelf and lost myself in Forties California, where men were men and broads were grateful.

It was only when I heard footsteps on the stairs that I looked up and noticed that it was starting to get dark outside.

I just managed to sweep the deed and the notebook into my top drawer before Joe Boyd walked into the office.

CHAPTER
Thirty-Three

JOE HAD a big grin on his face.

"Get your coat, you've pulled," he said. "I'm buying the drinks."

"What's happened? Did your lottery numbers come up?"

"Nope. Better than that. Crawford's prints were all over the Bowie knife. Case closed."

I didn't get out of my chair.

"Did you not hear me? Get a move on. I'm thirsty, and I'm buying," he said.

"Much as I like hearing those words, I can't join you," I said. "I'm working."

"A new client?"

I shook my head.

"The same one. Until I hear from her, Elsa Courtney is still my client."

Joe's smile disappeared. I was sorry about that, but I wasn't going to lie to him any more than I had to.

"Come on John," he said. "I know you knew more than I did about what went on at the Seventeenth, but we've got two bodies and a set of prints. The Chief Constable's happy, the press has moved on, and the lads down the station are having a great time sorting the porn into what's legal and what isn't. Don't go stirring things up."

"I'm just looking for my client," I said. He wasn't convinced, but then again, neither was I.

"Well, you'll not find her sitting here," he said. "Come on, just a couple of pints...I'm celebrating, I got my photo in the paper."

He took a newspaper from his pocket and showed me. There, on the front page, was a head and shoulders shot of him squinting into a camera.

"Very nice," I said. "Did you say cheese?"

"He caught me at a bad moment," Joe said.

"You never did take a good photo though," I replied. "Even at school you were always the one looking the wrong way."

"At least I wasn't making V signs behind the headmaster's head."

"That was just the once," I said. "Well, maybe twice."

"Come on John. Let's head for the Halt. We can drink beer, smoke fags and pretend we're seventeen again."

I stayed in my seat.

"I'm expecting a call."

He sighed, exasperated.

"I hope you're not going to go making a hash of things," he said. "The Chief patted me on the head earlier and told me what a good job it was. I don't want you shitting on that."

"You know me Joe," I replied, "All I'm interested in is truth and justice."

That at least brought his smile back.

"Aye, the American way," he said. "You're sure I can't tempt you?"

I shook my head.

"Okay then, your loss," he said. "Davy and Willie will be happy with more beer for them."

He turned and was almost out of the door when my civic duty finally made a move.

"I found out something about the case," I said.

He stopped. The smile was gone completely. He came back and sat down opposite me.

"If that's the case, I need another one of your fags."

We both lit up as I wondered how much to tell him.

"So, spill it buster," he said in an atrocious American accent that almost made me choke.

I decided on a little truth rather than a big lie.

"I heard a rumour," I started.

He rolled his eyes.

"Not again. If I had a penny for every one of your rumours that turned out to be worth something I'd have tuppence by now."

"No, I believe this one," I said. "This one's done the rounds, and it didn't come from Jessie at the café."

"That's a start then. Come on. Tell me. Ruin my night."

"When Crawford's blonde did a runner, she took two hundred grand with her."

"So? She was probably going to meet Crawford ..." he trailed off. He had seen the flaw in his own argument.

"You see," I said. "He had to know about the two hundred grand. So why would Crawford kill the Yank for a measly eight? And if she was running to meet him, why commit suicide?"

I'd got him thinking.

He took a long draw on the cigarette and let the smoke out slowly.

"Loose ends, that's all," he said finally.

I nodded.

"But I don't figure Crawford as a suicide," I said. "We both knew him too well. Come on. Do you <u>really</u> believe it?"

"I believe what the Chief tells me to believe," he said sadly. "I don't have the luxury of hindsight that you have. And now I'll have to drink twice as much to forget what you've just told me."

He stood.

"I'm warning you John. Don't go stirring up trouble."

I kept quiet as he left this time. He didn't repeat the offer of a drink, and I doubted that he'd enjoy his own much. I'd started him wondering, and that might come in handy later if I had to explain myself further. I still felt bad about lying to him, but it's bad form to tell cops everything at once … it just confuses them.

Besides, if I'd told him I meant to visit Johnson, he'd probably have locked me up for my own safety.

I CHECKED MY WATCH. FIVE O' clock. I left the laptop booting again and showered and shaved. I changed into my 'good' suit. It was real wool, a dark three-piece with a thick white pinstripe. It too had come from Oxfam, but it was in a lot better shape. I put on my best pair of black brogues and selected the blue tie with the dancing girl on the front. Once more I tried the fedora, and this time I decided to take it with me. I spent a while in front of the mirror, trying to smoke a cigarette without taking it out of my mouth, but all I got was smoke in my eyes.

By the time I got back to the laptop I could see the 'You have mail' icon flashing.

It came from Chuck.

"Here's the first installment," it said. "The genealogy will take a bit longer.

"Hank Courtney was born in Austin, TX, September 20th 1945. There's nothing much anywhere about his early years, His father was a grain merchant, and his mother taught at a junior school. Young Hank was a solid student, but nothing flashy, 'B' grades across the board. He played basketball, good enough for high school, not good enough for college. He worked for his father, getting primed for the family business, but that was shot to hell when the draft called. He served as a grunt in 'Nam, 1965 and 1966, before being invalided out with shrapnel in his back. He set up a roadside café with two other veterans in 1967 and has been doing that ever since. He never married. There's a story about a childhood sweetheart, but she didn't wait for him ... while Hank was off fighting the Cong he got a 'Dear John' letter from her. Word in the town is that he was heartbroken, and rarely looks at another woman. He's in hock to the bank for two thousand bucks, has three thousand in an account the IRS doesn't know about, and the locals reckon he hides his card winnings somewhere in the diner; it's led to the place being burgled five times in the last two years.

"He likes poker and golf, and hates to lose at either, but he doesn't seem to have a temper. He has no criminal record, not even a traffic violation. He drives a 70's Pontiac Firebird and likes snakeskin Cuban heels and leather bomber jackets in his spare time. In his working hours he's mostly behind the counter in the diner flipping burgers and jawing with his regulars. There's a recent picture attached."

I opened the picture. He looked healthier than when I'd last seen him. He stood outside a squat shack, 'Hank's Diner' in big letters above it. He wore a red, candy-striped apron and a chef's hat, which made him look even taller. He had a crooked grin as he squinted into the sun, and he looked happy.

I went back to the email.

"I got a local cop to ask around," Chuck continued. "Hank was excited about something, something to do with his trip to Scotland. But he didn't tell anybody what. He said he was 'Playing his cards close to his chest'. He flew out of Houston with his sister on Wednesday morning. No record of any incoming flights booked.

"As for the sister, Elsa Courtney was born Houston, TX, April 2nd 1947. She proved to be a hell-cat teenager, in trouble for being drunk and incapable at thirteen, an abortion at fifteen and another at seventeen. After that she 'dropped out' and bummed around the country with a gang of Angels called the Texas Steelmen. She stayed with them until they got busted for a fight with a rival gang from 'Frisco that resulted in three deaths. She must have hid out for a while, as there's no trace until '66.

"She turns up next working as an 'exotic dancer' in Frisco, hanging around Haight Ashbury and appearing at 'happenings' with various bands. I spoke to a guitarist who was around at the time, and he said she was a 'groovy chick', but I couldn't get much more out of him...he had more holes in his memory than there are in Blackburn, Lancashire. I did find a photo though. Have a look at attachment two."

Picture two showed a young, lean, girl, bare-chested, hair swinging wildly as she boogied on down and a guitar player leered behind her. It might have been Else Courtney, but it could have been anybody.

"Hubba hubba," Chuck continued. "She stayed in Frisco until '73. At one point she was rumoured to be pimping girls for bands, but that all stopped when she got busted for possession. Then there's a three year blank before she turns up again in Houston. She helped Hank buy out his partners in the diner, and the pair of them have run it ever since. Since that earlier bust she's been a pillar of the community.

"She has five grand in a personal account under her own name, and a further ten in the name of 'Dolores Mayqueen', her 'dancing' name. She never married, but she 'sees' one of the local doctors, a married man with three kids. It's all very discreet, and I had to dig deep to find out about it. I'd say even Hank doesn't know. She puts in time at various charities, and nobody has a bad word to say for her.

"Sorry there are no terrible secrets or bad guys here," the mail went on. "Maybe the genealogy will throw something up. Anyway, I'm off to find a man that likes to listen to a man that likes to talk. Later, Chuck."

I read it twice, but couldn't see anything germane to the case. I saved the email anyway. It might be that some fact in there would be useful later.

My Latin teacher was obviously still working on the legalese... there was nothing new from him.

I transferred the notebook from my desk drawer to my inside

pocket, but I left the deed where it was. My spider-sense told me it was important, somehow. It was just I couldn't see it yet. I closed down the laptop, put Billie Holliday on the turntable and began to get myself in the mood for the night out.

The darkness filled in around me, as I blew smoke rings towards the light from the street-lamps outside and tried to clear my mind. I had too much information clogging my thought processes, and it wasn't yet sorting itself out into any kind of pattern. Hopefully my trip tonight would bring some degree of enlightenment and a break in the case.

I needed to be careful with Johnson. As I've already said, I liked the man. But I'd sensed the undercurrents. He was used to getting his own way, and a temper bubbled under that wouldn't be pretty if it reached the surface. I'd already decided to give him the notebook. The only question was what I would get in return.

God knows I needed something.

CHAPTER
Thirty-Four

AROUND SIX-THIRTY, I got twitchy, and went to stand outside by the war memorial, watching the moon play on the water and listening to the waves splashing against the rocky outcrops just past the sea-life centre. Stars spread across a midnight blue sky, and young couples walked, hand in hand, along the path beside the sea wall. The shell-fish restaurant that had replaced the old bandstand was doing a roaring trade, and golfers, merry after a spell at the nineteenth hole, headed back to their hotels for more hospitality. Old Tom had a late client, and I saw through his window that he sat in his favourite seat, head back, eyes closed, lost in a long-ago memory.

A light breeze blew across from the Old Course, bringing the smell of newly mown grass and the first hint of a chill. On nights like this, when the town is quiet and the beach stretches away into the dim distance, I remembered why I stayed.

I lit another cigarette, pulled the fedora low over my eyes and leaned against a lamppost trying to look both nonchalant and hard.

A car, long sleek and German, pulled up and the driver's side window rolled down.

"You'll be Mr Royle," a small bald man said. "I can't imagine there's two dressed like you in the town."

"That's me," I said. "Are you from Johnson?"

He nodded.

"*Mr* Johnson told me to take you to the club. Hop in the back and help yourself to anything you fancy."

I got into a car more opulent than the best hotel room I'd ever been in. The seats were dark, sumptuous leather that threatened to engulf me. A glass screen separated me from the driver, and he didn't seem inclined to lower it. As he pulled away from the kerb, I looked for something to occupy me for the trip.

It didn't take me long to find some distractions. In the column between the seats, I found a bottle of Highland Park and a single crystal glass, along with a pack of twenty Camels. A DVD player and a twelve-inch screen were built into the back of the driver's seat, and a pouch with a collection of disks. Johnson showed off his influences; 'The Godfather', 'Goodfellas', 'Casino', 'The Untouchables', 'Once Upon a Time in America' and 'Heat'. It looked like he had a thing for De Niro.

I took out 'The Untouchables' and put it in the player, letting the car's sound system envelop me in the surround-sound experience. Sean Connery said 'Here endeth the leshon,' as we passed through Cupar, and had his big death scene as we hit the outskirts of Glasgow over an hour later. I felt proud of myself; I'd only drunk the one small glass of whisky.

THE WINDOW behind the driver rolled down as we approached the town centre.

"Are you all right there Mr Royle?" the man said. "I can go the long way round if you want to see the end of the film?"

"That's okay. I've seen it before," I said.

"Aye, me too," he said, and dropped into a perfect Costner impression; 'Never stop fighting until the fighting's done."

I laughed.

"Is it part of the job description?" I said. "To work at the club, you have to be an impressionist?"

"I wouldn't belong to any club that would have me as a member," he said in perfect Groucho.

"Have you worked for the big man long?"

"Five years now," he said, "Since I got out of the Bar L. I was away for four years for battering a policeman. Mr Johnson looked after me while I was inside and had a job waiting for me when I came out. I'll not have a bad word said about him."

"I'm not arguing with you there," I said. "Free whisky and fags works for me."

"Aye, he thought it might," the driver laughed. "He said you were old school. Like him. He said to tell you to keep the fags and have as much whisky as you like."

The car pulled up halfway down Union Street. I offered to tip him, but he was having none of it.

"Just doing my job Mr Royle," he said, and drove away, leaving me standing on the pavement.

I turned, and found my way blocked by a wall of bouncer. I looked up, and up further. He was about six-eight, and nearly the same wide. He looked like he would be more comfortable in wrestling gear, and he studied me with little interest.

"I'm here to see Mr Johnson," I said.

He didn't say a word, just moved sideways to let me squeeze past him.

"What, no token argument?" I said, "I'm disappointed."

He bent close to my face as I passed him.

"An argument can be easily arranged," he said softly. "Mr Johnson will let me know if you're going to get one."

"I'll look forward to it," I said, "It's been a while since a wall fell on me."

He only grunted as I moved on into the foyer, through a narrow corridor and into the club itself.

It was only just after eight o'clock, and the place hadn't

started to fill yet. Someone had spent a small fortune recreating the ambience of a twenties speakeasy, down to the uniformed serving girls, the ceiling fans, the chrome-laden bar and the wooden floorboards, tables and chairs. The place had a small, elevated stage, and a slightly larger dancing area, but it was the posters that caught your eye; larger than life black and white glossies; Raft, Bogart, Cagney, Brando, Pacino and, yes, De Niro.

I went across to the bar, but the barman waved me away.

"Take a table sir," he said, "A waitress will take your order."

"I'm looking for Mr Johnson."

He looked at me, seeing me for the first time.

"Ah. You'll be Mr Royle?"

"That's me."

"The boss said he had a wee call to make," he said. "He said that the drinks are on the house till he gets back. You're to have his usual table."

He snapped his fingers and a waitress appeared at my shoulder. She wore a starched white uniform that made her look a little like a nurse.

"Could you follow me please," she said. She tried for Mid-West, but her Glaswegian roots showed. She led me to a small table near the front, just to the side of the stage.

"Can I get you a drink?" she said.

"Beer please," I said, "A pint."

"American or Scottish?"

"Surprise me," I said.

She gave me a little salute and teetered off on heels that clacked on the hardwood floor.

The place started to fill, and the best dressed roadie I'd ever seen got busy setting up a piano, double-bass and drums. I took off my hat, lit up a cigarette, and settled down to some serious people watching.

CHAPTER
Thirty-Five

MOST OF THE clientele were older than me, but I didn't feel out of place; my clothing ensured that. They obviously dressed for the occasion in Glasgow, and there were couples and groups in a variety of styles ranging from twenties flapper up to fifties Teddy-Boy. But by far the dominant look in the room was gangster-chic; black tuxedo and white wing collar for the men, ankle-length ball gowns and cigarette holders for the women. And that's not to mention the slicked-back hair and the massive gold rings. I half expected to see someone picking their teeth with a flick-knife.

There were some pillars of the community in attendance; I counted three members of the Scottish parliament, two Edinburgh City councillors and at least three high-ranking police officers. And that was only the ones I recognised. The smell of wealth permeated everywhere. The sharks were out in force, recently fed, just cruising.

My drink arrived in a tall, continental lager glass.

"Samuel Adams Pilsner. Compliments of the house," the girl said.

I stopped her as she turned away.

"Is there anything to eat?" I asked.

"Not on music nights," she said, "Just nuts and crisps."

"Bring me a pile of each," I said.

She smiled, just with her mouth, and teetered off again.

A few of the customers looked my way, but nobody spoke to me. I guess sitting at the big man's table brought some compensations with it. I did my best to look enigmatic and blew smoke rings at anybody that looked sideways at me.

The snacks arrived as the lights went down and the band walked on stage. There were no announcements; some polite applause rippled around the room and got louder as a plump female struggled up the small steps onto the raised platform.

She reached no more than five feet tall and looked to weigh at least fifteen stone. Her ample bosom tried to escape from the gold lame ball-gown she'd been poured into; if it jiggled any further, she was going to blind the drummer. Her face showed up too white under the lights, and her mascara started to run as she stepped up to the front of the stage. The band struck up a slow blues.

I wasn't expecting much, but as soon as she launched into 'Cry me a River' she transfixed me, rooting me to the chair. She sang like an angel, her voice echoing around the room without the need of a mike. Nobody spoke, nobody ordered a drink. It was like a service at a funeral home as she poured her heart into the song and out again over us. When the band brought it down to a nearly whispered ending, we sat in the sudden silence, before erupting into loud applause.

For the next hour she held us captivated with a series of standards, culminating in a solo unaccompanied 'Summertime' that made grown men cry.

The lights went up. I had barely touched my beer and the small pile of snacks lay on the table unopened. Brian Johnson sat in the seat beside me. I had no idea how long he'd been there.

"She's something special, isn't she?" he said, still applauding.

I nodded.

"Where did you find her?"

"She found me," he said. "She came in for an audition one night three years ago, and she's been on every Wednesday ever since."

He motioned for a waitress. There was one at his side in less than five seconds.

"Two Highland Parks," he said, "And make them large ones."

"Not for me I said. I had a skin-full last night."

His smile faded. The shark had woken up, and he wasn't taking no for an answer.

"This is my night off," he said, "And I'm buying. So shut up and enjoy yourself."

"An offer I can't refuse, right?"

"Show me some respect," he mumbled in a very bad Brando impression, before lapsing into his normal voice. "And no business will be spoken until the punters go home."

"And when's that?"

"When the band stops playing," he said.

"And when's that… usually?" I asked.

"When the punters have gone home," he said, and his huge laugh bellowed out across the room.

AND SO THE long night began.

The stage got cleared quickly and a six-piece trad band came on and played Acker Bilk and Kenny Ball covers. Not my thing, but the punters lapped it up. Some of them even got up to dance on the small square of floor in front of the stage. By the time they'd finished I'd been served my second large malt and I started to feel mellow.

I tried to get Johnson to talk about last Friday and his golf game at St Andrews, but he refused point blank. And the smile left when he spoke.

"Listen Royle. I've told you once. This is my club, and I have rules. And top of the list is no 'shop' talk until the punters go home. Savvy?"

I 'savvied'. Johnson didn't tell anybody twice. I shut up and tried to relax.

We talked about jazz; Goodman and Krupa, Ella Fitzgerald and Dinah Washington, Coltrane and Mingus. He drank the whisky at twice the speed I did, but it didn't seem to be affecting him at all.

The third band of the night took up most of the stage with a ten-piece horn section alongside piano, bass and drums. As they swung into 'My Kind of Town' Johnson stood.

"I'm on," he said.

I sat, open mouthed, as he strode onto the stage. His was a different presence to the woman from the first band but no less adept at audience manipulation.

"I'm glad to see you all here tonight," he said. "It might not be Chicago, but let's get this joint swinging."

He had them singing along within two choruses. He brought the band to the end in perfect timing and soaked the applause for all it was worth.

"This next one's for my pal here," he said, pointing at me, "I've heard it's his favourite."

He launched into 'My Way'.

He wanted badly to be a 'Rat Pack' member, and had Sinatra's routine from that era off pat. He sang, he cajoled, he told jokes and he sweated until it dripped from his nose. And all the time he was lit up with a huge, shit-eating grin.

He stayed on for nearly an hour, and by the time he finished off with his Calloway impression on 'Minnie the Moocha' he even had me singing along. The applause afterward was loud and long, and he deserved it. He slumped back into the seat beside me, wiping his head with a handkerchief before downing his whisky in one gulp.

"You look like you enjoyed that," I said.

"I always do," he said. "It's the only time I feel alive."

He took one of my cigarettes.

"So, what do you think of my wee set up," he asked.

"I'm impressed," I said. "If I was you, I'd be here permanently."

He looked almost sad.

"I wish I could," he said. "But business needs to be done. And it has to be seen to be done. I've got a reputation to protect."

I checked my watch and was surprised to find it was nearly midnight.

He saw me looking.

"Just one more act," he said. "But I think you'll like this one."

The lights went out completely, just for a second, before a single spot lit up the centre of the stage.

THE SPOT PICKED out a pair of ivory stiletto heeled shoes, and panned up over sheer white-stockinged legs to a brilliant, dazzling, sequined dress and up further to a diaphanous top that you weren't sure whether was see-through or not.

A breathless voice said, "Hey Boss? Can I be your baby doll?"

The spot moved up to her face, red lips leaping from a white face fringed in soft blonde curls. It was only when she blew me a kiss that I realised I'd seen her before. It was Jill Crawford. The band eased slowly into "I'm through with love" and she played Monroe to perfection.

The image of the red kimono sprung back into my mind, and I took a long drink to push it away; it was obvious from the way she looked at the big man beside me that the grieving widow hadn't stayed grieving for long. Then another thought struck me, a nasty thought. I took another drink and pushed that one away as well...wondering whether the man beside you is a murderer is a dangerous business when you know the man can smell blood in the water over a distance.

She stepped off the stage for her next number, and I had a

moment's panic when I thought she might come for me, but she settled for ruffling my hair in passing before plonking herself down on Johnson's lap and singing "Lover Man" at him from a distance no further than an inch. She blew me a wet kiss on the way back to the stage, but I wasn't playing anymore, and that got me a little-girl pout.

"Hey Daddy," she breathed at Johnson, "Tell him to stop being a dick." The audience had a good laugh at my expense before she burlesqued her way through "Boogie-Woogie Bugle Boy'. Johnson got back up and joined her for a steamy "Baby it's cold outside" and "Somethin' Stupid," then she went back to Monroe for the big closing number, "Diamonds are a girl's best friend." The band reached a crescendo and she blew one, final, kiss to Johnson. The lights went out slowly, leaving the spot to focus, tighter and tighter, on those luscious red lips. With one final kiss they were gone into darkness.

The applause went on for a while, the lights came up and, slowly, the place started to empty.

"Is it time?" I asked.

"Not quite," he said. "Finish your drink. I'll be back in five minutes."

I sat and watched as all the tables were cleared and the band packed up. The barman turned the chairs up onto the tables, and all the lights went down except the one over my table. Soon there was only me and a solitary waitress left.

I lit a cigarette and tried for calm, but I wondered what had possessed me to come here in the first place. I felt old, tired, out of my league. I half considered getting up to go but had no time to get out of my chair. Johnson returned. He had a huge grin splattered all over his face.

"Sorry about that. I had a wee bit of business to attend to."

He had the waitress bring us two glasses and a bottle of malt then sent her home.

We were left alone, just a light over our table, with the rest of the club in silent darkness.

Suddenly I felt vulnerable.

"Did you like my wee surprise?" he asked as he poured me a whisky that nearly reached the top of the glass.

"Mrs Crawford? Oh yes, I liked her fine."

"I've got you to thank," he said. "I had her stopped getting off the ferry in Rotterdam. The stupid cow still had the money with her."

He smiled, but it was a cold thing now. It was business time. The teddy bear had gone, and the shark was back.

"Now she's all lovey-dovey for a while. Shameless hussy that she is, her with a man not even buried yet. And see that red lipstick?" he said, scratching his groin, "It itches something terrible."

His laugh echoed around the empty room. He waited until its reverberations faded before speaking.

"Let's talk business."

CHAPTER
Thirty-Six

I TOOK the notebook from my pocket.

"This was on Crawford," I said. "It's got the addresses of the stores he used for the porn." He leaned forward.

"Have the Polis seen it?"

I shook my head.

"Nope. If my mate Joe ever finds out that I've got it, I'll be a mate short."

"Aye," said Johnson, "But you'll have made a new one, so that evens things out."

He smiled again. Suddenly I wanted to leave. A friendship with this man wasn't anything I wanted to cultivate.

"The book also has the details of all the delivery points," I said. "You might want to have somebody contact 'The Dragon in the Basement' in Stirling. They're waiting for a shipment that's never going to come."

Johnson leaned over and took the notebook. He put it away in his pocket and took a long gulp of whisky. He lifted my hat and tried it on for size. It sat on the top of his head precariously.

"It doesn't suit you." I said. "I have you down for a bowler ... one of the James Bond models with the steel brim."

He laughed.

"I like you Royle," he said. "I could have a job for a man like you."

"No thanks," I said. "I'm happy with my wee office."

"How much did you make last year?" he asked. "Twenty grand? I could double that for you, easily."

"Aye, but my soul is worth more than that."

"Soul?" he said laughing. "I though you were a jazz man."

I laughed along with that one.

"All I need from you is what you talked to the Yank about," I said.

"Not much to pay you for saving me a fortune," he said. "We talked about property. He had some land he wanted to sell or develop, and he wanted some partners."

"How did he find you?" I asked.

"Through the lawyer," Johnson replied. "Taylor handles all my property business, and he's high profile in Edinburgh. The Yank found him, through a golf contact in Houston."

"And this land, it was in Pitlochry, right?"

He looked at me strangely, as if deciding what to tell me.

"No. It was much closer to you than that. He said he had twenty acres, next to the driving range beside the second fairway of the Old Course."

I sat, stunned.

"That's not possible."

Johnson grinned.

"That's what I said," he replied. "So, Taylor was going to have the Yank checked out? He never got far with it. The Yank turned up dead, and I decided it wouldn't be prudent to do any more digging."

"Did he offer you any proof?"

Johnson shook his head.

"He said he had some, but he wouldn't discuss it, not before we had a deal."

"And who did he take the phone call from during the round?"

He looked at me, the smile gone.

"You've been busy," he said. "He never told us. But he was a lot happier after he got it than before."

"And this land, he wanted to sell it?"

"Either that or build on it. He harboured visions of a new big hotel. Taylor and I told him there were major problems to be overcome, like planning permission, land rights, public outcry, all that happy shit. But he was full of the idea, and he was infectious. Can you imagine how much money would be involved if, and that's a big if, he actually had the land available?"

I nodded and fell silent.

"What are you thinking?" he said.

"A motive," I said. "A bloody huge motive that dwarfs the eight grand he took off Crawford."

"That's what I thought," Johnson said. "So now you understand why I've been keeping a low profile."

"And you've no idea who actually killed the Yank?"

He crossed his heart.

"And hope to die," he said. "It smelled like a set up from the start though."

"Tell me about it. I was the one who was supposed to be set up."

"I could have somebody watch your back for you?" Johnson said. "No charge. You've done me a favour."

I downed the last of my whisky.

"No thanks," I said. "I've got enough to worry about already."

HE INSISTED ON HAVING HIS 'MAN' drive me home again.

"We can't have you wandering the streets of Glasgow in the early hours of the morning dressed like that," he said, placing the fedora on my head. "You're liable to get beat up."

I got a different driver this time, a short thin man with cheeks like razor blades and eyes as dead as a bowl of used dishwater. I got in the back, and he took off like a maniac, doing fifty through the quiet night-time streets.

I lit a cigarette and tried to think, but the whisky and lack of food or sleep caught up on me, and my mind kept giving me pictures of Jill Crawford in that diaphanous dress. I put "The Godfather" in the DVD player but fell asleep before the wedding scene was finished.

I only woke when the driver rapped on the window.

"We're here," he said.

I struggled out of the car, and he headed off even before I was properly awake, engine revving away into the darkness. It was three-thirty in the morning, and it felt like I'd been awake for days. I dragged myself up to the flat, fought my way out of my clothes, and fell in a dead sleep into bed.

I DIDN'T WAKE until after midday, and even then, I didn't feel refreshed. A strong coffee and a cigarette got me kick started, and two pieces of toast began to assuage the growling in my stomach, but I felt in dire need of sustenance, something my empty fridge wasn't going to provide.

Before heading out I decided to check my email. Five minutes after booting up the laptop, all thoughts of food were forgotten for a while. The inbox contained one email, but it came from Chuck, and it suddenly made some things clearer.

"Hank Courtney is a fifth generation American," it began with no preamble. It went on to detail the Courtney lineage for the past two centuries, but the one that caught my attention was down near the bottom.

"His great, great, great grandfather, John McCourt, came from Scotland in 1822, having been the son of a rabbit farmer in St Andrews. His father, Tom, died in an accident at the age of 43, upon which John inherited the estate, sold the land, and brought the family to America, changing the family name to Courtney.

"There's more," Chuck's email said, "Going back to the Sixteenth Century in Perthshire, but your money's run out old buddy. Do you want me to dig further?"

I sent him back a reply.

"Thanks again Chuck. You've been comprehensive and useful as always. I've got more than enough to be going on with. I'll let you know how the case pans out. I've got a feeling things are coming to a head. Hopefully it'll be the stuff that dreams are made of. JR"

Indeed, I did have enough to be going on with. But I also needed the help of someone with some historical background.

I went downstairs and knocked on Tom's door.

He took a while getting to it.

"Tom. I need a word," I said.

He shook his head.

"Sorry John. I've got a customer, and another one later. Is it important?"

"I need some history, of the Old Course. It's about rabbit farms?"

"There's plenty of stories there, right enough," he said. "You could come back later? Or go and see old Willie Brown. He doesn't know as much as I do, but he'll know enough for you."

I headed once again for the Halt.

Willie and Davy sat in their normal places, playing Dave Turner at cribbage.

"Shit," Dave said to Davy. "You lucky wee bastard."

I guessed he was losing again.

I bought a round for the four of us and went to sit with them while they fleeced the reporter.

"You're twelve pegs down," Davy said. "Do you want to call it quits?"

Dave shook his head. "I'm just about to come good," he said. "I'll go double on the points."

Davy and Willie just smiled at that and set about taking Davy apart. By the end of the game Willie had won by three points from Davy, and thirty from Dave.

Dave sighed and counted three ten pound notes from his pocket.

"Remind me never to play them again," he said to me.

"I remind you every week," I said, "But you keep forgetting."

"I just figure that I'll be lucky enough to win one sometime," he said, shaking his head.

"There's your problem right there," Willie said, smiling. "You think its luck that's important, whereas Davy and I know that what you really need is skill."

Willie and Davy had big smiles on their faces as they turned their attention on me.

"So, you've sobered up a wee bit son?" Willie said. "Do you want to try balancing on the stool again?"

I smiled ruefully. To do anymore would just cause more ribbing.

"Nope. I've come for information. I need to know about those rabbit farms."

"Oh, so now you're interested," Willie said.

"What rabbit farms?" Dave asked.

"It's part of the case," I said. "I need to know about the rabbit farms and anything you know about George Roberts of Crail.

Willie did the disgusting thing with his false teeth again.

"George Roberts. Now there's a name to play with."

He took a long swig of his beer and got that far away look in his eyes. I settled back in my chair. A long story was coming.

CHAPTER
Thirty-Seven

THERE'S BEEN golf played on the old links as far back as the fifteen hundreds. But the rabbits were here long before that. Archaeologists have found evidence of the critters being used for food and clothing nearly as far back as there's evidence of man being here at all. Did you know that there was a dig out at the end of the point, in the 1940's? I worked as a labourer there as a boy. They found a burial site, exposed after a storm. There were skeletons and seashells, broken pottery and bits of flint. It was like a treasure trove to a wee boy. I remember..."

"Stick tae the point ye daft auld bugger," Davy said, "Otherwise we'll be here all day."

"And what's the problem with that?" Dave Turner said. I noticed for the first time that Dave had made an early start. His eyes slid in and out of focus, and he started to slur his words.

"Anyway," Willie said, glaring at Davy, "To cut a good story short, we found rabbit bones everywhere in that dig. And it was dated at nearly two thousand years old. The critters have been here for a while. And even when the 'gowf' started, they just played around the warrens, for in those days there was little concept of 'fair ways'. Some rabbit farming went on, but the town was quite small, and the players and the critters could safely live together.

"It went on that way for many a year. But the town grew steadily, so too did the pressure on the land. The golfers started cultivating the land, flattening out areas, digging in others. But even then, harmony might have been possible, but for an unforeseen circumstance. In 1797 the local council went bankrupt."

"Ah, the honourable gentlemen of the Town Council," Dave Turner said. He stood, raised his glass and said, too loudly, "A toast, to Master Bakers everywhere."

"Sit doon and haud yer wheesht son," Davy said. "You're making a fool of yourself."

Although Dave was over forty years old, he sat, as meekly as a chastened schoolboy. He raised his glass to his lips... and put it down again without drinking.

"Have you stopped showing off?" Willie said to him, and Dave nodded.

"Sorry Mr Brown."

Willie nodded and smiled.

"You can buy me a beer later. Now where were we?"

"The council," I said.

Willie drained half his beer and wiped the foam from his upper lip.

"Thirsty work this," he said.

I took the hint and motioned for George to bring another round as Willie continued.

"You know what the council are like. Back then, things weren't that different," he said. They had corruption, dodgy dealings, folk not paying their taxes, and too many fat councilmen with their noses in the trough. All of that, coupled with the Napoleonic wars and strife in the Empire meant that there was more flowing out of the coffers than was coming in.

"The council met and cast a furtive eye over the land that the golfers had 'claimed' as their own. And, like all councillors before or since, they knew a money-making opportunity when they saw one. They parcelled up the land into units, and started selling it off, slowly cutting the golfers down, a bit at a time. Local merchants also knew a good thing when they saw it, and they bought up the land with relish, and started raking in money hand over fist. They harvested the one thing the links had plenty of - rabbits. By 1799 there were over forty rabbit farms on the links, and the golfers had been more than marginalised ... they had become thrown off the land completely."

Willie stopped and took a swig of his beer.

"Round about the turn of the century, councillors started doing another thing they've always been good at: arguing amongst themselves. Even back then golf brought the rich and the gentrified to the town, and the University realised that it was in danger of losing its patronage as the landowners went elsewhere for their games; to Musselburgh and Guillane. So, the pressure group was set up, and started to apply force to the council.

"George Roberts was a local landowner...he owned most of what is the Botanic Gardens nowadays...and he was the figurehead for the University, and the driving force in the campaign to get golfers back on the links. He was also a keen golfer. He started buying back the land, surreptitiously at first, then more blatantly. Of course, the merchants were loath to lose their profitable farms, so there were many battles for Roberts, both legal and physical. But the University is a strong backer to have, and Roberts was never short of either money or muscle. By 1818 golf was back on the links, but there were several hardy farmers who still held prime sites. These banded into a coalition, holding back Roberts' plans. Their leader was one Tom McCourt."

I managed not to jump at the mention of the name; I'd learned some things over the years, playing cards with Willie and Davy. But Davy gave me a strange look anyway. I suspect he'd guessed some of the reasoning I was now starting to follow. I didn't have time to think about it then. Willie ploughed ahead.

"McCourt stood up to Roberts and the rest of the council.

Local legend has it that that there was a knock-down fight in the council chamber, with McCourt coming out on top. Roberts wanted him thrown in jail for that, but steadier heads prevailed. Roberts went back to trial by attrition.

"1819 and 1820 were hard years for the farmers. Roberts made sure that they had trouble selling their wares in the town, and suddenly there was no farm help available to hire when it was needed, and access to their farms across the golf course was denied, ancient rights of way being closed, forcing the farmers to walk the long way round the point up the beach. Many of them began thinking of giving in; especially as Roberts, backed by the University, started offering ever larger amounts of money for the land. But Tom McCourt held them firm.

"That all changed on the 1st of January 1821. McCourt was in the town drinking. It was in an old pub down at the North Gate, it's a coffee shop now, but I remember..."

It only took a look to get him back on track.

"There was another fight, one that threatened to turn nasty. Some of the students from the University started to taunt the farmers..."

"Nothing new there then," Dave Turner said. "I remember last year when..."

Now it was Willie's turn to be impatient.

"Just go back to sleep son," he said. "I'm telling a story here."

Dave went quiet again. He put his head in his hands and closed his eyes. I don't know if he went to sleep immediately, but light snoring came from his direction through the rest of Willie's tale.

"Anyway, the way the locals tell it, the students were sent back to their dormitory with lumps and bruises, and the farmers started the serious drinking. McCourt left the pub late. It being Ne'erday and all, he was three sheets into the wind, and it was a wild night. The last anybody saw of him he was heading for home."

"He never made it?" Dave Turner interrupted.

Willie gave him a withering look.

"He never made it," he said. "His body was found two days later, face down in the water near the cliffs under the castle. He had drowned, and the coroner's verdict was 'death by misadventure'. With his passing, the farmers' resistance fell away. Within three months the rest of them sold up and left the area forever. The golfers moved back onto the land. And the rest is history."

Willie went on, about how the links course developed over and around the old farms, and how you could still trace the farm boundaries on some of the holes, but I had confirmation of one part of my theory. Hank's perceived claim had something to do with his ancestor's hold on the land. And I became more convinced that the deed from Pitlochry had been planted on his body deliberately to throw either me, or the police, off the scent. I suspected there had been another document, something far closer to home.

CHAPTER
Thirty-Eight

A THEORY FORMED in my mind. I didn't like it, for it involved my client being party to the murder of her brother, and that I didn't want to believe. But a lot of money had to be involved; tens of millions, and that amount would turn the head of many, never mind the part-owner of a small roadside café in Texas. And to pull it off, to distract attention from herself, she'd have needed an accomplice; someone who could verify her claim, give her an alibi and provide the red herring to throw everybody in the wrong direction. I already knew she'd had a man in her room. Now I suspected I knew who. I had no way of finding Elsa Courtney, but I did know where to find the Professor.

I stood to leave and was stopped by a hand on my shoulder. Fraser, the young botanist stood behind me.

"Mr Royle. I've been looking for you. Did you read my results."

I shook my head.

"Sorry son," I said. "First I got drunk, then it didn't seem to matter."

He looked disappointed for a second, before coming to a decision.

"So, you don't know about the grass?"

"There are drugs involved?" I said.

He shook his head and dragged me away from the table. I saw Dave and Willie smile with amusement as he led me to a corner and leaned close, whispering.

"That was the important bit. I tried to tell you the other night, but you were too ... tired."

"Aye. Tired and emotional. So, tell me now. What's the big secret?"

He leaned even closer.

"The soil you gave me is just normal compost," he said. "But the pollen is far from normal. There are some huge flattened oval grains in the matrix, hundreds of them."

"Oval grains in the matrix," I said, trying to sound knowledgeable for all of five second before giving up. "And that's unusual?"

"Whatever left that amount of pollen in the soil had to have been growing close by. And the oval grains are huge. It is obviously a grass species," he said. "But I've never seen its like. At first, I thought it was one of the cereals, wheat maybe, but I couldn't find it in the standard reference works. I spent ten hours on the internet before I found it. It's *Spinocarpula Gigantica*."

He was as proud as a baby that has just filled its first nappy.

I must have looked as baffled as I felt.

"It's only one of the rarest grasses in the world. It's a giant black grass, growing to nearly eight feet high, native to the High Andes. The grains themselves are like rugby balls in shape, with symmetrical pores at the ends and...." he stopped when he saw that I'd glazed over again.

"Okay, I know. I tend to get over-enthusiastic. But the important thing is, there are hardly any of them in the country outside a botanic garden."

"So?" I asked. I felt particularly slow.

He sighed.

"The soil isn't anything a Botanic Garden would use. Ergo,

it's from a private garden. Find the grass, and you'll find where your soil came from."

He had a wide smile on his face.

"Congratulations kid," I said. "You're the only person I've met who has ever said 'Ergo'. Do you have a picture of this grass?"

He shook his head.

"I couldn't find one. It's…"

"Rare," I finished for him. "Yes, you said. How will I recognise it?"

"Well, it's black and…"

"Let me guess," I said. "This is just a wild stab in the dark. Is it big?"

He smiled apologetically.

"Sorry. It's got leaves about an inch wide, with sharp edges and thorny ridges every six inches or so. The flower heads are a bit like Pampas grass…you've seen that?"

"Is that the big blousy thing that's in all the gardens in Scotlandwell Road?"

That's the one. But the Spinocarpus flower heads are deep reddish brown. It should be easy to spot."

"All I've got to do is figure out where to look," I said.

He looked crestfallen again.

"You did good kid. You earned your fifty. If I ever need any grasses identified, I'll know where to come."

I NEEDED to talk to Foulkes, but before that, I needed to put some beef on my idea.

It was time for some lurking.

Luckily for me the sky loomed dark and grey overhead, and a scudding wind threw rain almost horizontally up North Street. Two pensioners saw me climb over the railings into the grounds of St Andrews Castle, but they quickly looked the other way.

I felt like fifteen again as I navigated the shrubbery and trees, keeping out of sight of the booth that charged the paying customers to the Castle. I was soon at the point I'd been heading for. I pulled myself up over the eight-foot wall to the south and dropped down into the Archivist's garden beyond.

I wasn't quite obscured by bushes, but I kept low and hid myself behind the biggest one. The bush opened out; just loose and open-branched enough for me to be able to see the whole of the garden without moving from my position.

To the north of me the house itself dominated the garden, but between me and it sat a large, extravagant greenhouse and a kidney-bean shaped pond, green and murky through lack of cleaning.

Someone moved behind the glass in the greenhouse, and I ducked instinctively. When I looked up again, I saw Foulkes, pottering amongst some tall palms. I could only see his back, and I didn't want to move from my position, but after ten minutes of balancing in a crouch my calves started to complain bitterly.

I crawled to my left. Joe Boyd would be proud of me; I used all the knowledge built up from stalking him during the cowboys and Indians games we played as a kid. I had a couple of scares when I was in the open and Foulkes looked like he might move, but I managed to get behind a large, thick, conifer. When I stood up my thighs cramped. They needed a couple of minutes of massage before I could straighten and poke my head round the tree.

He was still there, still with his back to me. He moved among the plants, and in a still moment when the traffic on the road died down, I heard him singing to himself, soft, nonsense words, like a lullaby to a baby.

Half an hour later he was still there. A wind got up, and I felt safe in sneaking a cigarette. Five minutes after that the rain really began to hammer down, and even pressed tight to the tree, my shirt started to stick to my body as cold water seeped down inside my collar. In less than ten minutes I got soaked through.

People see the job on the screen and think it's all thugs, blondes, bad cops and sudden leaps of intuition. In reality it's hours, days, sometimes weeks of tedium and bad weather. Over time I've developed strategies for dealing with it, playing games in my head; sometimes logic puzzles, sometimes compiling lists.

This afternoon I concentrated on connections in films. I tried to get from 'Bringing up Baby' to 'Pulp Fiction' in as few steps as possible... I went Katherine Hepburn, Spencer Tracy, Robert Wagner, Natalie Wood to Christopher Walken, but I needed to get it down to four. I got stuck on Hepburn, Poitier, looking for a link to Samuel L Jackson when things started to happen.

I poked my head round the tree once more to check up on him. As I looked, he straightened, and I almost pulled back, but he didn't turn. He pressed his hands to the small of his back and stretched. He put something down in front of him, then made his way up to the far end of the greenhouse, out into the garden, and across to the house itself. I gave him ten minutes, but he didn't come back.

I trotted across the patch of grass between the wall and the greenhouse. I looked for a patch of cover that would let me make my way to the house itself when I happened to look through the glass. There, close to where Foulkes had stood, was a tall, black, grass. Fraser was right; it stood about eight foot tall with thorns at six-inch intervals and deep red flower heads.

The choice was between checking out the house or the green-house. I knew the greenhouse was empty, so I decided to have a look round.

FOULKES HAD LEFT IT UNLOCKED. The iron handle turned loosely in my hand, and the door creaked loudly as if fell open an inch. I stood, stock-still, but there was no movement from the house.

The last of the sunshine leached out of the sky as I gently pushed the door open and went inside, flinching at the sudden burst of heat. It got gloomy fast, and the tall plants loomed and swayed over me as I made my way to where he'd stood. I started to perspire within a yard of the door and had to brush my hair back to stop it dripping into my eyes. Sweat ran inside my shirt, and my breathing became laboured. The last time I'd felt this hot was in a club in London in summer... I'd been younger then, and there had been scantily clad compensations. Here I only had the flowers for company.

I tried not to think about triffids and giant flytraps. My foot hit something soft, sending it sliding across the floor. It slid away from me, and I looked twice, making sure it was something inanimate before I bent to see what it was. I had to pull it out from under a bench, gingerly, just in case it wasn't what it seemed. It was Elsa Courtney's handbag.

A feeling of dread settled in my spine as I moved to the spot where I'd seen Foulkes.

When I had watched him, he'd stood in front of a raised bed. I lined up his position with the large conifer outside and turned to see what had kept him so occupied. Newly turned soil lay spread underneath a large, prehistoric-looking fern. A small trowel stuck out, point first in the earth. It came out with a little wiggling, and I used it to delve deeper.

I soon wished I hadn't. An inch below the surface I came across the first hint of pale, pink, skin. Within a minute I'd uncovered the waist area of a fleshy torso. I didn't have to move any more soil; I knew it would only confirm my fear; it was Elsa Courtney, face down, bereft of dignity at the last.

I gagged, and bent forward, holding down the gorge that rose involuntarily. I wiped my mouth with the back of my hand, stood up straight... and noticed the mirror, the small shaving mirror dangling in from the plant in front of me, framing a perfect reflection of the conifer I'd been behind.

There was little doubt about it. From where he'd stood there was no way I would have stayed hidden. He must have seen me.

Time to leave.

I turned away, too late. A grey shape came from my left, giving me no time to get my hands up to protect myself. It barrelled into me, knocking me sideways against the raised bed. I put out a hand to steady myself and touched the cold dead flesh of the body. I drew back instinctively, right into the path of my attacker.

A cudgel came down, a faster moving shadow in the gloom. White pain flared above my right ear. Hot blood ran into my eye, but I couldn't lift my arms to wipe it away. I tried to push against whoever was there, but my knees gave way beneath me.

He hit me again and things went black for a while.

CHAPTER
Thirty-Nine

I CAME AWAKE SLOWLY. Gene Krupa pounded a wild rhythm in my head, and my limbs were loose and refusing to cooperate. The right side of my head felt soft and pulpy where it rested on the stone and my right eye refused to open. It took a while for the left one to tell me it was almost full dark. Only the dim orange glow from a streetlamp beyond the garden reassured me I wasn't completely blind.

I tried to lift my head, but started to grey out, plants spinning and tumbling. I concentrated on breathing until the greenhouse stopped moving around me. All I could do was lie still for a while and try to check my situation.

It wasn't good. I'd been given a hefty clout on the head, and I couldn't check how bad it was; my arms and legs were bound tight with thin string – the kind gardeners use to tie up plants. I felt damp all the way through to the skin. A chill nestled in my bones, settling in my spine despite the warmth in the air around me. I lay almost underneath the large black grass, its flower heads throwing abstract shadows across the floor in front of me. This was where Hank had met his fate if the pollen sample was to be believed.

And that's what gave me impetus to get moving; that, and

the thought of the imitation Bowie knife in Elsa Courtney's handbag.

I had a bad moment when I couldn't see the bag. Panic set in, and I had visions of my attacker returning, pounding me to a pulp while I lay there bleeding on his shoes. I saw a darker spot about four feet away across the floor. I tried to get my legs under me, but they refused to respond. I rolled sideways, and eventually got my left eye accustomed to the dark enough to make out the amorphous shape of the handbag.

It took me five minutes to caterpillar-crawl to where the handbag lay, and another ten to manoeuvre myself into position to get it open. I rummaged in the bag, feeling for the keyring and finding everything but. A purse, lipstick, a pair of glasses, and a pile of tissues. I tired fast and had to stop several times for a rest. I'd started to shiver, and felt like lying down, letting sleep take me for a while.

I almost cried when the keyring fell into my hand.

I cut my fingers badly while trying to get through the string around my ankles, and the blood didn't make things any easier, but it's amazing what speed you can conjure up when you know that a murderer could be upon you at any minute. Within ten minutes I had my legs free. Getting myself upright took another five minutes and I came close to blacking out again several times, the greenhouse fading in and out of reality like a cheap Dr Who effect.

After that effort, the rest was simple in comparison. The trowel still sat in the soil, and it proved far more effective against the string. Two minutes later I leaned back against the raised bed, rubbing my hands, trying not to scream as the blood rushed back into them, trying not to bleed over the remaining clean portions of my suit.

I staggered to the door of the greenhouse. A wooden walking stick with a heavy silver bulb at the top leaned against the door. Only the knob wasn't silver at the moment. The polished surface had been coated; red, and slick with my blood. I wiped the knob on my shirt and used the stick to help me hobble out into the garden.

Cool air hit me, and I heard the sea crashing on the rocks below the house. Traffic passed slowly in the street. I began to remember that there might be life outside the jungle dampness of the greenhouse. I stood at the side of the large pond, taking deep breaths. Slowly the chill started to dissipate. I lit a cigarette with my left hand and leaned on the walking stick with my right until I felt capable of walking further.

The smart thing to do would be to get out of there and get Joe Boyd. But I've never been renowned for my smarts.

I headed for Foulkes' office.

HE DIDN'T SEEM TOO surprised to see me. He still wore the tweed suit, but with a different bow tie; green with yellow dots that hurt the eyes. The main thing that had changed about him was his hair; it looked to have mutated and grown new clumps at random places above his ears, He stood at the window looking out at the view and appeared calm, almost happy when I pushed open the door. He sat down heavily in his chair when I pointed the walking stick and motioned him away from the window.

He looked at my hands.

"That carpet cost fifty pounds a square yard," he said.

My fingers bled over the knob of the walking stick and heavy drops of blood dripped to the plush carpet.

"Lucky you don't pay for it yourself then."

"I hope I didn't make that mess of your hands," he said. "I didn't want to hurt you. Not yet anyway."

"You did a good job," I said. "I made the cuts myself. I had some trouble getting free."

"I'll need to get the more expensive string the next time," he said.

"Better still," I said, "Get a new gardener. The old one isn't letting the compost mature for long enough. It's still got bits in it."

He giggled, like a schoolgirl.

"Poor Elsa," he said. "She thought I was in love with her. You'd think a woman of her age would know better."

He made a move to reach for a drawer.

"Just sit still," I said. "Any sudden movements make me twitchy, and I'm not in a good mood."

He put his hands up.

"I was going for my pipe," he said. "That, and the bottle of whisky."

I liked the sound of that. I went round to his side of the desk. For the first time he looked frightened, and he flinched away from me.

"Don't worry," I said. "All I want is some answers."

"Just as long as you know the questions?"

He smiled. For some reason he seemed very happy with himself.

I opened his desk drawer and took out his pipe and tobacco, handing them both to him. I kept the bottle of Laphroig for myself.

"Keep yourself busy with that," I said. "I'll take care of this."

I sat in the chair opposite his desk, put the walking stick between my legs, lit up a cigarette, took a long swig of whisky, and watched him get the pipe going. Behind him rain splattered against the window, and the lights in the bay beyond danced and flickered in the droplets as they ran down the glass.

"Talk," I said.

And he did.

CHAPTER
Forty

"I FELT THERE WAS TROUBLE COMING," he started. "All last week I'd been on edge. I couldn't concentrate on work, and my poor PA bore the brunt of my anger with life.

"When he waltzed in here on Friday it was as if a dam had broken."

A cloud of smoke hung around him, starting to form in an inversion layer just above his head.

"I knew immediately he was trouble. He was far too loud for one thing. Why can't the colonials learn to be quiet?"

He wasn't really talking to me, so I didn't bother with an answer.

"It was five to eleven when he came in. He said he had something that was going to make him a fortune. He showed me the document. The stupid man didn't have the sense of a dog. What did he think I was going to do when I read it? Pat him on the back and let him get on with it?

"I nearly threw him out the window there and then. Of course, I knew straight away what it was, but I couldn't tell him that, now could I?"

"No, you couldn't tell him that. But you can tell me," I said.

"You don't know?" he said, astonished. "But I thought that was what brought you here."

"Indirectly," I said. "I know it has something to do with the rabbit farms, George Roberts, and Tom McCourt. I'm presuming there was some legal cock-up and that the Courtney's think they might have a claim on the land?"

"Oh, it was more than just a claim," he said. "Much more. May I?"

He motioned to his desk drawer again, and I gave him the nod. He rummaged and came out with some old-looking sheaves of paper.

"From the Scottish Antiquarian Society?" I asked.

He nodded.

"This is what really accompanied the letter they sent to Hank Courtney last year. Let me read it to you," he said, cradling the papers almost reverentially.

When he started to speak it was in that sing-song voice that academics always use when reading aloud.

"I, George Roberts, being of sound body and mind, do hereby bequeath this, my last testimonial, to the Almighty. May he forgive me my transgressions and avert his gaze from the foul deeds to which I am about to confess.

"It is five years since I left the Old Town, five long years during which even the sight of a club or ball has disgusted me. And still, I do not sleep, and still, he calls out to me in the night for mercy.

"For a time, I tried to convince myself that it was not my fault; that the blame lay with the town burghers who had so readily placed the monies in my hand to buy the land, who had so eagerly closed their businesses when the farmers came calling. But in truth, I cannot shy away from it; the sin was all mine.

"The councilmen had employed me for a singular purpose. To restore the game of golf to the links from which it had been so rudely usurped. And at first, I believed I might be successful. The farmers sold their land to me, and I passed it back to the council. Plans were being made for the layout of new holes, and councilmen practiced with the hickory in anticipation of the game returning.

"Then we ran into the McCourt family. For long years I tried to move the stubborn wretch from his land, but old man McCourt thwarted my ambitions at every turn.

"Matters came to a head at the council meeting in November. I made the farmers an offer, five times what the land itself was worth. And still McCourt would not be moved. He laughed at us, mocking our great game. He even had the temerity to hit me. Of course, I couldn't let that go. We tussled and wrestled across the council chamber, until I lost my footing. Even then I would have fought, but the council would not have it. They let the man walk free. Free! After insulting the council. He should have been flogged openly in the street!

"The council deferred a decision on their plans for the land, but I knew from their mood that they had reached the end. There would be no more money forthcoming. The farmers, that uncouth band of layabouts and vagabonds, had won.

"I was close to despair, that New Years Day, when I took myself to the sands to take the air and commune with my Lord. And my Lord spoke, in the air and the wind and waves as the storm grew and roared. And he delivered my enemy into my hands.

"I was walking back to town when I came across him, drunken wretch that he was, spewing out his guts across the rocks. Even then I might have tried reasoning with him, but when he saw me, he laughed at me, and spat at my feet. A red rage came over me, and I hit him, again, and again yet, pummelling him to the ground where I could more easily kick him. All the while he implored me for mercy and tears mingled with the rain, but my Lord was strong in me, and I kept punching. Blood ran, like a river, and I howled with the wind.

"My enemy died. And something of me died with him. I rolled the lifeless body into the raging surf and walked away.

"I said no words for him, nor did I look back.

"Afterwards, when the body was discovered, it was a simple matter for our fiscal to pronounce natural causes; after all, he was a golfer himself. The McCourt's were finally broken, but I couldn't find it in myself to celebrate.

"Within the year the good burghers had their golf course back, and the rabbit farmers were receding into memory. There was much rejoicing in the halls of Academe and council chambers. The links were full of the sound of club on ball. But not for me.

"I tried. When the ground was reworked and the great day came when golf came back to the links I stood on the first tee, the North wind caressing my face, the tang of salt on my lips. I took back my club for the strike. At that self-same moment, I could see his face, hear his cry. In my mind old Man McCourt bawled for a mercy that was never to come. I walked off the tee, and did not, could not, look back.

"I have not hit a single golf ball since that day. Indeed, the very sound of one being struck brings back to me my iniquity.

"I am not much longer for this world, but I cannot in all truth tell my tale to anyone, for to do so will bring shame to the very name of the game of golf, and coneys will once more rule over the glorious links.

"No, I will carry this burden within me, and let history, through this letter, judge me. I will have it sealed within the new fireplace. It may rot, it may fade, or the truth may somehow winkle itself out. In whatsoever manner it transpires, I leave the outcome to my Maker.

"Written in the year of our Lord Eighteen Hundred and Twenty-Six and signed, George Roberts, golfer."

"As you can see," Foulkes said, "I couldn't let that get out."

In truth, I couldn't see much of anything at all. My head throbbed like the bass speaker in a dance hall and my left eye threatened to close down in sympathy with the right. Nicotine and whisky were all that held me together.

"It's not a fake?" I said.

Foulkes sat forward at the desk and put the papers down, carefully.

"No, it's real enough," he said, "I have other documents by the man in the archives. The handwriting is very distinctive."

"And that's what you told Mr Courtney when you phoned him on Friday on the golf course," I said.

"My, you have been busier than I thought," he replied. "I kept the really interesting parts to myself. I told him just enough to get him excited; that it might be real, but that I'd have to do more work to prove it. I did intimate that he would indeed be looking at a large amount of money if the papers proved to be correct. I offered to provide him a certificate of authenticity to help him with his proof."

"That would work," I said.

"It did. I intimated that I would have a decision for him on Sunday and arranged a meeting. Even then a plot was forming in my mind. It took most of the weekend to set up."

"You can skip that bit," I said. I could feel tiredness seep through me. I needed to get this wrapped up. If I left it much longer, he'd be able to walk all over me and I would be able to stop him. "I know about the mobile phone, and your tryst with Ms Courtney at her hotel. Fast forward to Sunday."

His right eyebrow raised. That smile was back. I didn't like it. It told me the man felt confident. I wondered what I was missing.

"Courtney arrived right on time. He was like a dog with a squeaky toy. I couldn't take it anymore. He stood, just in front of the window. He talked about hotels and swimming pools, fast food resorts and dance halls. I took up the walking stick and hit him, hard behind the ear. He fell to the carpet, moaning and writhing. It was all just too messy, too upsetting. He started fumbling for the Bowie knife that was visible inside his boots. I took it from him easily, and stabbed him, in the chest."

Just like that. He showed no sign of emotion, just a little, pleased, smile.

"His sister helped me clean up. Can you imagine that? She was on her hands and knees, washing her own brother's blood from the carpet. She even helped me carry the body to the green-house. What kind of people are they?"

"So, she was in on it from the start?"

He nodded.

"Oh, it was mostly her idea. She had money in her sight, a lot of money, and she wanted it bad. It was my idea to send her to you though—I'd seen you around in the Halt, and you looked like somebody that could be manipulated easily."

He motioned towards the whisky bottle I was cradling in my right arm.

"I couldn't have some of that could I? It's thirsty work, all this confessing."

I pushed the bottle across the table to him. My head chose that moment to hit the pain button, and it was all I could do to stop myself screaming. He smiled that little smile again. Finally, I realised what it was. He thought he was the one in control here.

Then again, giving the way I felt, maybe he was right.

"I suppose Elsa helped you set Crawford up?"

"Oh, he was an innocent bystander," Foulkes said.

"Innocent? That's not a word Crawford knew."

"I noticed that. He barged in here on Monday afternoon," he said, "Shouting the odds about wanting to see the Texan. Said he'd followed him here. I placated him with whisky while Elsa planted the wrong deed on her brother."

"That was smart. The big man would never turn down a free drink," I said.

He nodded.

"I just kept giving him more. He was obviously too stupid to refuse and went out like a light quickly enough soon afterwards. We carried him out to the greenhouse and made sure his prints were on the knife. Elsa and I took a small risk in leaving him long enough to dump Hank in the bunker, but when the police were too stupid to catch you, we were glad we had done it."

"Why did you put his prints on the knife if you wanted to frame me?"

"That was just to confuse the police," he said. "We really wanted them to catch you at the Seventeenth. The fog saved you; stopped the plan working."

I nodded.

"So, after I got away, you thought you'd set up Crawford? How did you know about the garage?"

"Let's just say I have purchased some merchandise from the continent from the man. He was able to satisfy my particular needs."

"Putting him in the roller was a nice touch," I said.

"It was the first thing I thought of. It was just what that horrible, brash gorilla deserved."

"And the police bought it."

Again, he nodded. He took a small swig of whisky and handed it back to me. He went back to sending up smoke signals.

"After that was done and I had the deed I had no further need of poor Elsa. Disposing of her was easy. She just stood and looked at me in amazement. It never occurred to her that I might kill her too. And I always knew that walking stick would come in handy."

He laughed, as if inviting me to join him in seeing the funny side. I realised, way too late, that there was more than a hint of madness in the man.

"Okay, I understand the how, where and when," I said. "How about explaining to me why?"

The smile disappeared.

"I thought that was the bit you of all people would have no trouble with," he said.

He stood, fast enough to knock his chair backwards.

"Slowly," I said. "We don't want to frighten the horses."

He nodded, and turned, staring out over the bay. He moved to open the sliding door.

"Do you mind?" he said. "I'm used to my own tobacco smoke, but those American things of yours really are foul."

I waved my half-smoked Camel at him, and he slid open the window, letting the cold and the night in.

"I stand here most nights," he said, "Just staring out at it. It's one of the few oases of calm left in this modern world."

He turned back to me.

"I should have been born fifty, or even a hundred years ago. No cars, no television, none of this raucous rubbish that passes for music. Look at me. I'm forty-three and I'm already a grumpy old man. The only thing that soothes me, that comforts me in the long dark nights, is the thought that this place will still be here, still the same, after I'm long gone."

I finally got it.

"Eternal and unchanging?"

He beamed.

"Exactly. I knew you'd understand. Can I trust you to do the right thing with the document?"

I nodded.

"Then I will take my leave," he replied.

Before I had time to move from the chair, he took one step out onto the balcony, and a second, out into space. He seemed to hang in the air for a second.

I blinked, and he was gone, silently, out of sight.

CHAPTER
Forty-One

I FORCED myself upright and went to the balcony, gingerly. Heights and I have a mutual understanding...I don't bother with them if they don't bother with me. The rocks below swam in and out of focus as I peered over. So did Foulkes body.

He lay, just in the surf, washing gently against the foot of the cliff.

I pulled back from the edge and stood for a while, staring out at the bay, at the silver moonlight unrolling along the sands as the rain clouds passed and the stars came out. I smoked a cigarette and thought of tradition and history, and the dependability of landscape.

After a while I went back inside. I folded up the documents, went next door to the secretary's office and found an envelope and stamps. At the post box just down the road I posted it to myself. Finally, I went back to Foulkes' office and phoned Joe Boyd.

●

I FELL ASLEEP IN FOULKES' chair waiting for them to turn up. I woke looking up into Joe Boyd's frightened face.

"Christ John. I thought you were dead. What's happened?"

"The man floating at the foot of the cliffs killed my client, the American lady. She's buried in the greenhouse."

"I'll get a doctor."

"It's too late for that. They're both dead."

"It's for you, you idiot. For once I can tell you that you need your head examined without you giving me a smart comeback line."

The rest of the night passed in a blur as first Joe than the forensic team crawled all over the room. They had to get a boat out to pick up Foulkes body, and one of the young coppers threw up when they got to Elsa's body in the greenhouse. A police doctor stitched up my head and bandaged my fingers while I finished off Foulkes' whisky. I felt no pain.

"Just another quiet night on the force," Joe said grimly once things quietened down a bit. I was sat on the doorstep of the big house smoking a cigarette. Off to my left arc lights were set up around the garden. Out in the road beyond the press pack had already started to bay.

"So, the Professor killed the lady?" Joe asked. "Any idea why?"

I shook my head.

"I came up here looking for her," I said. "I heard that he had been visiting her in her hotel room."

"Any connection to the Crawford case?" he said. He sat down beside me and took one of my cigarettes.

I shook my head.

"Apart from the lady being the sister of the body in the bunker, your guess is as good as mine."

"I doubt that very much," Joe said, but he didn't push it. To his mind he had two murders and two suicides; he wasn't going to complicate matters any more than he had to.

"What are you going to tell the press?" I asked.

He smiled, and I saw the boy he had been.

"The Chief Constable is on his way. He was ticked off that I got the press attention on the Crawford case...he can take it this time. The newspaper boys will have plenty of theories to be going on with...that'll keep him out of my hair for a while."

"So, are we finished?" I said. My head pounded, my limbs ached, and I felt as tired as Mrs Curran's dog.

"For now," Joe said. "Go and get some sleep. I'll need you sooner or later for a formal statement."

"Make it later."

I crawled home and tried to sleep for a week.

Epilogue

THE REAL END of the case came a fortnight afterwards.

The document lay all that time in my top drawer while I wondered what to do with it. I only knew the answer to that one when I took delivery of a bottle of Highland Park, courtesy of Brian Johnson.

I took the bottle and the document downstairs.

"Tom," I said when he opened the door, "I've got a story to tell and a bottle to share."

"One of those I might be able to refuse, but not both," he said.

While Tom got the glasses I called Willie Brown, Davy Clark and Sandy Thomas.

"Get over here," I said to each. "The whisky's on me, and I'll tell you how the Yank ended up in the bunker."

Half an hour later we all met in Old Tom's museum. It took a while to get them settled. Every item on display in Tom's room reminded them of another story, and the evening threatened to get away from me as nostalgia took over.

"Quiet, please, gents," I said over the chatter. "Remember, it's my turn to entertain you."

"This had better be good," Willie said, "Dave Turner wanted to play crib. I could have been twenty quid up by now."

"Oh, this is worth more than that," I said. "This one's better than the German on Royal Wedding Day."

It was their turn to sit quietly while I told them the story and we polished off the malt.

"It started the day Elsa Courtney walked into my office," I said. "The day started like many another. I dressed, I made coffee, and I sat at my desk trying to magic up a client through the power of my will. All I managed to magic was a headache..."

I got remarkably few interruptions, and most of them were about Mrs Crawford and her red silk Kimono.

When I finally finished the whisky was almost gone. I passed round the document and Old Tom in particular treated it with as much reverence as a bible.

"I could buy this off you?" he said, pleading. "In lieu of rent for a couple of months?"

I was almost tempted. Then I remembered Foulkes. I shook my head.

"It's not for sale. We all know that this wee story is staying inside these four walls, don't we?"

They all looked at each other, and slowly nodded. To have the tale told around town would have just too many repercussions.

"So what are you going to do with it?" Davy Clark asked. "Are you going to give it to Joe Boyd?"

I shook my head.

"There's only one thing for it. Bring your glasses gents, let's go and propose a toast."

WE WALKED, almost in procession, to the Seventeenth green.

"What do you think?" I said, "Is this the right place?"

"I think it's the only right place," Old Tom said.

I handed him my glass.

"There's some left in there. Don't drink it. I'm going to need it."

I took the document from my pocket.

"Old George Stevens killed a man to preserve this place," I said. "Andrew Foulkes killed three for the same reason. Now the only people that know the secret are those of us here. We won't be talking about this again."

They all nodded.

I took out my lighter and lit the bottom of the document. The paper started to burn and thin wisps of black smoke rose and were taken away by the wind. When it was burning harder, I dropped it down into the bunker. It landed just where Hank's head had been.

We stood and watched it burn until there was nothing left but ash. Sandy Thomas lifted the bunker rake and scattered the remains into the sand until there was no sign it had been there.

"Here," Old Tom said, and handed me back my whisky glass. "It's time."

I looked around at the old men, then out over the links and finally to the lights of the town beyond.

"To St Andrews and the Old Course," I said raising the last of the whisky. "May she always remain, eternal and unchanging."

The old men joined me.

I may have had a tear in my eye as I turned away, but it might just have been spray from the sea.

As we walked down from the green to the road Davy Clark had a last look back.

"I used to bring Carol McGuigan down here," he said wistfully, "But I never did get into her knickers."

"I did," Willie said, and did the disgusting thing with his false teeth.

About the Author

I am a Scottish writer, now living in Canada, with over thirty novels published in the genre press and over 300 short story credits in thirteen countries.

I have books available from a variety of publishers including Dark Regions Press and Severed Press, and my work has appeared in a number of professional anthologies and magazines with recent sales to NATURE Futures, Penumbra and Buzzy Mag among others.

I live in Newfoundland with whales, bald eagles and icebergs for company and when I'm not writing I drink beer, play guitar and dream of fortune and glory.

You can find out more about me at https://www.williammeikle.com/.

9 798987 684733